THE DARKENING GLASS

THE DARKENING GLASS

Paul Doherty

headline

First published in Great Britain in 2009 by
HEADLINE PUBLISHING GROUP

WARWICKSHIRE LIB & INF
SERVICES

013440133 8	
HJ	2402374
AF	£19.99

ISBN 978 0 7553 3851 1 (hardback)
ISBN 978 0 7553 3852 8 (trade paperback)

Typeset in New Century Schoolbook by Palimpsest Book Production Ltd,
Grangemouth, Stirlingshire

Printed in the UK by CPI Mackays, Chatham ME5 8TD

HEADLINE PUBLISHING GROUP
An Hachette UK Company
338 Euston Road
London NW1 3BH

www.headline.co.uk
www.hachette.co.uk

For members of the Richard John Stephenson family
from the past, present and future
[Daryll Kelly]

Historical Personages

<u>ENGLAND</u>

Edward I:	warrior king (died 1307)
Eleanor of Castille:	first and most beloved wife of Edward (died 1296)
Edward II:	son of the above (crowned in 1308)
Peter Gaveston:	royal Gascon favourite, Earl of Cornwall
Margaret de Clare:	wife of the above
Isabella:	daughter of Philip IV of France, Edward II's queen
Margaret Queen Dowager:	second wife of Edward I, sister of Philip IV of France
Robert Winchelsea:	Archbishop of Canterbury

Aymer de Valence,
   Earl of Pembroke
Thomas,
   Earl of Lancaster
Guy de Beauchamp,
   Earl of Warwick   }   Great Lords
Humphrey de Bohun,
   Earl of Hereford
Henry de Lacey,
   Earl of Lincoln
Gilbert de Clare,
   Earl of Gloucester

Roger Mortimer of Wigmore:	Edward II's lieutenant in Ireland
Roger Mortimer of Chirk:	veteran fighter, uncle of the above
Hugh de Spencer:	nobleman, loyal to the crown
Henry Beaumont Isabella Beaumont, Lady Vesci Louis Beaumont	powerful family; related to the royal family, with estates in Scotland.
Stephen Dunheved:	Dominican confessor to both Edward II and Queen Isabella

FRANCE

Philip IV:	'Le Bel', King of France
Joanna (Jeanne) of Navarre:	wife of the above, now deceased
Louis Philippe Charles	sons of the above
Enguerrand de Marigny Guillaume de Nogaret Guillaume de Plaisans	Philip's principal ministers and lawyers
Clement V:	pope, who continued the papal exile in Avignon

THE TEMPLARS

Jacques de Molay: Grand Master of the Templar order

William de la More: master of the Templar order in England

SCOTLAND

Robert the Bruce: skilled Scottish war-leader against the English.

Foreword

In July 1307, Edward I died, to be immediatley succeeded by Edward of Caernarvon, Prince of Wales. In January 1308, the new King Edward married the young Isabella, daughter of Philip IV of France. Isabella, however, faced a rival, Peter (or Pierre) Gaveston, a young Gascon of lowly birth whom Edward immediately promoted to become a premier earl, granting him the lucrative Duchy of Cornwall. Between 1308 and the spring of 1312, Gaveston was hotly resisted by the great earls of England, who resented his status and his control over both king and crown. They issued ordinances against him, and tried to have him exiled but both the king and Gaveston fiercely resisted such opposition. In the early spring of 1312, both sides slipped towards civil war at the very time Isabella began to proclaim her own power as both queen and wife. The kingdom tensed itself: the question of power and government was to be decided by the sword, bloody intrigue and gruesome murder.

The quotations at the beginning of each chapter come

from the *Vita Edwarde Secundi* – the Life of Edward II, a contemporary chronicle. An author's note at the end gives the historical context of the stirring events of Mathilde's account.

Prologue

He who loses the most . . .
is judged the more brave and the stronger.

I awake. The dark fell of night presses down. I lie and seethe against the dying light in my own life. Shadows shroud the mountains and deep valleys of my soul, all peopled by ghosts of yesteryear. I listen to the patter of feet as the sacristan and his escort, lanterns in hand, keep strict vigil between Compline and Matins here in the Priory of Grey Friars, nestling like some bird beneath the soaring glory of St Paul's. If I rise and peer out of the window, I can glimpse the jutting belfry of the cathedral, its beacon light glowing above the night-shadowed lanes and trackways of Cheapside, with its cross, tun and standard. The busy heart of the buzzing beehive of London. Bells, echoing sombrely, mark the passing of the hours and the creeping approach of dawn. When the call for Matins is proclaimed, I leave my bed and wash fastidiously. I dress in my heavy tunic and linen shift, with thick wool stockings over my old legs, dark leather sandals protecting my feet. Over all I put my anchorite gown to cloak myself like one of the good brothers. My hair, now white as snow, I hide behind a tight-fitting pale-blue wimple, then, vanity of vanities, I stare into a mirror of polished brass. I glimpse my face as it is now and I remember how I was when life blazed in me like a fiery torch. The ghosts of the past cluster around me, drifting up from so many, many years ago, when I was *clerica medica atque domicella reginae camerae* – clerk, physician and lady of the chamber – to Isabella, wife of Edward II. A time of chaos, when God and his angels slept. A hurling season when fortune's wheel spun dizzyingly, bringing down kings and princes, a veritable litany of names of those who met horrid death on the battlefield, in lonely dungeons or high on some public scaffold.

I, Mathilde de Clairebon, Mathilde de Ferrers and Mathilde of Westminster, wake to greet these memories. The good brothers shelter me here deep in their cavernous priory. When I slip like a ghost along its vaulted passageways, the gargoyles and babewyns grin down at me as if they know why I am really here. Edward of England, third of that name, son of Isabella the so-called 'She-wolf' and her fox-like mate, has ordered me to be immured here. He calls it a living death. He does not want me to wander abroad like some fey creature with a stone in her head, babbling all my secrets. The Iron King, with his dagger-like eyes and that once beautiful face, his golden hair now streaked a dirty grey, desired to hear my confession. I refused. The sea will give up its dead before I share my secrets. God knows he has tried to seduce my loyalty with his tray of baubles, but I'm content to be locked away. I observe the long holy hours from Matins through Lauds to Compline song, but at least I'm with her, Isabella. She lies interred in the choir of Grey Friars church, an exquisite table tomb that contains the remains of her beautiful body, garbed for burial in its wedding dress, close to where Mortimer, the great lord of her heart, also lies buried. Mortimer the Warrior, who ended his brief span of glory dangling naked for three days at the Elms. I eventually cut his cold cadaver down and brought it here for the good brothers to sheathe in its silken shroud. When was that? Oh, so long ago – thirty years and more!

Now I'm here. Father Guardian, young and austere, with a harsh face but a kindly heart, has provided me with a vaulted chamber overlooking the cemetery, a quiet place rich with wild flowers in the summer. The breezes, thickened with the fragrance of fresh grass, cleanse and purify my cell as they caress my face. I have a little scriptorium beneath the window where I write my secret chronicle. A lay brother, Simon of the Stocks as he calls himself, his whimsical face ever smiling under its shock of sprouting hair, now looks after my needs. He brings me food and all I require. He even walks with me out amongst the faded gravestones and weather-beaten crosses. Simon loves to point out the graves of the various brothers, accompanied by a litany of their peccadilloes, virtues and skills. He asks me what I write. What can I tell such a simple soul about the landscape of hell I've crossed? The clash of arms and the silent malevolent intrigue of Isabella's court? Filthy assassins, capuchined and visored, daggers glinting, slipping through the dusk? Or cups of wine brimming at their jewelled rims, neatly coated with the most noxious of poisons? Battlefields like that at Bannockburn, where the chivalry of England in all its emblazoned colours lay like a tapestry across the soil drenched in a shifting sea of blood? Leeds Castle, stormed and sacked, its defenders dancing against the walls as the nooses tightened around their throats? Lord Badlesmere, hanged and drawn, the steaming quarters of his corpse boiled and pickled, displayed like lumps of meat above the gates of Canterbury? And those other secrets contained in the coffer of my mind, bound, tied and clasped?

A strange one, Simon of the Stocks! After Lauds last Candlemas, it was he who gave me the idea of asking Father Guardian if I could paint a fresco along the gloomy plastered wall that runs down the vaulted passageway outside my chamber. Now, I am a magister in physic, as skilled as any practitioner *cum laude* from the universities of Montpellier or Salerno. I was given firm grounding in medicine, skilled and disciplined by my uncle Reginald, physician-general in the order of the Templars before Philip, King of France, that prince of hell, attacked and dissolved the order in a welter of blood. I am also a painter with a sharp eye for colour, though not possessing the skill I, and perhaps others, would like. Frescoes, painted panels and decorated walls fascinate me.

I remember the tap room of the Boar's Head in Kings Street, Westminster, where we stopped when the royal guards brought me down to Grey Friars. The walls of the tavern were lustily painted with red lead worked in oil, decorated with gilt motifs provided by a dozen stencils and cups of gold dust. The tavern master explained it all to me as I sipped a stoup of ale and tried to ignore the foul chatter of my escort, Edward's bully boys, a group of household knights with a penchant for lechery; hotter they were than a flock of sparrows in spring. Such paintings like that in the tavern absorb and distract me. I wondered if I could do my own, a parable on the harrowing of my own hell. Father Guardian kindly agreed and had the wall freshly plastered. He supplied me with lime water and sinopia, that blood-red chalky material, to draw the outlines. A generous man, Father Guardian also supplied the paints and coloured dishes, as well as a clutch of squirrel and hog-haired brushes.

I ground my colours and worked as busily as any itinerant painter in a parish church. I found such activity a soothing balm to my soul. I chose as my theme the parable of Belshazzar's feast in Babylon, as described in the Book of Daniel. A searing tale in which God's finger scrawled on a wall that ominous warning to the king and princes of Babylon: 'Mene, Mene Tekel and Parsin – I have numbered, I have weighed in the balance and I have found wanting.' Oh yes, the truth indeed! Father Guardian and the brothers came down to stare. God bless Francis of Assisi and his brethren. If they laughed behind their hands, they did not show it. Of course Belshazzar's feast was simply an image to summon up my own past. The people who throng this painting are those nightmare wraiths lurking in the memory chambers of my soul. As in life, so in death, these demons rub shoulders with the angels, those souls who touched me gently and healed my wounds. Grey-haired, kindly uncle Reginald de Deynecourt, physician-general in Paris; Bertrand Demontaigu, the Templar priest who hid in the household of my mistress as a clerk, the only man I have ever really loved. I certainly remember the one I cannot see. I cannot accurately paint his face, but I recall it so well: long, sallow and severe, with close-cropped black hair. A preacher's face, swiftly redeemed by beautiful, kindly sea-grey eyes and those deep laughter lines around his mouth.

Demontaigu sits at the end of the banqueting table gowned in dark-blue murrey and Cordovan riding boots; long fingers grasp a quill pen, and around his neck hangs a reddish Templar cross. He sits next to Uncle Reginald and the dark-featured Ap Ythel, captain of Edward's bodyguard. They dine apart from the rest on wholesome foods, sweet viands and manchet bread. The rest of my guests are hidden behind fantastic details, a mosaic of different symbols, foolish forms and countless chimeras. Belshazzar's palace is no hall of light and life, but a stretch of the dark lands, the vestibule of Hades, the gloomy enclosures that house the tombs of hell. I have summoned up the smoke spirits, the wraiths, the pallid, bloodless ghosts to drift in my painting along that cold, lifeless passageway. The food for these demons is foul scorpions and fiery toads, whilst the wine pouring from the jugs looks like stagnant water from a sewer. Servants hover like black-feathered demons. These wait in attendance on the Great Lords. First, Philip of France, killer of his own wife, Jeanne of Navarre, with his silver-white hair and soul-less blue eyes, and a face that looks almost pious if it wasn't for the smirk twisting his lips. On either side, his three sons: Louis, reddish as a weasel; Philippe, long and gangly, fingers scratching his face, mouth half open, as it was in life when he believed his dead, dread father constantly walked by his side; next to Philippe, Charles, blond and fat, one hand as ever going out to grasp the wine flagon, the other beneath the table stroking a pig playing the bagpipes. Behind the King of France are his three familiars, those human boars and bloodhounds, Philip's mole-men. The demons who worked constantly in the dark to bring down the Templar order in shattering ruin and send my uncle and other innocents to the yawning scaffold over the great pit at Montfaucon. Oh yes, Philip's lawyers, who believed they could plunder hell and return unscathed. They stand there in their scalloped jerkins lined with rat's fur. I gave them hoods with monkey ears, whilst a whetstone and a jordan, a dripping urinal, hang clasped around their necks as their every breath was crooked. Foremost amongst these is red-haired Enguerrand de Marigny, Lord Renard, Philip's first minister and leading councillor; then his other two minions of murder: Guillaume de Nogaret, with his face fat like a bag of dung, and Guillaume de Plaisans, blond-haired and mastiff-featured. On another table sit the Lords of England. Edward of Caernarvon, king yet a fool, with his lustrous blond hair, moustache and beard. Beside Edward, dark-haired Peter Gaveston, his woman-like features, gentle eyes and laughing mouth hiding a heart full of murderous deceit. On a bar above their heads stands a magpie, its black and white feathers all ruffled, sharp yellow beak ready to jab.

I finished this part of my own harrowing of hell on the eve of the Annunciation, when dying winter meets a strengthening spring. The scenes took me back to my chronicle, to that time of blood so long ago, that egg-ripe Easter of 1312, when a hideous massacre on the ghost-haunted wastelands outside York ushered in a season of murderous betrayal.

Chapter 1

Dearest and most powerful lady.

By the spring of 1312, my mistress Queen Isabella was on the verge of full ripeness. Sixteen summers old, she had matured rich and fertile, a fairy-tale Queen from the romances she so ardently read. A beautiful woman, tall, willowy and slender, her face as perfect as an angel, with lustrous blonde hair, rose-kissed lips and eyes that could dazzle with life. Strange eyes, light blue and sloe-shaped, a legacy from her Navarrese mother. Isabella presided over a court in chaos. The great earls were in fierce rebellion against Gaveston, the king's favourite, who had been created Earl of Cornwall and placed at the right hand of the power. Gaveston's banner, a gorgeous red eagle, its wings spread, constantly fluttered over the English court and sparked the flames of civil war. The great earls assembled in this church or that, hands extended, to swear the most sacred of oaths that Gaveston's banner and coat of arms must be reversed, torn and ground into the dust. Thomas, Earl of Lancaster, cousin of the king, and the other Great Lords whistled up their levies and, with banners displayed, marched on London, only to find that the king and his hen-groper – as the great earls mockingly called Gaveston – had fled north to the fastness of York. King, queen, favourite and their households sheltered at the Franciscan friary opposite St Mary's on Hetergate, which lay between Castlegate and the river Ouse. The Franciscan house was a splendid sprawling complex of buildings around a stately church with a lofty bell tower. I still recall its nave and sanctuary, places of hallowed light, with their altars to the Resurrection and the Trinity, all shrouded in the glow from a thousand tapers. How can I forget, when that house of God soon became the haunt of murder? Most of the royal servitors lay quartered in other establishments, stretching from Bootham Bar to Fishergate; my mistress and I, however, occupied the Arcella chambers above the main cloister garden of the friary.

Isabella had changed, and so had I. A few years older than the queen, I was now recognised as a lady of the inner household, the queen's own chamber; in fact, its only member. Others gossiped that I was Isabella's shadow, with my long pale face and mousy hair. True, I was, I am, no beauty, though Demontaigu always claimed my eyes were clear and merry, my face an ivory pale, with lips meant for kissing. Flatterer! An honourable man; was it just a lovely lie? I was the queen's physician, adviser and clerk. I attended meetings of the king's chamber council. Sometimes Gaveston and even the king would ask my voice on certain matters. My relationship with the queen had certainly deepened: in public her lady and handmaid, in private the closest of kin. My duties were not only in the kitchen and spicery but generally in the household, whether it be the scullery, the hanaper or the great wardrobe. I was Isabella's trusted *domicella*, in charge of the jewel chests and the great coffers containing her robes. I paid messengers like John de Moigne, presented the high altar of the Franciscan chapel with cloths of gold, supervised the purchase of five hundred Galloway pears, a great delicacy much loved by the queen, together with Gruyère cheese, which her father sent from Paris along with a spate of advice on how she should behave, especially towards Gaveston, the king's favourite. Gaveston, pretty-faced, with a dagger-like wit! What was Isabella's relationship with the king's minion? Many have asked me. To be true, it's still a mystery, even now, tens of years later. I can only suspect the truth, not demonstrate it. In public or in private, be it courtyard or secret chamber, they acted like sweet cousins, with soft words and pretty compliments towards each other. I detected no tension between king and queen, or between Gaveston and Isabella, at least not until that fateful Easter.

In the February of 1312, the favourite's wife, that little mouse, the sanctimonious and ever pious Margaret de Clare, gave birth to a girl child. Six weeks later, Isabella announced to a delighted court that she too was expecting a child. I had known this since the Feast of the Epiphany. I advised the queen that she was to be a mother: her courses had stopped for at least three months, whilst the swelling of her stomach and thighs and the tenderness of her breasts confirmed this. Isabella suffered slight sickness in the early hours. I begged her not to take any potion except a little camomile sprinkled in pure water, boiled then left to cool. In truth, she had come into her own. She proclaimed that the child would be a boy, a future king. Edward was beside himself with pleasure, for the heralded proclamation confirmed his own virility and put paid to the filthy rumours that he was nothing better than a capon nestling with his lover Gaveston. Of course, the curious ask if there was any truth in such scandalous rumours. I can only answer on what I perceived. In my eyes, Gaveston was the king's brother, sister, mother and father. Edward was a lonely man, and he pined for Gaveston as a man would for the staples of life.

And my place in all this? Well, it was not all leisurely strolls along closed walks; sitting in a carrel enjoying the rich smell of roses from the cloister garden; riding in a litter or astride some gentle palfrey as the royal cavalcade, under a forest of brilliant banners and pennants, moved from one palace to another. So how can I describe it? It's like looking back down a torchlit passageway where the shadows dance and the light picks out certain gleaming objects to catch the eye. Or like breasting a hill, when your gaze sweeps the horizon, searching for a spire or the crenellated battlements of a tower. So it was looking back at that Easter of 1312,

when the Saviour's Resurrection was greeted with a clash
of steel as swords and daggers were unsheathed, banners
unfurled and war horses harnessed for battle. The great
earls, the lords of Lancaster, Warwick, Pembroke and
Hereford, began the hunt. Edward might be king, Isabella
might be pregnant, the French might be threatening
Gascony, the Wolf Pope, Philip's creature Clement V, might
nestle in Avignon and hurl imprecations against the great
Templar order, but the chaos and crisis in England only
deepened, more specks against the darkening glass.
Gaveston was marked for the slaughter. In the last four
years he had been exiled, judged and condemned. He and
the king, however, remained obdurate, bargaining for a place
in the sun. In the end, negotiations in shady porticoes and
flower-filled alcoves, with their consequent indentures, prom-
ises, proclamations and schedules, all proved fruitless.
Gaveston's status was to be settled by the sword.

We waited at York whilst a host of scurriers and messengers galloped the length and breadth of the kingdom as
Edward and Gaveston sought support. So desperate were
they that Gaveston even sent one of his Aquilae into Scotland
to treat secretly with Robert the Bruce, the Scottish rebel,
whose ragged troops had overrun most of Edward's castles
and fortresses and now threatened the northern marches.
Scottish raiding parties drove like daggers through the soft
meadowlands south of the great wall. I pause in my writing
and stare at the word 'Aquilae', the name given to Gaveston's
squires, his trusted henchmen and household guard. Yes,
there were five in number: Philip Leygrave, Robert
Kennington, Geoffrey Lanercost, Nicholas Middleton and

John Rosselin. All of mixed parentage: English fathers and Gascon mothers. Men-at-arms trained in war, the Aquilae reminded me of lurcher hounds, ready to hunt at their master's whistle. Handsome young men, swaggering in their short jerkins, cambric shirts and tight hose, yet deadly all the same, despite their foppish ways, curled coiffed hair, painted eyes and fastidious manners. They strutted about in their long high-heeled boots of ox-blood Cordova, yet the war-belts slung like a woman's girdle around their slim waists carried dagger, poignard and sword, expertly sheathed and ready to be drawn. They boasted Gaveston's arms, especially the blood-red spread-eagle. They lounged and settled outside his chamber, bejewelled fingers not far from dagger hilts. They called themselves the Aquilae Petri, 'Peter's Eagles', and others responded by playing further on the Latin tag, as *aquilae petri* was also the name given to a precious jewel. Edward's favourite jester, a dwarf clad in Lincoln green from head to toe, like Robin of the Hood, teased them with that, so what began as a slight insult was eventually accepted as a compliment.

It was one of these Gemstones, Geoffrey Lanercost, who had been sent north of the border to treat with Bruce. God knows what madcap scheme the king had dreamed up. Scottish help against his own earls? A refuge for Gaveston? In return for what? Recognition of Bruce's claims? Isabella prayed that it remained a secret. If the great seigneurs of the kingdom could prove that Edward was ready to surrender their estates in Scotland for his Gascon hen-groper, then all of England would betray him. Such fey schemes didn't concern me. Isabella's well-being did.

On that afternoon in Easter week, I sat in the cloister of the Franciscan house. My mistress was sleeping. Bertrand Demontaigu and I, with other members of the secret Templar coven, planned to go out and meet some of their brethren fresh from Scotland. We were to assemble at Devil's Hollow, a deserted farmstead out in the moors, well beyond the bar and gates of York. The friary had fallen silent. April in all its trimness was making itself felt in bursts of greenery and brilliantly coloured flowers. A shadow fell across me. I glanced up. Brother Stephen Dunheved, Dominican confessor to both the king and, quite lately, Isabella, stood staring down at me. From the very beginning Dunheved was a strange one, with his neat tonsure, smooth, round, olive-coloured face, gentle eyes and soft mouth above a slightly jutting jaw. A wolf disguised as a lamb! The way he held his head betrayed the fanaticism burning like a firebrand in his devious soul.

'*Benedicite, mea filia.*' Dunheved threaded his Ave beads through soft, plump fingers.

'*Benedicite, Pater,*' I replied. Dunheved sat down next to me as he always did, as if we were fellow conspirators. He then turned to whisper in my ear, his breath hot against my face.

'Are you at peace, Mathilde?'

'I was, Brother!'

He smiled, patted my hand then glanced around.

I recalled how this Dominican often sought me out. He pointed at the stout riding boots peeping from beneath my kirtle.

'You are travelling? Her grace is sending you . . . ?'

'Her grace is resting,' I interrupted. 'I wish to God I could.'

'Will this ever end, Mathilde?' Dunheved lifted his Ave beads and gestured at the Pity, a carving of the Virgin, the crucified Christ lying across her lap; above them both soared an empty black cross. 'The Resurrection,' he breathed. 'Mathilde de Clairebon, Mathilde de Ferrers,' he smiled, 'or have you taken the title now usually given to you: Mathilde of Westminster? Ah well.' He didn't wait for an answer; he rarely did.

'We are being crucified now, but when will the green shoots of our passion bear fruit?' He edged closer. 'Mathilde,' he whispered hoarsely, 'advise the queen. Tell her to persuade the king that my lord Gaveston must go into exile.'

'It's finished,' I retorted without thinking. 'The king is tired of demands. He does not want the likes of Lancaster and Pembroke dictating what is to happen.'

'Then *consummatum est*,' the Dominican whispered. 'Is that what you are saying, Mathilde? Who will defend us if civil war breaks out? I thought I'd left my soldiering days behind! I am God's priest now, not His squire.' He paused as the bells clanged in the high tower of the church. 'Slightly askew,' he murmured.

'What is?' I asked.

'Nothing, nothing!' he replied, and patted me once again on the hand.

I turned and studied this enigmatic Dominican: the high cheekbones, the wary eyes, the firm chin, neatly shaved, the dimple in his right cheek. A man, I thought at the time, who saw his will as God's and rested serene in that final judgement. A soul very much at peace with himself, determined on his course. Dunheved gathered his black and white robes more tightly around him. He fingered the cord around his waist, moving to the three knots representing his solemn vows of obedience, poverty and chastity. Then he murmured something about God's will being done, rose and pattered away. I watched him leave. A man to be kept under careful scrutiny, I reflected. A conviction that lasted for at least fifteen years after that fatal Easter of 1312.

'Mathilde, Mathilde!'

I glanced around. Demontaigu, cloaked, booted and spurred, stood in the doorway leading off from the cloisters to the chapter house.

'We must go.' He gestured.

I joined him and the others in the stable yard. Cowled and cloaked, they looked like a group of monks preparing to go on pilgrimage, though their dark and sombre attire hid weapons, whilst from the saddle horns on their horses hung arbalests and battle axes. These were once Templars, but now, by royal and papal decree, they were outlaws and wolf's-heads. Those who'd survived capture had moved north, and had entered into secret negotiations with Robert the Bruce. They wanted sanctuary and refuge with the Scottish war-leader, who had the grace and good sense to welcome these battle-hardened warriors. Jewels, records and other movables of those Templar houses that had escaped forfeiture had already been dispatched across the northern march for safe keeping. Five Templar serjeants had recently been sent into Scotland with more chests and coffers. Demontaigu and the rest were to meet these men out on the moors at Devil's Hollow and find out what reception had been accorded before leading them back into York. Nothing was done in writing, as Bruce had been publicly judged a traitor to the English crown. Despite Gaveston's own secret negotiations with the Scots, anyone convicted of treating with the Bruce would suffer the full rigours of the law for treason, being hanged, drawn and quartered.

Demontaigu had explained all this to me. I was to accompany them, as I carried warrants under the privy and secret seals allowing safe passage wherever I wished. The former Templars had come to the friary and were now ready to go. They greeted me with grunts and nods. I recognised a few: Simon Estivet, acting grand master in England after William de la More's imprisonment in Canterbury; next to him, Ausel the Irishman, who liked to exaggerate what he called his Celtic charm and temperament. In truth a killer to the bone, Ausel was dedicated to revenge for what the Templars had suffered. Because of Demontaigu, as well as my status with the queen, I was not so much accepted as tolerated by these hunted men. Ausel was the only one to greet me by name and courteously helped me with the stirrups of my horse. To break the tense, sombre mood, he swung himself into the saddle and immediately insisted on proclaiming a bawdy story about a monastery near Clontarf outside Dublin, where the monks could fly and their abbot could only summon them back by beating the bare round bottoms of novice nuns. The story provoked some laughter. Ausel scrutinised me for blushes. I tartly informed him that lechery at the English court was as common as his stories. He laughed and pushed his horse ahead.

I rode alongside Demontaigu, who was lost in his own

thoughts. I left him to it as we passed under the friary gate-house, turning right along King's Staith, which would take us to the bridge across the Ouse on to Micklegate Bar. The day had promised rich sunshine, but now this was beginning to fade. Nevertheless, the good citizens of York, powerful burgesses with baggy cheeks as soft as clay, accompanied by their harsh-faced, barrel-bottomed wives, were parading in all their fineries. A thin, stinking mist seeped in from the Ouse, carrying the stench of tar, salt, pickle and dried fish. Such smells mingled with the rich odours from the pie shops, bakeries and smithies as well as the shabby stalls offering a range of food to those who worked along the river and its quayside. A busy, motley throng of the living and the dead, for it was early afternoon, and funeral parties carrying staves, candles and tawdry banners escorted coffins from the river down to the various churches where the death watch would be kept until the final requiem mass the following morning. The track-ways were clogged with mud and ordure drying hard under the sun. All of York seemed to have emptied itself on to the streets. A surge of people of every type and rank, busily intent on reaching the markets or simply strolling in the not so fresh air, enjoying the sun after winter's bleak blackness.

We left King's Staith because of the crush, going along an alleyway on to a broad paved thoroughfare, which proved just as frenetic, clogged with carts, barrows and litters as well as traders of every kind, eager to pluck at your sleeve or catch your eye. Tinkers and tailors, the bars above their stalls displaying their products, shouted against the calls and cries of furriers, goldsmiths, hempen sellers, butchers and fruiterers. Beggars pleaded, stretching out their battered ladles for coins. A swarm of beadles and bailiffs tried to impose order amongst unlicensed pedlars with horn and staff. These nimble-witted traders simply packed up their wares and moved to any free space between houses, doorways, the steps of churches or the backs of carts. Peasants and farmers, heads shaded by straw hats, offered hens, piglets and ducks, 'all fresh and lively for sale'. We had to muffle our mouths and noses as the stink from the runnels and sewers grew offensive, the refuse piles and offerings from the sewer pots being cooked to ripeness under the sun. Little wonder they call Satan lord of the latrines! I took some comfort that in such chaos no one would pay us special attention. Indeed, the royal city of York seemed totally oblivious to the growing confrontation between the king and his leading earls, being more concerned with selling a collection of buttons for a farthing or a litter of piglets for a quarter of a mark. York was immersed in commerce to the exclusion of everything. The citizens even jostled the coped priests who carried the viaticum to the sick. The glow of hallowed candles, the tinkle of bells and the smoke of burning incense did little to smooth the priests' path through the turbulent crowd, who were more interested in challenging a relic seller offering a wing from a seraphim or the nail from the big toe of the Trinity. York was living proof that 'love does much, but money does everything'.

We finally crossed the bridge, going along Micklegate to the Bar, its lofty crenellations decorated with the tarred severed heads of Scottish rebels. These grisly relics stared blindly down at the great stocks on either side packed full of miscreants, their heads and faces plastered with horse dung and honey. Eventually we passed through the yawning gateway, following the road leading to Tadcaster, which was crowded with carts, plodding peasants, wandering friars, preachers and story-tellers. One of these, desperate to solicit custom, had stopped on the steps of a crumbling wayside cross to proclaim that verse from Isaiah: 'I said in the midst of my days, I should go through the portals of hell.' Little did we realise how true that was of us! We journeyed on for a little while, pausing whilst Ausel checked the map he had drawn. Demontaigu pulled the muffler from his mouth, leaned over and apologised for being withdrawn. He explained the urgency of what we were doing.

'The serjeants will bring us news out of Scotland. They met Bruce personally; soon, Mathilde, we'll have sanctuary.'

My heart skipped a beat, as it always did at the prospect of his departure.

'No, no!' Demontaigu recognised my fear. 'No, *ma doucette*.' He smiled. 'I shall not be going into Scotland with the rest. My duties keep me here with you in England. I am well pleased,' he added impishly, 'to keep both eye and ear open to what is happening.'

I was about to reply when Ausel called out at us to follow, and we cantered on to what our companions called 'the great wastelands of Yorkshire', empty, bleak moors still recovering from the great burning by the Conqueror hundreds of years before. A wild, lonely place, a tapestry of shifting colour: greens of many hues; gold and black; the occasional dash of purple where sprouts of wild heather burst up through the grass. Gathering clouds blacked out the sun. The sky became swiftly overcast. We moved across the rain-misted landscape through stubborn gorse and tough heather, our garrons choosing their steps wisely. An eerie land with ancient rocks darker than iron. Above us wild birds shrieked like lost souls against the wind. We trooped in silence for a while through a dense copse of gnarled trees, then began to climb. I felt deeply uneasy. Perhaps it was the contrast between the noisy, turbulent city and this place of utter, miserable silence, which harboured its own grisly secrets.

We breasted the rise and stared down at a scene from hell. Devil's Hollow was a broad, deep-bowled basin in that rough landscape. At its centre rose the ruins of an old house built of grey moor-stone, its thatched roof long gone. Around it stood stunted trees, probably the relic of some ancient forest where the murderous pagan gods used to shelter. The poet writes: 'Who paints a rose cannot paint its fragrant soul.' That also applies to those who describe demons; they cannot summon up the true terrors of hell, which was what Devil's Hollow had become. The ancient cottar's place lay silent, but from the branches of the nearby trees hung five corpses. The scene was cruel and hard. We rode swiftly down, dismounted and searched around. We found traces of battle: the ground had been scuffed by many horsemen, and the blood-splattered grass was littered with grim straps of leather, armour and a broken dagger. There was nothing else. No horses, no baggage, nothing but those five corpses, their eyes gouged out, dressed solely in jerkins and hose, feet bare, their bodies swaying slightly in the breeze, the branches creaking under their weight. Some had died before they were hanged. Horrid blue-black wounds to the chests and guts; their mangled mouths and shattered skulls told their own macabre tale. Certain places reek of terrible evil. Devil's Hollow certainly did. The way the ground abruptly dipped, the abandoned cottar's house of rough stone and those gnarled trees rich with their grisly fruit.

I walked into the old cottage. It stank, fetid and sour, a dark cave of stone with a floor of beaten earth. Outside echoed the curses of my companions as they cut the corpses down. I searched the cottage but found nothing except the spent embers of a fire. A shadow darkened the door.

'They are ready,' Demontaigu declared. 'God have mercy on them, Mathilde.'

I went out. Estivet, a priest Templar, was crouching by a corpse, whispering the words of absolution into the dead man's ear, in the hope that the living soul would gain some comfort on its journey towards the light.

'Go forth, Christian soul.' Estivet's horror and anger at what had happened thrilled his words. 'Go forth like a soldier to meet your God. May Michael and all his angels come forth to meet you. May you not fall into the hands of the enemy, the evil one, and so I absolve you from . . .'

I waited until he had finished, then I inspected the corpses. Everything of value had been stripped off them: belts, buckles, boots, armour and weapons. Three had died in vicious hand-to-hand fighting, with deep, ugly wounds to the face, neck and chest. Two of them, in my judgement, had still been alive when hanged. All had been abused: noses slit as if they were felons, with the added indignity of having their eyes gouged out, and their gaping mouths stuffed with dirt and the excrement of wild animals, a blasphemous mockery of the viaticum. Ausel and the others were now in deep conversation, heatedly discussing what had happened. I stared down at the faces of the dead men, then up at the rim of the hollow. I could visualise how these Templars had been trapped and slaughtered.

'Noctales!' Ausel spat the word out.

I nodded in agreement.

'Scots?' someone called.

'Nonsense!' Demontaigu snapped, face all pallid. 'We have a treaty with them, they wouldn't . . .'

'Outlaws? Wolf's-heads?' another called.

'No!' I replied loudly. My companions were sorely frightened. So terrified they wanted to ignore the obvious menace: Alexander of Lisbon and his comitatus. A free company of murderers, specially commissioned by Clement V of Avignon and Philip of Paris to hunt down Templars and kill them. Edward of England, to his eternal shame, had also issued them licence under letters patent to pursue their quarry in England.

Some of the Templars shook their heads, muttering at the opinion of a woman. I walked towards them.

'These corpses are cold,' I declared. 'They were killed early today, perhaps just before dawn.' I pointed to the rim of the hollow. 'A safe place most times, but the Noctales ringed them in here and rode down. Your comrades were surprised and massacred. Well,' I brushed the dust from my gloves, 'that is what I think.'

'But how did the Noctales know about them?' Ausel asked. 'Here, out in the wilderness?'

A spate of answers greeted the question. Demontaigu took

me by the shoulder and led me towards the cottage. Estivet joined us.

'Alexander of Lisbon and his Noctales: you are sure, Mathilde?'

'Who else, Bertrand, for the love of God?' I shivered. Such a gloomy place: those corpses lying sprawled on the barren earth, the tree branches twisting out as if waiting for fresher fruit, the edge of that hollow, its long grass bending gently in the breeze. Ravens screeched above us as they fought the strengthening winds. I wanted to be gone. Cold fear pricked my heart and twisted my stomach. 'They may return,' I whispered.

'Not now.' Demontaigu shook his head. 'I don't think so, not in daylight: the land is too flat and open. They could not surprise us.' He breathed in deeply. 'Alexander of Lisbon must have learnt about this place and led his demons here before dawn. They did their bloody work and left. They'll be long gone now.'

I disagreed, but I did not wish to argue the point.

'The corpses?' I asked.

'We'll leave them here.' Estivet called over one of his companions and gave him instructions. 'I'll pay the good brothers at the friary,' he continued. 'They'll see it as an act of mercy and give them proper burial in the poor man's lot in God's Acre.'

'This,' Demontaigu gestured at the dead, 'is finished. Their bodies are for the soil, their souls to God, but who betrayed us, Mathilde? Alexander of Lisbon must have been told how our men were coming out of Scotland. He must have been given the exact time and place those serjeants would arrive here, but how, who?' he whispered hoarsely.

Ausel, seeing us deep in conversation, drifted across as the others carried the corpses into the cottage, cloaks being offered as shrouds, stones quickly collected to protect the dead from wild animals.

'You are probably asking the same as we all do.' Ausel's usually laughing face was grim and his keen green eyes were cold and hard, while a nervous tic high in his right cheek muscle betrayed his simmering fury. 'How did this happen, Demontaigu? The only people who knew were you, me and Estivet.'

'And myself,' I added, 'but only two days ago. Demontaigu will swear to that.'

'I do,' Demontaigu murmured. He raised his hand to his companions and led us up the side of the hollow. We stood on the rim. I stared out across the patchwork landscape of heather, gorse, brambles, marsh, stagnant pools and the occasional copse of trees.

'How did your companions know to come here?' I asked.

'Some of them were local men.' Demontaigu replied.

'Their names?' I asked.

'Morseby, Thorpe, Rippenhale, Lanercost and Easterbury.'

'Lanercost?' I queried.

'Yes, John Lanercost,' Demontaigu agreed. 'Why?'

'Any relation or kin to one of the Aquilae Petri?'

'The Gemstones?' Demontaigu faced me squarely. 'One of Gaveston's creatures?' He pulled a face. 'Our Lanercost was an experienced squire, a serjeant. He was born in these parts. He might be related to Gaveston's minion. Yes, yes.' He blinked across the breeze. 'Our man sheltered in a garret close to the Shambles in York. Lanercost organised sanctuary for others.

26

Most Templars moved north. York is a good place to hide. What are you saying, Mathilde? That Lanercost told his kinsman, who informed Gaveston, who then betrayed them all to Alexander of Lisbon and his Noctales?'

'Impossible!' I replied. 'Templar power in England has been shattered. Everything worth seizing has been taken. Why should the king or Gaveston be interested in betraying harassed Templars to the Noctales?' I turned away, uneasy, and stared across at a thick copse of wood, the path we'd taken from York snaking through it. I was about to look away when I started at a glint of steel.

'*Jesu miserere!*' I exclaimed, plucking at Demontaigu's sleeve. I looked up at the sky, then back again: nothing. Yet . . .

'What it is?' Demontaigu grasped my wrist.

I walked down into the shelter of the hollow, my abrupt departure attracting Ausel, who came hurrying over.

'What is the matter?' Demontaigu insisted.

'Those trees.' I waited until we'd walked a little deeper. 'I am sure mailed men lurk there.'

'No, no.' Ausel shook his head.

'Why not?' I retorted. 'I am not mad, Ausel, some maid calfing at the moon, full of fanciful notions that every bush is a bear. I am not hare-hearted; I know what I glimpsed. Who else would be hiding out here in the heathland?'

'Mathilde is keen-eyed.' Demontaigu, for all his doubts, believed me. 'It's logical. The Noctales must know we were coming here. They withdrew, waited and watched, just as they did when the others arrived here yesterday evening. A scout would alert them, and then they closed in.'

27

Demontaigu was convinced. He gestured back at the rim. 'We could return and gape, but that would warn them. It's best if we were gone from here as quickly as possible.'

'Might they attack us here?' I asked.

'No.' Demontaigu tightened the buckle on his belt. 'We are too many, armed and ready. They hope we will take the same road back, then they will trap us. They'll be waiting, all harnessed for war.'

I recalled the Noctales: a troop of killers, mercenaries, the scum from various cities, armed like men of war. They were accompanied by battle-dogs, great mastiffs with sharp teeth and crushing jaws, spiked collars around their muscle-thick necks. A swift riding horde of the sons of Cain.

'We'll warn the rest.' Demontaigu pointed across the hollow. 'It's best if we return by different paths. Once we are off the moors and reach the villages, the Noctales will withdraw. They do not want any witnesses to their murderous slaughter.'

Demontaigu hastily summoned the others. He stilled protests and objections, declaring that swiftness not battle was their prayer for the hour. The group would leave, separate, seek out travelling merchant groups or the outlying villages, and meet again in York. It was quickly agreed. Estivet murmured a brief benediction and we all remounted to the heart-tingling jingle of harness, the creak of leather and the ominous slither of weapons being loosened in their sheaths. Estivet again murmured a blessing, to which Ausel spat out a curse that the tongues of demons would pierce the Noctales' souls and they would grill in hell like bacon fat for all eternity. His sally provoked a few smiles. Hands were clasped, farewells made and we guided our horses out of the hollow and over the rim and scattered in a desperate, frenetic gallop.

Demontaigu and Ausel rode either side of me as we broke into a canter, streaming from the hollow in a thunder of hooves and flying dust. The stiff cold breeze whipped at my face. The ground beneath me became a blur, as did my two companions. My world was reduced to the thunder of our horses' hooves, a deep sense of danger, the blood drumming in my ears, my throat narrowing as if to cut off its breath. I gripped the reins and murmured a prayer at the swift and dread turn of events. I had to remind myself that I was *Domicella reginae*, yet fleeing for my life across a wilderness as bleak as the souls who hunted me. Killers who would cut my throat only a few miles from the king's own chamber. Eventually I calmed; I even wondered if I had been mistaken, then I heard the bell-like bark of great hunting dogs, a hollow, soul-searing sound that seemed to echo up from the caves of hell. Our horses began to slow, and we halted on the brow of a hill and turned. I caught my gasp of terror; it was not a time for the weak-hearted. Below us unfurled a scene from a nightmare. Men fleeing, swift shadows across the sun-dappled heath, whilst from the nearby woods streamed others, already breaking up as the hunting pack chose their quarry. More terrifying, before or alongside each cluster of horsemen, were those black racing shapes, the great war-hounds of the Noctales. Terror seized me. A group of four riders and a hound had already singled us out for pursuit. Demontaigu sat and stared, gauntleted fingers to his lips as if he might retch.

Ausel, however, leaned forward in the saddle, eyes narrowed, clicking his tongue.

'Our garrons,' he patted his horse's neck, 'are not as swift as theirs, but they are sturdier and more sure-footed. Those riders will never bring us to bay, which is why they have brought the dogs. They will close, panic our mounts and savage their legs. The dogs will bring us down. I've seen chieftains in Ireland do the same. Ah well.' Ausel grasped the reins and pulled his horse round. 'There is only one thing we can do.'

We continued our headlong gallop. Behind us the baying of the hound grew stronger as one of those long, sloping, ghastly shapes began to close. Ausel, however, led us on to a track-way that rose slightly between a marshy stagnant pool on our left and thick barbed gorse to our right. The moorland path was slightly off our general direction, but he urged us on up the track-way as it narrowed between two ancient, craggy outcrops of lichen-covered rock. We cantered through and down the path. Ausel reined in and dismounted, shouting at us to do likewise and demanding we prime the arbalests we carried. I fumbled with mine; Ausel collected it and Demontaigu's, then waved us back. He crouched at a kneel, two arbalests beside him; the other he raised, pointing at the gap between those rocks. He was as calm and assured as any Brabantine mercenary. A loud howl rang out above the sound of drumming hooves. In a flurry of dust, the war-dog leapt between the rocks, ears flapping, huge jaws bared, a charging mass of muscular black flesh, terrible in its fearful beauty. It seemed unaware of Ausel; trained to pursue horses, it charged directly on. Ausel released the catch, and the squat barbed bolt whirred like some deadly bird. The hound, struck in his jaw, was maddened enough to carry on. Ausel raised the second arbalest, primed and ready. The hound rose in a leap. Again, the click of the catch. This time the bolt shattered the beast's throat, yet still it hurtled on, its muscular body twisting to one side in a flurry of dust as it crashed into Ausel. Man and dog whirled in a dust cloud sprinkled with spurts of blood. They turned and rolled, Ausel's war cry drowned by an ominous snarling, then it was over. The hound lay on its side. Ausel sprawled face down. I tried to shout, but my mouth was too dry. Then Ausel lifted his grinning, blood-splattered face and pulled himself up, brushing the dirt off his clothes.

'No harm, no harm. Praise be to God.' His smile faded. He gestured at the arbalests and ordered us to prime them again. Demontaigu had recovered. Only later did I learn about his deep fear of dogs after being attacked by one in his childhood. He gathered his crossbow and mine, our whole existence taken up by the threatening drumming of approaching hooves, and had a swift word with Ausel. Armed with arbalests, the two Templars separated just as the horsemen, cloaks billowing, breasted the rise, charging so furiously they had little time to realise what had happened. Ausel and Demontaigu knelt, crossbows up. The catches clicked and the bolts spun out, cutting the air to bring down the two leading riders. The ensuing chaos and confusion tipped a third out of his saddle as his horse reared in terror. The two Templars sped forward, sword and dagger out. Demontaigu was a skilled knight, but Ausel was a warrior born and bred, one of those men who knew no fear and relished the song of battle. The hunters became trapped in a lure of their own making. The three fallen riders were quickly dispatched with shrieks, groans and spurts of hot blood. The fourth, desperate to control his mount, turned to flee, but he was trapped on both sides, and dragged off his horse. Ausel, kneeling on his chest, roared as he plunged his dagger time and again into the man's throat. Then he rose, staggered away and half crouched, staring strangely at Demontaigu, who moved along the corpses ensuring they were dead before whispering a requiem and sketching a blessing in the air. I walked over and stared down at one of the Noctales, his scarred face made uglier in death: the blood-spattered gaping lips, the blackening stumps of teeth.

'You'll kill no more!' I whispered to him.

'Go away!' Ausel had snatched a battle axe from his saddle horn.

I stared around.

'Their valuables?' I asked. 'Are you going to strip them . . . ?'

'And what?' Ausel sneered. 'Sell them in York? No, I want Alexander of Lisbon to see what I've done. So go.' He pointed back to our horses. 'Demontaigu, take your lady away. What she doesn't see she will not remember.' He lifted himself up. 'Hell has devoured these sinners like wolves devour sheep. Satan's henchmen will fill their gaping mouths with molten lead. I wish to leave Lisbon fair warning that he too will melt like wax before the fire.' He was almost talking to himself, his usually good-natured face tense and pallid.

Demontaigu took me by the elbow and steered me further down the track-way, where our horses were hobbled. I went to look back but he almost pushed me into a small culvert between the straggling gorse. I sat down on a rock. Demontaigu collected his small wineskin and made me take a couple of mouthfuls, then we waited in silence. Sounds echoed from up the track-way. The terrors began to leave me. I grew aware of the wine taste in my mouth, how heavy my legs felt. The trees and bushes of the wastelands were bending under a breeze. I smelt a mingle of horse sweat, leather and the fragrance of wild flowers. A cormorant cried, to be answered by the raucous call of circling crows. Time passed. Demontaigu sat, eyes closed, mouth moving wordlessly in silent prayer. Ausel joined us. He'd used the clothes of one of the dead men as an apron. Now he tore these blood-soaked garments off and threw them into a bush.

'I'm done,' he murmured. 'It's finished.'

Demontaigu gathered the horses and we mounted. Ausel loudly announced that the Noctales would still be involved in their pursuit of the others. He proved correct. We rode safely out across the deserted heathland, reached a village and joined a line of carts taking produce to the Minster from one of its outlying farms. Ausel and Demontaigu rode ahead, talking quietly amongst themselves. I drifted gently into a half-sleep, shaken awake by the sounds around me. We reached Micklegate Bar, and went up its main thorough-fare and on to Ouse Bridge. Beggars clustered on the steps of St Michael's chapel at the entrance to the bridge. One of these darted forward and grasped Ausel's bridle, pleading for alms. I noticed how strong and muscular he was, his skin burnt dark by the sun of Outremer rather than the freezing wind of York. He was undoubtedly a Templar in disguise, passing on information. Ausel searched for a penny, tossed it at the mendicant then urged his horse on.

We stabled our mounts at The Road to Damascus, a stately pilgrims' tavern fronted by a broad cobbled yard and flanked on either side by flower gardens. The tap room was high-ceilinged; no mush of dried reeds covered the floor; its black and yellow lozenge-shaped tiles were clean and polished. At the far end stood a long counter of burnished oak, gleaming in the light of pure oil lamps and beeswax candles. Barrels and buckets all ribbed with ash, hazel and iron lined one wall. Smoked ham hanging from the broad-beamed roof gave the room a pleasant tasty smell. We hired a table in an alcove with a small oriel window overlooking the garden. I remember such details well. The customers were a few guildsmen, wealthy travellers and pilgrims. Mine host wore a felt hat and a clean cloth apron with spotless white napkins criss-crossed over his chest. Around his muscular wrists hung two more to keep his fingers clean. He took our custom: stoups of ale, amber-glazed bowls of meat and vegetable broth, manchet loaves, still warm and wrapped in a linen cloth, as well as a small pot of butter. We cleaned our hands in the rosewater provided. Ausel quickly blessed the food. I went to talk, to break the silence, but Ausel leaned across. He still looked battle-crazed, eyes large and dark in his pale face.

'The tongue,' he whispered. 'How small it is, yet a petty flame can consume a forest. The tongue,' he continued, taking out his horn spoon, 'is a whole wicked world in itself. It can infect the entire body with poison. It can catch fire from hell and set the world ablaze.' His eyes were staring over my shoulder.

I turned. A hooded man had wandered over but then shifted away. We ate in silence. Ausel got up, nodded at me, patted Demontaigu on the shoulder and left.

'What is it?' I asked.

Demontaigu lifted a finger to his lips. I glanced around. The hooded man had come drifting over again. I stared hard at this individual dressed in dark green buckram and short leather boots. The cowl he wore was deep; I could only glimpse pinched white features. He turned to face us squarely; shadow-rimmed eyes stared out from a ghost-white face.

'Your friend has left?' the hooded man murmured. 'Has he gone looking for the Key of David?'

'No, friend.' Demontaigu lifted his stoup of ale in toast. 'The Key is not needed. The Tabernacle of Solomon is gone!'

The hooded man startled. 'Gone?' The whisper was hoarse.

'Destroyed,' Demontaigu replied tersely, 'out on the heathland.'

'Then, friend,' the hooded man lifted his hand, palm extended in peace, 'I'll be gone.' And he slipped across the tap room and out through the door.

'Who?' I asked.

'Roger Furnival,' Demontaigu replied. 'Outlaw, wolf's-head, defrocked priest. He was to meet us here with our comrades out of Scotland. Now . . .' He shrugged.

'And Ausel's strange words about the tongue?'

'Someone betrayed us, Mathilde, perhaps not intentionally. Ausel wants us to return and question Geoffrey Lanercost.'

He collected his gloves and made to rise.

'Bertrand.' I gripped his wrist. 'Ausel, what did he do out there on the track-way?'

'Ausel's words are like silver from a furnace,' Demontaigu whispered, 'seven times refined. He has sworn terrible vengeance against Alexander of Lisbon.'

'On the track-way?' I insisted.

'He severed the head of that war-dog and those of its four dead masters. He placed them along the track-way where it narrows between the outcrops.' Demontaigu paused. He glanced pityingly at me from the corner of his eye. 'A Celtic thing,' he murmured. 'He also removed their genitals and thrust them between their gaping dead lips. Ausel has sent warning to Lisbon that our fight is *lutte à l'outrance* – to the death . . .'

Chapter 2

There was no safe place in England for Gaveston.

Living at court was a dappled existence of colours ranging from the brightest silver-gold to the deepest black. Glorious displays of power as brilliantly hued banners and pennants flapped bravely under a searing blue sky. Tables covered with the purest damask groaning under jewelled plate, bowls and goblets all brimming with the sweetest viands, succulent fruits and the richest wines from Bordeaux and the Rhine. Brilliant, dazzling tapestries decorated walls hanging down to floors tiled in the most exquisite fashion. Along such rich galleries, princes, ladies and lords paraded all dressed in cloth of gold and costly jewel-encrusted fabrics. In the courtyards outside, powerful destriers, splendidly harnessed, reared and neighed as knights in glittering mail prepared to break lances, jousting in nearby tilt-yards where the sand glowed like amber. Trumpets blew. Horns sounded. Bells chimed. In the courtly sanctuaries, priests in splendid copes under soaring rood screens offered the risen Christ back to His Father. Light poured through windows illuminated with flashing colours. Incense, thick and white, fragranced the air. Choirs intoned 'Christus Vincit'. Close by, clerks in oak-panelled chambers grasped pens to write important letters of state sealed with purple wax. Outside the chamber clustered mailed knights and armoured men-at-arms eager to do the king's will. Yet there were other aspects of life at court, like the sides of fortune's dice just waiting to be turned. Ghastly killings out on lonely heathlands or in filthy alleyways, dingy taverns or rat-infested garrets. A world where assassins, capuchined and visored, flitted like shadows through the door, dagger or garrotte at the ready. Poisoned wine served with tainted meats. Scaffolds soaring dark against the sky, heavy with corpses, whilst across the square severed heads above lofty gateways dripped blood to patter to the ground like rain. Treason and treachery, bloodshed and betrayal, hypocrisy and hubris came wandering like twin demons garbed in all the horrors of death and the anguish of the tomb. I'd seen it all, be it in gorgeous pavilions with exquisite chambers or cobwebbed closets and garrets where the vermin came creeping under the doors.

This contrast in mood weighed heavily on me when we

returned to the Franciscan priory with its hallowed, peaceful cloisters all fresh with the herbal potion the good brothers used to scrub the grey flagstones. I made enquiries of Boudon the steward, to be arrogantly informed that the queen was closeted with the king and his councillors, in other words Gaveston. After further enquiries I discovered that Geoffrey Lanercost and the other Aquilae Petri were gathered in the prior's rose garden to celebrate Lanercost's recent return from Scotland. A lay brother led us to that serene, lovely place with its flower beds and lawns, neatly tended herb plots, garlanded arbours and shady walks. In the centre was a circle of white pavestone with cushioned benches and quilted turf seats. Close by, a fountain carved in the shape of a Jesse tree, its water gushing into a grey-stone bowl, where small golden carp darted amongst the fresh leaves. All five Aquilae were seated there, talking and laughing with Brother Stephen Dunheved, who sat plucking at a viol. The Dominican was skilfully mimicking and ridiculing the professional gleemen, who could pull their faces into a smile or a grimace depending on what song they were singing. Dunheved was most skilled in that. Others were there too. Oh yes, in those early months of 1312, I came to know more closely that unholy trinity, those imps of Satan, falseness incarnate, the Beaumonts! Henry, his brother Louis and their sister Isabella, known more popularly as Lady Vesci after her marriage, of sorts, to some hapless nobleman. The Beaumonts were the spoilt children of Europe, with the royal blood of England, France, Spain and Sicily in their veins. Rumour whispered that they also had Satan's blood. They could be charming, courteous, chivalrous and brave – when they wanted. They were cats who would lick your face but scratch your back. They'd ransack hell for a gold piece and skin a nag for a farthing.

On that particular day, the Beaumont coven sat close together in the rose garden. Henry wore a green tunic sporting golden fleur-de-lis over a snow-white cambric shirt, its neck, cuffs and waistband of cloth of gold; black hose cased his muscular legs and Castilian boots, still spurred, his feet. Lady Vesci was dressed in a gown proclaiming the same heraldic device with silver edging, a cloak of deep murrey around her shoulders, her hair bound up in a white wimple under a light blue veil. She dressed like a nun but had the heart of a courtesan. Louis, the churchman, was slightly fatter, garbed in the black gown of an Augustinian canon, though the fabric was of the purest wool and his shoes were of soft leather, whilst the silver cord around his plump waist boasted golden love-knots. The three all looked the same: flaring red hair and white skin, their freckled faces full of impudence, slightly slanted light green eyes that made you think they were quietly laughing at you; they usually were! The Aquilae Petri lounged on either side of them, half dressed in shirts, tunics and multicoloured hose. Jerkins and cloaks, war-belts and boots lay about. Gaveston's fighting boys, relaxing in the late afternoon sun after they'd eaten and drunk deeply. Jugs, goblets and platters were stacked on the ground. Two of Gaveston's greyhounds nosed amongst the remnants of roast quail, slices of cooked ham and half-ripe fruit. Somewhere behind a trellis fence a peacock shrieked, whilst the first swallows of the year darted above the gurgling fountain. Dunheved smiled as we came through the wicket gate and continued with his song of nonsense.

>'When salmon hunt in the wood
>And herring fly and blow the horn . . .'

The lines were greeted with laughter. Dunheved was about to continue when, sharp-eyed as a hawk, he sensed our grimness.

'Like ghosts at the feast,' he murmured. 'Why, Mistress Mathilde, Master Bertrand, what is it? News about Lancaster?'

Henry Beaumont leapt to his feet, head slightly tilted back. 'Is that whoreson on the march?' He glanced at his sister and brother; the family were the king's body and soul. Thomas of Lancaster wanted them exiled because they exercised 'a perfidious and malignant influence over the king, providing evil council on affairs of the Crown'. In truth, they simply revelled in basking in the royal sun and snatching whatever trifles came their way.

'Lancaster is not on the march,' Demontaigu replied wearily. 'Not yet. We look for Geoffrey Lanercost. I have news about his kinsman John.'

'I am Lanercost.' One of the Aquilae rose lazily to his feet. He was dark-haired, thickset, with a slightly hooked nose in a full, wine-flushed face. Shadows ringed deep-set eyes and sweat glistened above the points of his loosened shirt. A man who had travelled far and fast, then drunk deep to refresh himself. I studied him. I recalled the horror-struck face of one of those dead Templars and saw a close likeness.

41

'Well, sir.' Lanercost lifted his hands. 'You have news about my brother?'

'Perhaps in private, sir?'

'Here is private.' Lanercost's reply provoked laughter. 'My friends are private. What news?'

'Your brother John.' I spoke up, wishing to end this nonsense. 'Your brother John,' I repeated, 'God have mercy, is dead.'

All the arrogance and hauteur disappeared. Lanercost's face sagged. Such a stricken look, it cut me to the heart. One of the others, I think it was fair-haired Rosselin, sprang to his feet as Lanercost, hand to his head, swayed slightly.

'No, no,' Lanercost whispered, 'no, no.' He gestured at us. 'You'd best come away.'

We left the glories of the rose garden for a grey-stone porch in the prior's cloisters. Demontaigu tried to be gentle, but murder is murder. Violent death shatters everything. Lanercost heard him out, head in hands; when he glanced up, his face was soaked with tears.

'You're a Templar, Demontaigu, aren't you?' He forced a laugh. 'Your secret is not really a secret, but who cares? Many in court have kin in that order. Poor John.' His voice grew stronger as anger curdled his grief. 'Alexander of Lisbon,' he breathed, 'and his Noctales. I'll provoke the blood feud. I'll see them all hang.'

'Hush now.' Demontaigu drew closer. 'Leave Lisbon to the Templars. He is tainted and marked for the sword. More importantly, your brother was of these parts, a citizen of York, yes?'

Lanercost nodded.

'He was guide for the others,' Demontaigu continued. 'Ausel, one of my comrades, told me that. Your brother knew Devil's Hollow; did he tell you what he was doing?'

Lanercost bit his lip, his mind swirling like a lurcher. A look of anguish as memories came flooding back. He realised the implication of what Demontaigu was saying. He should have told us the truth, but of course he felt deeply ashamed, guilty.

'He told,' he whispered. 'Yes, he told me.'

'And did you tell anyone else?'

'No, no.' Lanercost sprang to his feet, all agitated. 'I . . . I . . .' he stammered, 'I may have told someone, one of the others. I cannot . . .' He made to walk away. I caught his arm; he did not resist. He just stared in rank despair at me.

'Did you tell . . . ?'

'Tell?' he muttered. 'I told no one.' He broke free of my grip and strode away.

There was little more we could do. Demontaigu and I kissed in the shadows and went our separate ways. I rarely saw him over the next few days. He withdrew from the queen's chancery with this excuse or that, busy with his brethren, or so I learnt later. Most of them had escaped the Noctales, but three of their companions simply vanished, never to be seen again. God have mercy on their poor souls. They must have been trapped and their corpses tossed into some peat bog. The other cadavers out in the hollow also disappeared, an act of malignant vindictiveness by Lisbon, who had used them as bait. Lanercost returned to ask Demontaigu about his brother's corpse, and when he learnt the truth became even more sorrowful. Such tragedies, however, were drowned by other news. The great earls had mustered their troops, both foot and horse, moving slowly north. My mistress was rarely seen, being closeted with Edward and Gaveston. We would meet in the evening, when I would anxiously enquire of her health, but Isabella, though beautiful and graceful, was sturdy as an oak. Sixteen she was, of full height, sophisticated and elegant in all her mannerisms. Pregnancy had brought a fresh bloom to those blue eyes and that golden face; her hair seemed more like spun gold, and her body, when I bathed it, glowed with health. The queen's abdomen grew swollen to 'a slight thickness', as she laughingly described it. She was more concerned at the dangers threatening. Only once did she lose her temper, snapping at me like an angry crow as she ranted about Edward's fecklessness and Gaveston's futile attempts to resist exile.

'My lord Gaveston,' Isabella whispered through clenched teeth as she sat on the edge of the great bed one evening, 'should go once more on his travels and stay there. Now listen, Mathilde.' She plucked at the gold-fringed tassels of the counterpane. 'The earls will try to trap us. We must, at all times, be ready to flee.'

'Your meetings with the king?' I asked.

'A dialogue with fools,' Isabella retorted. 'Schemes to bring the great earls to battle, to ally with the Scottish rebels, even . . .' She paused. 'Yes, Edward has even asked my beloved father for troops from France. Nonsense!' She waved a hand. 'Mathilde, I am *enceinte*. I should be relaxing in flowery bowers at Sheen, Windsor or Westminster, not scuttling across the heathland like some rabbit darting from hole to hole.' She glanced directly at me. 'The glass is darkening; we must bring an end to this foolery.'

So she said it, that brief remark. The dice, cogged or not, had rolled and Isabella was committed. Little did I realise then how the game might end. Now my duties at the court were to advise and protect my mistress. Sometimes this involved sinister secrets and murderous shadows, but these swirled through a tangle of other ordinary matters that filled my days, for my mistress now ruled a great household. She was *domina* of extensive estates, be it the manors of Torpel and Upton in England or the county of Ponthieu in France. She presided over an exchequer, a chancery and accounts chambers. The great departments of her household were headed by royal clerks such as William Boudon, John de Fleet and Ebulo de Montibus. She employed three cooks, two apothecaries, a number of butlers, pantlers, spicerers and marshals of the hall, grooms for the stables, laundresses and washerwomen. The large coffers, chests and caskets of her household were crammed with precious items, be it the ring of St Dunstan or exquisite embroidered cloths from Flemish looms. Isabella owned falcons, lanniers, hawks, greyhounds and a string of horses: sumpter, palfreys and destriers. My task was not to get involved in petty details but to survey and assist as my mistress directed. I ensured that after Easter Sunday no fires were lit, that the hearths be cleared and decorated with garlands, whilst linen curtains were to be hung over windows to keep out the spring draughts. I kept a particularly sharp eye on the kitchen, buttery and spicery. The most serious threat to Isabella's health was tainted food or practices. I insisted that all who served the queen above the Nef, that gorgeous gold salt-cellar carved in the shape of a ship, regularly clean and scrub both their hands and all vessels and cutlery intended for her table.

Other tasks outside the household also concerned me. The arrival of the court at the priory attracted a legion of beggars, some genuine, others counterfeit. They would cluster at the gates pleading for alms. I was responsible for disbursements of 'queen's bread' and 'queen's pence'. I would often supervise such charity after the Angelus bell; other times I would delegate it to others. One beggar, however, caught my attention. He called himself 'the Pilgrim from the Wastelands', a grim, dark-featured, slender individual, easily noticeable because of his wild staring eyes and the birthmark on the right of his face, a large mulberry-coloured stain. He'd definitely been in Outremer under the scorching sun of Palestine, deep-voiced with a commanding presence. I glimpsed him on a number of occasions, especially as the queen's almoner reported how the Pilgrim had the audacity to petition 'to see the queen or one of her ilk'. Of course, he was refused. Other urgent business dominated our days, nevertheless I could not forget his pleading eyes and strident voice. However, at the time, I did not know what part he had to play in the murderous mystery play unfolding around us, whilst the busy routine of each day left little time for such petitions even to be considered.

Such ordinary tasks kept me busy for the first few days after my return from the moors, but that day had not been forgotten. A harvest of evil had been sown, and sin is a fertile shoot. My mistress and I were attending the Jesus mass in the friary church. We knelt on prie-dieus just within the rood screen. Brother Stephen Dunheved, resplendent in the robes of the Easter liturgy, was bringing the mass to an end. The tower bells were tolling; Dunheved was raising his hand in benediction. I was lost in my own thoughts, staring at the carved wooden statue of Judas used to hold twelve candles that were extinguished during Tenebrae on Maundy Thursday, a symbol of the Apostles' desertion of Christ, when piercing screams from the cobbled yard outside carried through the church. Dunheved quickly finished his blessing. I glanced at the queen; she nodded and I joined the others who hurried through the corpse door out into the great courtyard that stretched alongside the church. Lanercost lay there in a tangle of cloak, boots sticking out, head eerily turned, skull shattered so that the blood seeped out in rivulets. A serjeant-at-arms came hurrying over. I ordered him to keep back the crowds while I approached the grisly scene. Of course Lanercost was dead, his neck broken, his skull smashed.

'What happened?' I stood up and walked away as Dunheved, who'd been informed about the incident, came hurrying out of the church still in his vestments, a phial of holy oils in his hands.

'What happened?' I repeated.

Dunheved was kneeling by the corpse, swiftly anointing the stricken man. I murmured a requiem and glanced around. A crowd was now gathering to gape at the corpse. Some were pointing to the top of the steepled bell tower built on the south side of the church. According to the serjeant, Lanercost had fallen from there. I glanced up. The tower rose sheer above me. Small arrow-slit windows on its sides, and in the bell chamber itself, two great oblong windows on each of the four walls. The bells had ceased tolling but the birds nesting in the tower still fluttered noisily. I glanced down at Lanercost. He was dressed in a brown cloak over shirt and hose; his boots were unspurred and he wore no war-belt. The serjeant-at-arms pushed back the crowds. I glanced over my shoulder, to where Isabella and two of her ladies-in-waiting clustered at the church door. The queen stared bleakly across. I quietly gestured with my hand that she should not approach. She nodded, turned and went back into the church. I abruptly realised then how my mistress' mood had recently changed, to become more withdrawn and reflective. A trumpet sounded, a sharp, braying blast that brought everyone to their knees, myself included, as Edward and Gaveston came striding across, Father Prior hurrying behind them.

Dunheved finished his ministrations. He murmured about changing his vestments and hastily left. Both king and favourite had apparently dressed hurriedly in long purple velvet sleeveless robes over shirt and hose, their feet pushed into soft buskins. They slipped and slithered on the muck-strewn yard. Both men were unshaven, hair bedraggled, their eyes bleary as if they'd spent the previous evening deep in their cups. Gaveston crouched beside the corpse. He moved Lanercost's head and fingered the ghastly bruises on the face, neck, chest and legs. I had already concluded that Lanercost must have fallen sheer from the tower and hit the sloping roof of the church before tumbling over for the second long fall to the ground. Gaveston stretched across and tipped me under the chin; tears brimmed his eyes.

'A fall?' he asked.

'Presumably, my lord.'

'Presumably!' Gaveston sneered. 'Or murder, or suicide? I suppose I will have to accept whatever that coxcomb of a coroner Ingelram Berenger decides.'

I stared back. I shared the same low opinion of Berenger as he did but I had the sense to keep a still tongue in my head. The king's coroner was the king's coroner; he would do what he had to and so would I.

'My lord,' I whispered, 'can you tell me why Lanercost should be in the bell tower?'

Gaveston glanced up. 'I don't know,' he replied. 'I haven't talked to him for the last two days.'

Gaveston could be a liar, but I sensed he was telling the truth. Yet there was something else, a look of guilt mingled with his compassion. As if to avoid my scrutiny, he returned to the corpse. I got to my feet. Two knight bannerets from the king's chamber arrived, fully harnessed and armoured, as if the Scots had attacked, to disperse the crowd. The morning was chilly after a long night's rain. Lay brothers had wheeled fiery braziers into the great yard. The charcoal crackled noisily, the sparks flying up. A bell tolled deep in the friary. Oveners from a nearby bakery drifted across whilst I studied the mangled corpse of that young man who'd fallen, been pushed or jumped. Gaveston rose to his feet. I caught a look of profound sadness in those beautiful eyes, lips twisted as he fought back his grief. I sensed the Gascon's deep desolation. Here he was, 'the king's own brother', Earl of Cornwall, royal favourite, yet he was hiding deep in a Franciscan friary in York. Nevertheless, even here he wasn't safe. I had no proof, just a suspicion that murder had followed Lanercost into that tower and sent him whirling to his death. Gaveston sensed the same. Three years ago he had been cock of the walk, Lord of Westminster, a man who could bring anyone down, but now even his own squires were not safe. Isabella was correct: the glass was darkening. God knows what the future held!

A scurrier came hurrying across. He knelt on the rain-soaked cobbles before the king and whispered his message. 'My lord.' Edward stepped closer, one ringed hand extended to grasp his favourite. 'Peter, my brother.' His voice carried an urgency. 'Other matters await; we have news from the south. Mathilde, *ma coeur*.' Edward's face grew soft, smiling, full of that lazy charm that could so easily disarm you. 'For me, Mathilde,' he whispered. He fumbled in the wallet beneath his coat, drew out a small cast of the secret seal and handed it to me. 'Your licence. Search, Mathilde, find the truth behind this. Now, Peter . . .'

Gaveston crouched down again. He pressed his lips against Lanercost's blood-splattered hair, a mother's kiss. He stroked the side of the dead man's face, smiled tearfully up at me, rose and followed the king across the yard. Father Prior agreed to have Lanercost's corpse taken to the corpse house. I slipped the wax seal into my gown pocket and walked back into the church. As far as I could see, the nave stretching up to the sanctuary was deserted. Isabella and her companions must have left by the coffin door. I walked deeper into the darkness and stared round. An ancient, hallowed place, the shadows lurking in the corner ready to creep out once the light faded. The incensed air was full of memories of plainchant, bells and the sacred words of the mass. All now lay deathly quiet. Battered statues of angels and saints, their faces bathed in candle-glow, stared stonily down at me. Gargoyles grimaced through the gloom. I closed my eyes. Earlier today Lanercost came into this church. He walked across into the gloomy recess and up those tower steps to the belfry. Why? Did he feel guilty at his brother's murder and committed suicide? Or had he been enticed in, trapped and hurled to his death? But why should someone murder Lanercost, one of the Aquilae Petri? I started. The squeak and slither of mice scurrying in the shadowed light echoed eerily.

'Good morrow, Mistress Mathilde.'

I whirled round, hand to my mouth, as the Beaumonts sauntered out from the gloomy corner where the baptismal font stood. All three were swathed in rich green cloaks. I realised they must have been meeting secretly in that deserted nook of the church.

'My lords, my lady.' I bowed, using courtesy to mask my alarm.

'We were here in the church.' Henry pulled the muffler down from across his mouth.

'Of course you were, my lord. Praying?'

'We all must pray, Mathilde.'

'Some more than others, my lord?'

'True.' Lady Vesci smiled. She came forward and grasped my hands tightly as if in friendship. In truth she wanted me to stay. She pulled her face into a look of concern. 'That poor squire, one of Gaveston's henchmen?' Her voice betrayed duplicity; she was in the same camp as Gaveston, but I doubted if she was his friend.

51

'What happened?' Louis asked in that sanctimonious voice some priests adopt, as if they consider the laity as witless as a flock of pigeons.

'*Domine*,' I replied, freeing my hands. 'Lanercost apparently fell from the belfry.'

'Why was he there?' Louis whispered.

'He did not tell me,' I retorted. 'I have yet to search, but surely, if you were in church, my lords, you must have seen him enter the bell tower?'

All three shook their heads in unison. On any other occasion I would have found it amusing, but the Beaumonts were never amusing, just dangerous in their vaulting ambition. I bowed.

'I must go.'

'My lady.' Sir Henry moved closer, green eyes sharp and unsmiling. 'Is my lord Gaveston secretly treating with the Scots?'

'For all I know,' I replied, 'he could be treating with the lord Satan. He does not discuss such matters with me. I have other duties.'

'So do we all.' Henry smiled. 'But . . .' He just shrugged and gestured dismissively at me.

Again I bowed and walked over to the darkening recess leading to the door of the bell tower. I paused, my hand on the latch, then turned and glanced back. All three Beaumonts had followed me and were now standing close, scrutinising me carefully. I recalled certain information Isabella had given me. The Beaumonts were powerful lords north of the border. During the old king's time they'd been given extensive estates, manor houses, castles, barns and granges.

I realised why they were interested in Gaveston. If Edward settled with Bruce, what would happen to their estates?

'I recognise your interest, my lord, about Gaveston and Scottish affairs, but that does not concern me.'

Henry shrugged. 'One day, Mathilde, it might! My lord Gaveston's hours are surely numbered. His grace the king cannot wander up and down the roads of this country like some witless pilgrim or hapless mendicant. He should be in the south, at Westminster.'

'Then, my lord,' I retorted, 'that is a matter for you to tell him, not me. I bid you adieu.'

I pressed down the latch, the door swung open and I walked in. The stairwell was so dark I almost screamed at the shape that rose out of the gloom. I stepped back. The grey-garbed lay brother looked like a gargoyle come down from the wall: a long, thin, bony face, popping eyes, a mouth that never kept still and ears sticking out from the side of his head like the handles of a jug. He scratched his bald head.

'My lady, I'm sorry, I'm sorry.' Again the mouth moved as if he was talking to himself.

'Who are you?' I asked, stepping closer.

'Brother Eusebius. I am the bell man. I ring the bell of the church. I always do. I always have.'

'So you know what's happened?' I asked. 'Why did you not come out?'

'I was frightened.' The man's voice trembled. 'I was truly frightened, my lady. I did come out. I peered through the door. I saw the king and my lord Gaveston. I realised that the fallen man was one of theirs. They might suspect I had done something. I'm sorry.'

53

'Hush now.' I stretched out and touched one vein-streaked, spotted hand. 'You are the bell-keeper, Brother Eusebius?'

'No, the assistant bell-keeper.' Eusebius gestured at the heavy, thick ropes that hung down. 'I ring these before the Jesus mass.' He smiled foolishly. 'Peter and Paul we call the bells. I'm also,' he declared, 'keeper of the charnel house, which you can find in the transept. Look for the wall painting, the Harrowing of Hell.' He gestured with his hand. 'You are most welcome to come in. I have few visitors here.'

I closed the door and looked around. Eusebius' chamber was really nothing more than a closet containing a pallet bed, a stool and a rickety table. A dingy, shabby place, its corners laced with dust-laden cobwebs. I gave him a coin; he chattered like a magpie, describing his duties. I peered up at the thick wooden flap pulled down to reveal a square opening in the middle of the roof for the ropes to hang through. Access was provided by a stout wooden ladder. The tower was ancient, a soaring four-sided edifice. The floors were of hard oak. Five levels in all, with the sixth serving as the belfry. Eusebius explained how the masons had dispensed with a stone floor as too unwiedly. I nodded in understanding. Such constructions were highly dangerous. Stone platforms were heavy and difficult to construct, and if one collapsed, the consequences would be hideous. He then described how he rang the Jesus bell, the bell at the end of mass and other peals, as well as the calls for Vespers and Compline. No, he shook his head as he used his foot to shove away a beer jug peeping from the beneath the cot bed, he did not live here, though he often used the tower to rest and meditate. He explained how earlier that morning he'd arrived just before mass, but had found nothing untoward. He had tolled the bell at the introit and the consecration, as well as to mark the final blessing. He'd kept the door open because he knew enough of the Latin rite to hear Brother Stephen (no, Eusebius assured me, he did not really know the Dominican) pronounce the *ite missa est* – the mass is ended. The tolling of Peter and Paul was coming to an end when he heard the screaming outside.

'*Pax et pax et pax* – peace and peace and peace – all shattered. Fly he did, like poor Brother Theobald.'

'Theobald?'

'Theobald was a novice here many, many years ago,' Eusebius gossiped on. 'He fell in love, he did, with a moonmaid who became his leman. When she left him, Theobald climbed to the top of the tower and tried to fly like an eagle. Before he fell, he carved some words in the belfry. You can see them there.'

'You mean he committed suicide?'

'Now, you hush!' Eusebius raised one black-nailed finger to his lips. 'You hush! Theobald's ghost haunts this place, so be careful what you say.'

I thanked him and took heed of his warning about how the swinging bells could be dangerous. I climbed the ladder to the first floor. A grim, chilling experience, the cold air seeping through the arrow-slit windows. Eusebius, his voice like that of a ghost, echoed up, reminding me to be careful and telling me that he was now leaving for the buttery to break his fast. Each of the floors of the tower was the same: dirt-filled, cobwebbed, nothing but shards of rubbish and heaps of bird droppings. At last I reached the bell chamber.

The ceiling rose to a cavernous vault above me. The heavy
bells, and the wood and cordage to which they were attached,
looked like some grim engine of war. There was hardly any
room to move. The windows in each of the four walls now
looked much bigger than the apertures glimpsed from the
courtyard below; each was about two yards high, the same
across, the brickwork on either side about two feet in thickness. The slate ledges, slightly sloping away to drain any
rainwater, were broad enough to allow a man to stand on.
The sills were at the same level as the two bells hanging
side by side, so if these were swung, anyone standing between
them and the ledges would be struck. Had this happened
to Lanercost? I walked carefully around, examining the floor,
studying the droppings and clumps of rotting feathers as
well as spots of oil, paint and polish used to grease the bells
and the apparatus that carried them. The bells themselves
were massive, their yawning bronze mouths tinged a greyish-
blue due to the elements. The sharp rims of both were decorated with the lettering of their names, carved by some
ancient smith above the date on which they had been consecrated.

I can still recall that bell chamber. A lonely, sinister place
made even more so by some bird, wings splayed, swooping
in to dim the light, only to wheel away with raucous screeching.
Was it also an abode of murder? Had someone been up here
with Lanercost? What had truly happened here? Using my
hand to rest against the wall, I edged carefully around to the
window that Lanercost must have fallen from. I examined
the slippery, sloping ledge but could detect nothing untoward.
I leaned over to inspect the heart-stopping drop, first to the

black-slated roof of the nave, then to the great courtyard below, where the occasional friar hurrying across looked so small. I eased myself back and stared at the rough, undressed walls of ashlar, those bells hanging so silently, the corners choked with the dust of centuries. I recalled Eusebius' remark about Theobald. I found nothing until I returned to the window from which Lanercost must have fallen. High on the smooth lintel stone, I detected some letters carved so many years previously: 'Theobald, who loved so much and lost so much'. My fingers traced the inscription. I wondered if Lanercost had known of such a story. Had he been so overcome with guilt at the death of his brother that he'd climbed up here and committed suicide? Yet Lanercost was a young warrior hardened in the service of Gaveston – so was it murder? Yet again, he was a man of war and would have defended himself vigorously, and if murder was the explanation, why had he scaled the ladder up into this narrow forbidden room in the first place? Surely he wouldn't have come up here with an enemy. This was the root of the mystery.

I startled at a creak, steadied myself then gazed in horror – the bells were moving slightly, swinging backwards and forwards. I was still standing at the window where Lanercost must have fallen. The bells were slowly swaying as if in a dream, like monsters roused from their slumber. They swung, dipped and came out towards me; their sharp rims seemed more like teeth. I glimpsed the heavy metal clappers even as I realised that if I stayed there, as Lanercost might have done, the bells would tip me over the rim. Why were they moving? It was about Nones, yet no peals should mark such an hour. I edged around the wall even as the bells began to move faster, their heavy metal edges skimming the air like deadly sharpened blades. They did not move in accord but one in either direction. I was in no real danger as long as I did not panic or make a mistake. I reached the opening and clambered down the ladder to the floor below.

'Brother Eusebius!' I screamed.

The first faint toll struck, then fell silent. I glanced at the ropes that fell through the gap to the floor below. Whoever was pulling them had now stopped. I reached the bottom breathless, the sweat on my coarse woollen kirtle cooling in the icy air of the tower. For a brief moment memories surged back of running down a ladder in my father's farm while he urged me to be careful, shouting so loudly my mother came rushing out of the house, clothes flapping. I blinked. I felt feverish and agitated. I drew my dagger from its concealed sheath on the belt beneath my cloak. I turned to the left and right but no one was there. The ropes were still moving slightly. The door leading back into the church hung half open. I went through. The nave held so many gloomy corners a host of enemies could lurk there unseen. I opened the main door of the church and went out on to the porch. The Aquilae Petri stood at the bottom of the steps, staring up at me.

'Have you been in the church?' I accused. I gazed around. The great cobbled square was busy with the good brothers going about their usual duties. Barrows stood piled high with vegetables; a cart of manure from the stables trundled across. A lay brother, raucously singing a hymn, pushed bracken into the braziers. I could see no one hurrying away.

I felt unsteady, as if I was in a dream. The horrors of that lonely belfry contrasted so sharply with the normal duties of a busy friary and those four young men staring up at me curiously.

'Mistress what is wrong?' Rosselin, blond-haired and ruddy-faced, his thickset body swathed in a cloak, stepped forward. The others had their cloaks thrown back. They were all harnessed and armed, wearing leather breastplates, war-belts strapped on as if ready for combat. 'Mistress,' Rosselin walked up the steps, spurs clinking, 'we came to see where Lanercost died. What is the matter? We have not been in the church.' He pointed back at Middleton, whose head was completely shaven. 'Nicholas believed he heard the bell chime.' I stared at Rosselin's companion, the strangest of the Aquilae. Middleton's jerkin was festooned with medals and amulets, a pair of Ave beads twined round his war-belt.

'Nothing, nothing.' I leaned against the stone pillar of the church door and glanced up at the babewyn glaring down at me; it had the face of a monkey, with pointed ears, protuberant eyes and popping tongue.

'Come away,' I murmured. I turned and walked back into the church. The Aquilae followed in a jingle of spurs, a creak of leather and a slither of steel as two of them unsheathed their swords and daggers. I sat at the foot of a squat, drum-like pillar. Further up the church I heard a door open and the patter of sandalled feet as the sacristan and his assistants pruned the candles in the sanctuary. I gestured at the squires to join me. Despite their wariness and war-like appearance, they squatted down. Gaveston must have told them about the king's commission to me under the secret seal.

I made myself comfortable. It was so strange to discuss such matters like farmers gathering in the nave of a church to do business, but the order, harmony and etiquette of the English court had been violently shattered. The king and his favourite were like fugitives fleeing from one sanctuary to another. Fortune had turned her wheel yet again. The Aquilae also sensed such a change, a sense of loss that their days of power, of strutting around the throne, were over. They too were marked men, hotly pursued by the forces of the earls, and now one of their coven had been mysteriously killed. They were both curious and highly nervous.

'How did Lanercost die?' Rosselin voiced their thoughts. He spoke louder than he intended, his words echoing through that cavernous place.

'I don't know,' I replied wearily. 'He may, God forbid, have taken his own life.' My words were greeted with shakes of the head and loud objections.

'Or he may have been murdered.'

They fell silent.

'If so,' I continued, 'why, how and by whom? Did someone invite him into that belfry? If so, why did he go? Whom was he meeting? In addition, was it one attacker or more? Yet,' I shrugged, 'I have examined the belfry; it is narrow and close, a place where more than one assailant would find it difficult to hide. You see the problem, sirs: why, how, who?' My voice trailed away. I was tired, and could make little sense of what I'd seen and heard.

'He carried no arms,' Kennington murmured. Small and wiry, Kennington reminded me of a fighting dog, with his pugnacious jaw and close-set eyes. His black hair was cropped short, and he had a scar on his right cheek. He was nervous and ill at ease, fingers never far from the hilt of his dagger.

'And?' I asked.

'So, if he met someone, it must have been someone he trusted. I mean, to take off his war-belt . . .'

'And whom would he trust?' I asked. 'Whom do *you* trust?' Kennington didn't answer.

'Lord Gaveston?' I offered. 'His grace the king?' I paused. 'And, of course, you, his brothers in arms?'

Again silence. I stared beyond the Aquilae at a faded wall panel ridiculing the idiocy of life. From the neck of a white lily sprouted the head of a crane with a fish between its teeth; from its feathers protruded a monkey's face sporting horns and spitting fire. Murder, I suppose, is life's supreme idiocy, especially murder of a friend by a soul turned Judas.

'Well?' I asked.

'We know nothing!' Philip Leygrave, his girlish pink face framed by wispy blond hair, grasped his war-belt and clambered to his feet. 'Remember, mistress, we were in the rose garden when you brought news of poor John Lanercost's death. After that . . .' He shrugged and buckled on his war-belt, making a sign for his companions to do likewise.

'After that what?' I snapped.

'Geoffrey withdrew from our company, mouthing threats against Alexander of Lisbon. He kept to himself. He came here to pray. Well,' he pulled a face, 'what does it matter?'

The rest also rose, those who'd taken off their sword belts strapping them on.

'Do you fear an attack?' I asked. 'Here in this friary that

has become the king's own chamber? What do you really fear, masters?'

'Nothing,' Leygrave replied over his shoulder.

'I am trying to help,' I pleaded. 'Sirs, I am not your enemy!'

'You're a woman.' Kennington's foppish remark provoked a few sniggers.

I recalled the gossip that the Aquilae Petri were homosexuals, imitating David in scripture, whose love for Jonathan 'surpassed that of any love for a woman'.

'A woman?' I conceded. 'Like your mothers, your sisters, her grace the queen? What does that matter? My heart is good and my will is sound. Woman or not, I offer you this advice. If Lanercost was murdered, could not one of you be next? Is that why you are all harnessed for war like bullyboys in Cheapside?'

Rosselin swaggered across and stood over me. The others called him back. I shaded my eyes against the light pouring in through the coloured pane window on the opposite wall. I was determined to show no fear. I expected Rosselin to be aggressive but his face was full of fear. The others kept calling him away. He took a small scroll from his wallet and handed it to me. I unrolled it.

'Aquilae Petri,' I mouthed the words, 'fly not so bold, for Gaveston your master has been both bought and sold.'

The letters were perfectly formed. I did not recognise the script, nor, when I asked, did Rosselin or the others.

'When was this delivered?'

'We share chambers in the friary guest house.' Rosselin crouched down. 'Lanercost, as was his custom, rose early and left long before dawn. We were still in bed when the Jesus mass bell sounded.' He glanced away, embarrassed. 'We are more concerned, mistress, about our bodies than our souls. Anyway,' he gestured at the parchment, 'that was pinned to our chamber door. God knows who sent it. Ah well, you may keep it.' He rose, bowed and sauntered out with the rest.

I stayed to collect myself. The morning was drawing on. Eventually I felt calmer, more resilient. I left the church and crossed the yard to the buttery to collect some milk and bread. Brother Eusebius was there, face almost hidden in a huge bowl of oatmeal. He quickly finished, wiped his mouth on the back of his hand, assured me that the church and bell tower were deserted when he left, then volunteered to show me to the corpse house, where Lanercost's body had been taken. I forgot the food and gladly accepted. Eusebius chattered all the way as he led me along grey flagstoned passageways, around the great cloisters and the small, through the apple yards and baking yards, past the scriptorium and library, the prior's chancery and the almoner's chambers, then through a small orchard ripe with sweet-smelling white blossom to the corpse house, a one-storey, red-tiled, barn-like building with a rough-hewn crucifix nailed to its door. Inside, the whitewashed walls were decorated with herbal sprays pushed into crevices. The beaten-earth floor was clean and sprinkled with flower petals. In the centre stood a huge table, with smaller ones around the walls. On some of these lay corpses under their shrouds, from which feet and arms dangled. Eusebius handed me over to the corpse dresser, Brother Malachi, a burly Franciscan, head bald as an egg, his face almost hidden by a thick white moustache and beard. A jovial soul, Malachi, with a wave of his hand, proudly introduced me to his 'visitors', as he called them. At my request he took me over to the centre table and removed the shroud to reveal Lanercost's naked body beneath. Brother Malachi had done his best to clean and anoint the corpse, but a mass of ugly wounds and bruises marked both the head and body, eloquent witness to Lanercost's horrific fall.

I inspected the cadaver most closely. I noticed how the back and sides of the head were staved in. I heard a sound and turned. Demontaigu stood in the doorway. I lifted a hand and beckoned him over. He walked across, stared at the corpse, crossed himself and said he would wait for me outside. I inspected the corpse once more, whispered the requiem, thanked Brother Malachi and joined Demontaigu. He simply shook his head at my questions about where he had been and, clutching my wrist, led me across the friary grounds to his cell in the Sienna gallery, which lay near the refectory. The cell was a small whitewashed chamber with a bed and a few sticks of furniture, its only luxury being a painted wall cloth displaying a golden cross against a red background. Demontaigu had emptied the contents of his saddle bag on to the bed. He now sat down and sifted amongst these. I watched him curiously as he listed them, mementos of his previous life. A small relic; a psalter embossed with the five wounds of Christ displayed in silver; little leather pouches containing a medal his mother had given him, a lock of her hair and that of his long-dead sister. Next to these a flute, a childhood toy, as well as badges and amulets from the various shrines and Templar houses Demontaigu had visited.

'My heirlooms,' he declared without glancing up. 'I heard about Lanercost's death but I had to face more pressing matters. Ausel and the rest have gone to Scotland. They've accepted the Bruce's writ and his claim to the Throne of Scone. The Noctales have severed any loyalty and fealty my brethren had for the English crown. They've taken everything with them, including all my possessions except these.' He scooped them up and placed them in a pannier. 'Memories,' he murmured, 'of a former life, as a boy in a farm near Lilleshall, as a novice at the New Temple, of service in Outremer.' He rose to his feet and grasped my hands. 'Now you have my full obeisance.'

I smiled at his chivalrous play-acting. Demontaigu, however, gazed sadly back.

'I'm not leaving, Mathilde, but the world has changed. My life as a Templar is no longer a secret. People may have suspected before, but now they know the truth. I enjoy the queen's protection. Lisbon might wish me harm, but whilst I am here, I am safe. Moreover, his massacre out on the moors is now well known. In his heart, his grace cannot be pleased at such an abuse of his authority. In the old king's days, Lisbon would have been hanged out of hand.'

'There again,' I added bitterly, 'in the old king's days, Lisbon would never have been allowed into the realm.'

'True.' Demontaigu heaved a sigh. 'He is certainly not welcome at court.'

'Where is he now?' I asked.

'Before he left, Ausel discovered that the devil and his minions shelter at Tynemouth Priory, further up the coast.' Demontaigu paused. 'I've just come from the city. Rumour runs like flame through stubble. The earls are advancing fast. God knows what will happen next. Now, as regards to Lanercost, my brethren have asked me . . .'

I told him succinctly what had happened, voicing my suspicion that somehow Lanercost had been inveigled up into that tower and murdered. I did not add what had happened to me. I wanted to remain cold and alert as deep suspicions gnawed my heart. Lanercost had been murdered soon after we informed him about his brother's death. We had raised the suspicion that Geoffrey had, unwittingly perhaps, passed information he'd learnt from his brother John to someone else, who'd informed Lisbon and so provoked that bloody massacre. Did a mysterious unknown party blame Lanercost and decide to carry out vengeance? Was it the Templars? Had they sent an assassin into the friary to exact summary justice? I stared into Demontaigu's face; those lovely eyes gazed shrewdly back. God forgive me, for a while I wondered about the Templars, until a second Aquilae fell to his death.

Chapter 3

Finally the kingdom of Scotland was freely
offered to Robert de Bruce.

The next two days were taken up with household affairs. Isabella, alarmed at the news from the south, ordered her officers to be ready to leave at a moment's notice. I supervised the packing of the wardrobe, items such as £6 worth of silk for stitching on robes, £20 of silver thread, four dozen mantlets, thirty pairs of stockings, ten bodices, a tunic of triple Sindon, heavy linen, as well as forty tunics of Lucca. The queen's jewel caskets were crammed with rubies, sapphires, emeralds and other precious stones then locked, sealed and placed on carts. At the same time Isabella had letters drawn up and dispatched, whether it be to her officials in the exchequer at Westminster or to the Royal Hospital of St Katherine's by the Tower, which she so generously patronised. She wanted everyone to realise that, although exiled in the north, she still kept a sharp eye on her interests, be it in Westminster, London or elsewhere. I also had medical duties: the preparation of electuaries on a broad sheet of lead with an oak base, mixing grains of paradise with cinnamon, or the various potions for my ointment pots. Isabella herself was in vigorous health, though she remained quiet and withdrawn, as if silently brooding over a grievance she could not share with me.

A few days after Lanercost's death, following the Aquilae's requiem mass and hasty burial in the commoners' side of God's Land in the Franciscan cemetery, Edward called a meeting of his chamber council in the prior's parlour. I remember the detail so vividly. The parlour was truly a magnificent room, with a hooded fireplace of marble built against the outside wall. Despite the late date, pine logs dusted with dried herbs crackled merrily and gave off a perfumed smell. The weather had certainly turned bitter. Icy rain pelted the small oriel windows with their painted mullions and transepts, making the brightly decorated linen curtains dance in the draught. Settles, stools and benches had been pushed away, leaving the room dominated by a great oak table with leather-upholstered seats placed around it. The tiles on the floor, decorated with heraldic devices, were covered in thick, lush Turkey cloths, whilst on the walls, tapestries and hangings extolled the joys of the chase alongside brilliantly coloured murals describing scenes from the life of St Francis. On a great open aumbry directly opposite the fireplace, jewelled plate, Venetian glass and metalwork of Damascus glittered in the light of a host of beeswax candles, as well as torches burning fiercely in cressets driven high into the wall. This was the king's chamber, where Edward and Gaveston closeted themselves to discuss the eternal crisis. They talked and talked but did so little. They were suspicious of everybody so they preferred to lurk deep in some place they considered safe. The prior's parlour, large and cavernous, was ideal: its walls were thick, the door heavy. There were no eyelets or gaps in the wall for eavesdroppers, whilst above was no other chamber; just brightly painted beams decorated with banners and pennants of the royal household. A huge chest near the table, its lid thrown back, was crammed with documents, most of them letters and memoranda sent to the king by his spies in the south, informing him about what was happening.

On that particular day, Edward had apparently made a decision, a rare event. Both king and favourite, as usual, were dressed alike in heavy blue and scarlet surcotes fringed with gold and lined at the neck and cuff with costliest ermine. Both had shaved and oiled their faces, their hair neatly combed and tidied. The king sat at one end of the great table, Gaveston at the other. On Edward's right was Isabella, dressed in a sleeveless cyclas of green-gold decorated with silver-gilt love-knots over a pure white undergown; a gauze veil across netted cauls hid her lovely hair. On the other side of the table sat Lady Vesci, Dunheved and myself next to Henry Beaumont and his brother, all cloaked and muffled against the seeping cold. I watched my mistress intently; she kept looking down at the table, slipping a sapphire ring on and off the middle finger of her left hand, as Edward explained his reasons for the meeting. He had, he announced, made a dreadful mistake. He made the declaration in a slurred voice, then gazed sadly down at Gaveston.

'His grace,' the favourite chose his words carefully, 'now realises that we are trapped here in the north. Our couriers report how the earls completely control the roads south as well as all bridges and river crossings.'

'So no help can come north.' Henry Beaumont stated the obvious. He undid the cloth button of his cloak, which displayed the royal heraldic device he was so proud of: silver lilies on a green background. He threw off the cloak, revealing a costly green jerkin underneath, then shook his shoulders and gestured at the door. 'We have no troops. Only Ap Ythel and his Welsh archers, our own retinues and whatever local levies we can summon.'

'Yes, yes.' Gaveston's half-whisper was a chilling indictment of Edward's incompetence. He'd locked himself in York and could summon no troops; little wonder he had to tolerate mercenaries such as the Noctales, turn a blind eye to massacre and murder and ignore the death of Lanercost. I had been so immersed in my own troubles that only then did the real danger besetting the Crown and my mistress seep in like a river, swollen with rain, that abruptly rises and breaks its banks. Edward was not only a fugitive in his own kingdom but in grave danger of losing his crown.

'No help out of France?' Lady Vesci murmured.

Edward just shook his head.

'And Scotland?' Dunheved asked.

'To even treat with them is dangerous and treasonable,' Beaumont bellowed. 'So what is to be done?'

'Your grace.' Dunheved rose, pushing back his chair. 'I beg you,' the Dominican had a powerful preacher's voice, 'as confessor to both your grace and the queen, I can come to only one conclusion. My lord Gaveston, the Earl of Cornwall, should he not leave the kingdom for a while, shelter well away from the king?'

'You mean exile, Brother Stephen?' Edward glared at the Dominican. 'For what purpose? How can I be king yet allow my subjects to dictate who sits at my council board?'

No one dared answer him. Edward's rages were sudden and furious. I glanced at Isabella. She sat motionless, still playing with that ring, lost in her own thoughts.

'I have,' Gaveston stirred in his chair, 'ordered Scarborough Castle on the coast to be provisioned and fortified. It's only a short journey to the east.' He paused as Dunheved quietly clapped his hands in approval. *Sic tempora* – such are the times! Scarborough! A place of refuge! Oh, so true are the words of the psalmist: *My ways are not your ways. My thoughts are not your thoughts, yea, even as high as heavens are above the earth, so are my thoughts above yours!* Gaveston had unwittingly chosen the stage for the rest of that murderous charade to be played out. At the time, however, the prospect of refuge in a castle was seized on by the Beaumonts as a compromise. Scarborough, so we thought, could be easily defended. More importantly, it boasted a small port, and if Gaveston changed his mind, it was an ideal place from which to slip into exile.

The favourite then moved to the question of supplies for the journey to the coast. He was explaining how he would use his own henchmen, the Aquilae, to scour the roads to Scarborough when the harmony of the friary was shattered by the clanging of the tocsin, a constant tolling of the church bells. Edward sprang to his feet, shouting for Ap Ythel. The Welsh captain and his company threw open the door and thronged into the chamber, swords already drawn. Beaumont yelled for his own war-harness to be brought, while his brother Louis quickly donned a stole, a sign that he was a cleric and carried no sword. For a while we thought that Lancaster and the earls had, through forced marches, secretly slipped into York and reached the friary. The parlour became a scene of shouting and mayhem. Only my mistress remained seated; she'd taken ivory and mother-of-pearl Ave beads out of her purse and was sifting them carefully through her fingers. I went and crouched by her chair. She smiled down at me and gently stroked my head.

'My lady, you are silent?'

'*Video atque taceo*,' she murmured. 'I watch and keep silent, as will you, Mathilde. Watch!' A hand bell, raucously rung, stilled the clamour in the parlour. A young Franciscan, gasping for breath, forced himself through the crowd to kneel before the king, who stood, arms outstretched, as Ap Ythel strapped on the royal sword-belt.

'Your grace.' The friar spoke in the local patois, then changed to Norman French. 'Your grace, there is no danger, but,' he lifted his head, 'one of my lord Gaveston's squires, Master Leygrave, he's been found in the same way . . .'

The rest of his statement was drowned by shouts of consternation. Gaveston undid his own sword-belt and sat down on his chair, fingers to his lips like a frightened child. Edward glanced at me and gestured with his head to leave.

'Go,' Isabella hissed, not lifting her face. 'Go, Mathilde! *Vide atque tace* – watch and keep silent!'

Escorted by a dark-faced Ap Ythel and three of his archers, all dressed in their leather breastplates, faces almost hidden by their deep cowls, I left the prior's parlour. We went down hollow-sounding galleries, across the garden plots into the great yard or bailey, its cobbles sparkling in the rain. A crowd had gathered. The three Aquilae clustered around Leygrave's corpse which was sprawled grotesquely, the blood from his cracked head mingling with the muddy rain. I forced my way through. Leygrave lay almost in the same spot as Lanercost. I glanced quickly up at the tower, those ominous windows . . .

'Mistress.' Brother Eusebius shuffled forward. 'I rang the Angelus bell, I recited the prayer: *Angelus Domini annuntiavit Mariae* – the Angel of the Lord declared unto Mary—'

'Yes, yes,' I interrupted.

'Well, I had reached the seventh toll,' he squinted up at the sky, 'and the screaming began outside.'

'We were close by,' Rosselin added. 'In fact we were looking for Philip; he'd been with us when we broke our fast, then left.'

Rosselin's hair and face were soaked with rain, his leather

73

jerkin and those of his two companions drenched black by the downpour. They were agitated, frightened men. They'd donned their war-belts, though, like Lanercost, Leygrave hadn't.

'Where,' I asked, thanking Eusebius with a nod of my head, 'are his sword and dagger?'

'God knows.' Rosselin abruptly got to his feet.

He and the others were expressing their fear by yelling at the curious to stand back. Dunheved came bustling through, stole around his neck, a jar of holy oils in his hand. I let him administer extreme unction over the corpse and stared back towards the church. Demontaigu stood in the doorway. I beckoned him over as Brother Eusebius whispered hoarsely in my ear, 'They were the ones!'

'What?' I asked.

The lay brother pointed a bony finger across to the main door leading into the yard, where the Beaumonts sheltered against the rain.

'What did they do?' I asked.

'Talked to the dead man.'

'You mean Leygrave?' I drew closer, aware of Dunheved's voice murmuring the absolution.

'No, the other one, the first to fly like an eagle.'

I glanced at Eusebius' foolish face and realised his wits were sharper than had first appeared.

'Saw them speaking to him, the morning he fell,' Eusebius added, 'out in the apple orchard.' His voice grew hoarser. 'Sees a lot, does Brother Eusebius, and for some coins, he could tell you much more.' Then he scuttled away.

Dunheved finished his anointing, then he rose, smiled and

hurried off. The Aquilae clustered around the battered corpse. I inspected it carefully: a gruesome mass of bruises and shattered bones, cracks to the skull and ghastly wounds disfiguring his face. One arm was no more than a coil of thick hardening flesh, his right leg horribly twisted.

'Did anyone see him fall?' I asked.

Rosselin called across a young lad clutching a bundle of sticks. By the flour on his apron, he was the fire boy from the nearby bakery, sent out to the wood stall to collect kindling. I beckoned him closer and spoke to him. In halting phrases and an accent I could scarcely understand, the fire boy explained how he collected wood for the master baker. He'd left the wood stall and glanced up at the tower because of the gossip and chatter, then he'd seen it. I offered a coin; it was snatched away. The boy grew animated, chattering like a sparrow. I had to urge him to speak slower as he described how he saw something black, 'like a monstrous raven', fall from the tower. The body dropped like a stone. No, declared the boy, he saw no movement of the legs or arms. He heard no scream. All he saw was the body spin, hit the sloping roof of the church then bounce like a ball along the tiles and over and down into the cobbled yard. I tweaked his cheek, thanked him and said his kindling might get wet, so he hurried off.

The Aquilae had also heard the boy's tale. They could tell me little about Leygrave except that he was Lanercost's close friend, deeply downcast at the death of his comrade. Accompanied by Demontaigu, I led them away from the eavesdroppers up into the deep porch of the church. As I did so, I glimpsed the Beaumonts sloping across to watch a group of lay brothers lift Leygrave on to a stretcher brought from the infirmary. I ignored them. We sheltered from the rain beneath the tympanum showing Christ on the Last Day carrying out judgement above the phrase carved in stone: *Hic est locus terribilis! Domus Dei et Porta Caeli*: This is a terrible place! The House of God and the Gate of Heaven.

'Mistress,' Rosselin rubbed a thumbnail around his lips, 'we must attend to Leygrave's corpse. What do you want?'

'An assassin is hunting you,' I replied. 'Who it is and why, I don't know. Two of your comrades have been barbarously murdered. All of you may well be marked for slaughter. So I ask you, I beg you, why?'

Those three young men, who'd flown so high and basked in all of Gaveston's glory, could only stare sullenly back. Rosselin handed across a piece of parchment.

'I found that, tucked into the rim of Leygrave's boot.'

I knew what it contained even before I undid the small roll of vellum.

'Aquilae Petri, fly not so bold, for Gaveston your master has been both bought and sold.'

'Is that all?' I asked. 'Is that all you can offer me?'

'It is all I can say; it is all we can tell you.' Rosselin tucked his thumbs into his war-belt gleaming with glittering studs. 'True, we are frightened, mistress. The case against us presses hard. We take your warning, we heed your advice. This is a matter, *À l'outrance* – to the death.' He bowed and, followed by the rest, left the porch.

I took Demontaigu deeper into the church. There I stopped and leaned against a pillar, staring down at the gorgeously decorated rood screen.

'Is this the work of the Templars, Bertrand?'

'No.' He drew closer, crossing himself. 'I understand your suspicions, Mathilde, but no.' He glanced away. 'I don't think so. We should leave.'

I winked at him. 'We'll have other visitors soon.'

'Who?'

I lifted my finger to my lips, even as the door latch snapped and the Beaumonts came into the church, stamping and shaking the rainwater from their cloaks and boots.

'We meet again, mistress.' Henry Beaumont swaggered forward. He sketched a courteous bow and glanced sharply at Demontaigu. 'The queen's clerk,' he murmured, 'deep in conversation with the queen's shadow.'

'We are all shadows under God's sun,' I retorted.

The Beaumonts simply stared back.

'So why have you followed me here?' I asked. 'To discover what I know? That is very little! Or to tell me what you and Lanercost were discussing out in the apple orchard on the morning he died?'

Lady Vesci's smile faded. Louis coughed and turned away. Henry remained ebullient as ever.

'Direct, mistress, so I will be equally direct back.' He gazed quickly at Demontaigu. 'Take your hand away from your dagger, Templar; you are only here by the queen's grace.'

'And God's,' Demontaigu retorted.

'Perhaps,' Beaumont replied, 'but God seems to have deserted your order. Now, Mistress Mathilde, I'll be honest.' He was standing so close I could smell the wine on his breath. 'I met Lanercost because I wanted to know what he took into Scotland, what the king truly intends. Rumours about possible Scottish help buzz around like bees.'

'In which case, that's the king's business, secret to him.'

'Is it?' Beaumont snapped his fingers. 'I wonder. Think, woman! Gaveston is in great danger. The hawks circle. Your mistress, God save her, is *enceinte*. Does Gaveston politic for her, for the king or just for himself? Gaveston's business could be a threat not only to me but to us all.' He stepped back, bowed and, followed by his kin, sauntered out of the church.

'We'll know soon enough,' Demontaigu said thoughtfully, 'if Bruce will help or not.'

I nodded and glanced down that sombre nave. The vigorous wall paintings, proclaiming the punishments of hell and the glories of heaven, seemed to press in on me. My mind was caught by the depiction of a king and queen thronged in glory.

'Court life is like a body,' I replied, 'full of all sorts of strange humours. I want to study the particular symptoms of what is now happening.' I crossed over and opened the door to the bell tower. Inside it was deserted. Asking Demontaigu to accompany me, I grasped the ladder and was about to climb when I caught the glint of a stud. I picked it up and recognised that I'd seen the same on the ostentatious war-belts the Aquilae liked to wear. I handed it to Demontaigu.

'Why should it be lying here?'

Demontaigu grinned. 'Because,' he unstrapped his own belt, tossed it to the floor then indicated the ladder, 'it is hard enough to climb through so narrow an opening; sword and dagger would make it very clumsy.'

'So that is why Lanercost and Leygrave weren't wearing theirs.' I stared around. 'Brother Eusebius has more to answer for.'

We climbed the ladder into the bell tower. We searched and probed, but that dusty ancient chamber refused to yield its secrets about the mysterious deaths of those two young men. I scrutinised the slippery, sloping window slab very carefully. I found no trace of blood, but I did detect very clearly the marks of boots, the broad sole and narrow heel of the Cordovan type much favoured by Gaveston and his Aquilae. The slab was smooth and the imprint of drying mud in the centre of the ledge quite pronounced. God forgive me, I should have been sharper. I put aside any closer scrutiny and reached the obvious conclusion that Leygrave must have stood on that ledge and then . . . what? If he had stood there then he must have been contemplating suicide. Or was he pushed, forced, blackmailed? Yet why did he come up here in the first place, unarmed, to this lonely, stark belfry where his close companion and comrade had also died so mysteriously? Someone else had definitely been involved in their deaths; hence that cryptic, jibing message. I looked over my shoulder. Demontaigu was staring at me strangely. I voiced my suspicions. He walked around the wooden platform and stretched out a hand.

'I cannot help you, Mathilde, but come, come.' He grasped my fingers and escorted me back to the ladder.

We reached the storey below, but instead of continuing down, Demontaigu took me into a shadowy, crumbling corner that stank of wetness and bird droppings.

'Bertrand, what is it?'

79

He let go of my hand and stared at a point beyond me. I suppressed the shiver that prickled my spine and shoulders.

'You asked whether any of my brethren could be involved in these mysterious deaths.' He rubbed his mouth on the back of his hand. 'I said we were not, but I speak for the brethren, not for any individual. There could be one, mingling in disguise amongst the good friars.'

'Ausel!' I exclaimed. 'But you said he'd gone into Scotland?'

'I was sworn to secrecy, Mathilde.' Demontaigu held my gaze, then sighed. 'But you are also my secret. Ausel defied the master's instructions. He said he would not leave England until he was avenged on Lisbon for that massacre. Eye for eye, tooth for tooth, life for life; you know Ausel . . .' He squeezed my hand. 'You saw him out on the heathland. He will not rest, not until he's had blood.' He walked to the ladder and stared down. 'Ausel believes that Lanercost told Gaveston about the meeting at Devil's Hollow, and that Gaveston, for God knows what reason, told Alexander of Lisbon.' He grasped the sides of the ladder. 'Ausel could be responsible for these deaths.'

We reached the bottom of the tower. Demontaigu collected his war-belt and declared he would search out Ausel. I grasped him by the arm. 'Bertrand, let us walk a while.' We left the church. A chamberlain, all flustered, came hurrying over to announce that the council meeting was adjourned but that her grace the queen needed me. I thanked the chamberlain and waited till he left.

'Mathilde?'

'Bertrand.' I took him over to stand in the shelter of a porch.

'That message left on each of the corpses? It mocks Gaveston, it declares he is finished – bought and sold.'

'And so he is.' Demontaigu squinted up at the sky. 'Oh, I've heard the rumours about possible help from the Bruce. Publicly Gaveston says he is negotiating with Edward's allies in Scotland.' He pulled a face. 'What allies? Secretly he may, on behalf of the king, be pleading for help from Bruce, but none of that will be in writing – too dangerous.'

'And?'

'It shows how desperate Gaveston is. Mathilde, this mummer's play will end, but how?' He shrugged, kissed me full on the lips and left.

The rest of the day was taken up with my mistress, who was silent but forceful. She had written a number of letters that I did not see, though I had to supervise their dispatch to Hull and other ports. Isabella was intent on leaving, so the rest of that day and the following morning were taken up with preparations. Only after the Angelus bell was I free to return to the mysteries confronting me and what I should do next. I remembered Eusebius. I left messages for Demontaigu about where I was going and went back into the church. The bell tower was empty, so I crossed the nave and went up the transept towards the shrine to St Francis. Sounds echoed through that vaulted space. I passed altars and chantry chapels all ghostly in the dim light. Occasionally a host of burning candles would pick out a wall painting of angels ascending into heaven, or St Francis embracing a leper, a disgusting figure depicted in all the horror of flaking snow-white skin, red mouth and blood-rimmed eyes. Statues and carvings glared sightlessly down at me. I became a little flustered, even frightened.

I recalled Eusebius telling me that the entrance to the charnel house lay directly beneath a mural depicting Christ's Harrowing of Hell. I found that: a scrawling but vigorous depiction of Le Bon Seigneur standing on the shores of hell, hands outstretched to the legion of souls awaiting resurrection. The entrance was easy enough to find: a trap door of oaken slats smoothed to run level with the flagstones. Two hooks, through which a wooden bolt was passed, kept the trap door locked to its frame. The bolt had been withdrawn and lay to one side. I lifted the door. A glow of light from a lantern horn on the bottom step greeted me. 'Eusebius,' I called. 'Eusebius?' I went down the steps. I reached the bottom, lifted the lantern and stared around that macabre hall. A long passageway stretched before me. On either side were shelves crammed with the dead, tightly packed together. Row after row of skulls, some shiny white, others yellowy-black with decay, and beneath these, bones stacked like bundles of fire sticks. 'Eusebius?' I called. The charnel house held a chill that bit the flesh. My voice rang loud, echoing off the heavy stone. A rat scurried across my path, screeching at this intrusion on its hunting run. I walked down, raising the lantern, passing alcoves and recesses full of darkness. I did not stop. I was drawn by the glint of metal at the end of the passageway. On either side, stack after stack of skulls gazed at me. I reached the end, lifted the lantern and stared. Brother Eusebius was propped against the wall, his skull smashed by the thick bone tossed on to his lap, his grotesque face masked by blood through which sightless eyes glared bleakly at me. I crouched beside him. One hand still gripped a sword, the other a war-belt. On a shelf to my right the bones had been cleared away; there were oil lamps, which had guttered out, as well as a baking tin heaped with scraps of ribbon, coins, small medals and crosses.

'You poor, poor magpie.' I crossed myself. Eusebius had apparently used this place as a hideaway for the little items he'd been given or found in the church, including the war-belts of the two Aquilae. I found the second one behind his back. This half-witted lay brother had apparently been surprised by his killer; he'd made some pathetic attempt to defend himself, all to no avail. He'd been trapped in this macabre place and his skull staved in. God knows the reason why. I murmured a prayer, then spun round, alarmed at a sound behind me. I grabbed the lantern and raised it high, my other hand searching for my dagger. My imaginings deceived me, then I saw a shape move. At first I thought it was hurtling towards me, but that was a trick of the light. In truth it was moving away. I shouted at it to stop, but the wraith-like figure sped into the gloom. I pursued it as fast as I could, lantern in one hand, dagger in the other. It was fruitless. There was a pounding on the steps, then the trap door was raised and came crashing closed. Sweat-soaked, I put the lantern down and hurried up, but the door had been bolted shut. I crouched on the steps and stared across at the mounds of bones. The dead did not frighten me. I was more concerned about Eusebius' murder. I went back to search again, but found nothing new. I returned to the steps, listening for the brothers. A short while passed. I heard footsteps and called out. Demontaigu replied. He drew back the bolt and helped me out. As he did so, I glimpsed a piece of fabric with a green and gold button attached to it. The device embroidered on it was a silver-gold fleur-de-lis against a dark green background, the one so proudly worn by the Beaumonts. I put that into my wallet and went and crouched at the foot of a pillar. The lantern horn created a pool of light before me. Demontaigu joined me, full of questions. I told him what had happened and what I'd found.

'Not now!' I protested at his questions. 'I see no sense in all of this.' I clambered to my feet. 'Ausel?'

'Disappeared,' Demontaigu replied. 'Gone into hiding. Ausel is adept at disguise; he will show himself when he wants to.' He pointed across at the trap door. 'I don't think he had anything to do with that.'

I made no answer. We left the church, and I immediately informed the prior about what I'd found. Then Demontaigu and I helped the brothers remove Eusebius to the corpse house. I also collected the war-belts of the two dead Aquilae and had them dispatched to Rosselin with a message that they'd been found in a shadowy nook in the church. Father Prior had the good sense to realise that Eusebius' murder was connected to the deaths of Gaveston's henchmen. He wisely informed his shocked community that poor Eusebius had been killed by some wandering intruder and left it at that.

It was late in the day by the time I was free. The king and queen had left the friary for a banquet at the Guildhall. Demontaigu returned to his search for Ausel, whilst I adjourned to my own chamber close to the queen's. I washed

84

and changed and rested a while to calm my humours, then distilled some powders and potions. I remember beating egg white in preparation for a treatment for open sores and wounds, mixing musk and amber for heavy coughs, theriac and valerian for agitation and finally preparing hellebore for fumigation, a potion that was constantly in use. As I worked, memories floated through my mind. Gaveston's fear. Edward's agitation. Isabella white as a statue. Leygrave, his broken corpse sprawled like some animal carcass. Eusebius' busy whispers and sly, knowing smile. The bootprints on that slab so clear for me to see. The gloomy charnel house where Eusebius' cunning had been silenced for ever. That shadow flitting through the murk, and finally the scrap of cloth and the ornamental button displaying the coat of arms so beloved by the Beaumonts. A series of images with no logic to them.

Once I had finished distilling the herbs, I sat at my small writing desk and began to list everything I knew. I chose a large sheet of costly vellum, the type Isabella used for her letters, and wrote down what I'd seen, heard and reflected upon. The great Trotula maintains that the fundamental syllogism of medicine is that if the human body was perfect, all its senses would be keener. We would, for example, have the power of smell of a dog or the eyesight of a cat. The human body, however, is not perfect, so we can observe what is wrong in the symptoms of all its functions, be it the twenty-nine for the urine or the five signs of approaching death. Now, the detection of murder and the diagnosis of disease have a great deal in common. I decided it was time to list these symptoms and study them carefully.

Primo: The massacre at Devil's Hollow was carried out by the Noctales, but who had told them that a party of Templars fresh out of Scotland would be there at that time? Was it Geoffrey Lanercost, who'd learnt it from his brother? Or someone else who knew the precise details? Yet who could that be?

Secundo: Lanercost himself. He took his war-belt off and went up into that bell tower. Why? Whom did he meet? If the person was his murderer, how could he, or possibly they, overcome a young, vigorous warrior and throw him to his death. And why there?

Tertio: Leygrave. Why did he go up to the same place where his comrade had been killed? Apparently he too felt safe enough to leave his war-belt behind. Again, a young warrior. If he'd stood on the edge, why? Was he forced? Did he jump, or was he pushed? Yet the fire boy from the bakery heard no scream; he simply saw Leygrave fall like a stone.

Quarto: Why the bell tower, that dirty, narrow chamber, those bells swinging out? I had been in danger there. So who had watched me go up? Was it out of mischief or malice that those bell ropes were pulled? Eusebius or the assassin?

Quinto: Eusebius. Why was he murdered? Someone followed him down into that charnel house and shattered his skull to silence his gossiping mouth for ever. Why? What did the lay brother know?

Sexto: The cryptic message to the Aquilae about Gaveston being bought and sold. The writer was warning Gaveston's henchmen that their lord was finished. Was the assassin punishing the Aquilae, or was it part of a devious plot to destroy Gaveston and all his coven? If so, when would the assassin strike at Gaveston himself?

Septimo: The Beaumonts. That rent of cloth and the button pointed to their possible involvement in Eusebius' death, but why? And what did Beaumont really discuss with Lanercost?

Octavo: Isabella and her stony-still attitude. What was she plotting?

Nono: Edward and Gaveston, trapped here in York with the earls closing in. What could they do? What would happen if both king and favourite were apprehended by the earls?

I reviewed what I'd written whilst from outside drifted the sounds of the friary as the brothers prepared for prayer and the onset of darkness. My own eyes grew heavy, my mind tired, my body begging for sleep. I rested easy that night; it was just as well. The following day, Edward and Gaveston began their own descent into hell. Scurriers, coated in mud, their horses dropping with exhaustion, galloped through the friary gatehouse. The news they brought was dire. The earls were much closer to York then the king had ever suspected. Lanercost and Leygrave's deaths were swept aside by the thunderous roar of that hurling time. The court fell into a panic. Edward and Gaveston had no choice but to flee. Carts were hitched, sumpter ponies and pack animals trotted out. The great hunt had begun. The earls were determined to trap Gaveston and send him into eternal night. In their proclamations there was no tolerance, no mention of compromise. If Gaveston was taken, Gaveston would die. Hell opened its maw to spit out all forms of troubles. The weather turned changeable. Rain storms and lashing winds clogged the muddy roads. Gaveston and Edward were forced to move swiftly, leaving Isabella to follow slowly behind. A long trail of carts and horses moved across desolate moorlands in weather that had abruptly changed from the sweetness of spring to the icy memories of winter, with sleeting rains and biting winds. A harsh time. We were caught out in the open like tired, dispirited troops fleeing from a battlefield. We warmed ourselves before weak camp-fires, wore sodden clothes and groaned and itched at our saddle sores. We gobbled ill-cooked food and drank brackish water and wine more bitter than vinegar. We were like deer trapped in a hunting run. Isabella and the remains of her household desperately followed the king, whilst to the rear and flanks our pursuers crowded us like hungry hounds: the retinues of Lancaster, Hereford, Warwick and Pembroke, their banners and pennants displaying the various coats of arms. The hunting pack were in full flow. They did not close in but waited to see what would happen. Chaos descended.

Edward and Gaveston eventually decided to wait for the queen. A hasty council was convened in some wayside tavern. The die was cast. There, in a dirty tap room, its windows covered with filthy rags, rotting onions hanging from the blackened rafters, the tawdry settle stools and tables glistening with grease, a smoky fire shooting out foulsome fumes, the decision was made. Around the tavern were camped Ap Ythel and his comitatus loyal to the king; there was no one else. The great earls were winning the day; their outriders clashed with our scouts, whilst the sheriffs and great manor lords of Northumbria either did not receive the royal writs summoning troops or pretended they hadn't. Worse news came hot on our heels. A powerful Scottish war band had crossed the northern march: mounted mailed men and a host on foot. Bruce was not only winning in Scotland but was ruthlessly determined to exploit Edward's weaknesses. My mistress looked exhausted, and to be fair to Edward, he sensed that she could no longer continue. In the dim light of that tavern it was agreed. Edward and Gaveston would continue north. Isabella and her retinue, guarded by the Aquilae and their henchmen, would shelter at Tynemouth. Alexander of Lisbon was already there to bolster the garrison. All non-combatants, household retainers, priests and chaplains, including Dunheved, would accompany the queen.

We approached Tynemouth late the next morning. A long line of carts and horses moving along a narrow track-way up towards the great castle built round a Benedictine priory, which perched on a sheer headland overlooking the Tyne estuary and the sullen northern seas. Tynemouth! A great craggy, jutting monument of stone with its high curtain wall on the land side, the rest guarded by sheer cliffs. The western approach was heavily fortified, not only by the curtain wall but by a three-storey fortified gatehouse and barbican. A fearsome, brooding place of war, which dominated the surrounding countryside and kept a sharp eye on the coastal routes. Stark in its purpose, Tynemouth was no country manor or royal palace, but a place built for strife. The day we entered was bright and clear, yet even this could not dispel a sense of brooding menace. I glimpsed archers high on the crenellated walls, and the tops of mangonels and catapults alongside the royal standards and pennants flapping vigorously, their colours bright against the light morning sky. As we entered the castle, we passed one of those ancient crosses covered in mysterious symbols and carvings. A local anchorite, hearing of our approach, had come out to lecture us as we passed.

'What is man but snow under the sun, dust in the breeze, a flurry upon the water? We flash like an arrow through light to dark! A short-lit spark! A common reed! Frail grass! A delicate flower! Mist on the ground! Smoke in the air! Foam on the wave!'

Oh, I remember those words as we cantered on under the yawning gatehouse and into the great bailey, where dark-garbed Alexander of Lisbon and his Noctales, together with the Castellan and his retinue, were waiting to greet us. I had to curb my tongue, control my feelings at the sight of these mercenaries, some three score in all, lounging around in their half-armour, all harnessed and ready for war. These men, warming themselves around braziers as they fed their faces, had tried to kill me. I avoided their arrogant gazes and tried to ignore their golden-black war pennants and banners attached to poles stuck in the ground. Beneath these sprawled their war-dogs, lounging in the weak morning sun. The Castellan a veteran soldier from the old king's days, hastily stepped forward, as if aware of Isabella's distaste for Lisbon and his ilk. The queen was welcomed in a brief but courteous speech. Afterwards we were quickly escorted out of the bailey and up to what used to be called the Prior's Lodgings, high on the south wall. The Castellan, God bless him, tried his best to make the queen comfortable, but it was an eagle's eyrie. On the land side it overlooked the castle; on the other three sides the lashing waves and dark swollen sea groaning under a lowering sky. Around the arrow-slit windows seagulls and other birds provided a strident chorus from dawn to dusk. The wind, when it swung from the north, was bitter, sharp and heavily salted, keen to penetrate the thickest shutters or heaviest hangings. Outside the castle stretched wild moorlands you would be only too happy to escape from and, inside, pressing in, curling and twisting, a thick veil of mist which could deepen swiftly to cover Tynemouth like a heavy shroud, dulling sound, turning that castle and its turrets, walls and towers into a place of shifting shapes.

Messengers came and went, clattering across the drawbridge. Edward and Gaveston had totally misjudged the situation. The earls had, like some vengeful river, swept by York and were pursuing the king north to Novo Castro. Neither the Crown nor the earls seemed concerned about the Scottish war party still moving south, whilst Bruce's allies, a fleet of Flemish privateers, threatened the coastline. The Castellan heard all this, so Tynemouth was put on a war footing. The Beaumonts, who had accompanied us, tried to exercise their authority, but the Castellan refused to bow either to them or the Aquilae. Instead he encouraged the royal favourites to participate in the constant watches, in the end they had no choice but to agree. The Noctales chose the gatehouse and barbican; the Beaumonts were given the Prior's lodgings; whilst the Aquilae and their retinues stationed themselves in Duckett's Tower, which stood above the eastern cliffs overlooking the sea.

Days passed. Isabella rested secure in her chamber. Demontaigu believed that Ausel was one of those who crowded into the castle: tinkers, traders, wanderers, as well as local people fearful about what was happening. Then it happened: the great silence. No more couriers or messengers. No further carts heaped with fresh supplies. No wandering preachers, tinkers or traders. Scouts were dispatched but they never returned. At night the dark was lit by fires glowing eerily across the heathland as well as through the heavy mist out at sea. The Castellan sought an audience with Isabella. She received him in her private apartments, swathed in woollen robes, fur boots on her feet, a mantle around her neck and chest. The stark chamber was warmed and lit by flickering cressets, chafing dishes and sparkling braziers. These kept back the cold, ghostly wraiths of the ever-seeping mist. Despite Isabella's invitation, the stern-faced old soldier insisted on kneeling before her footstool. He gazed beseechingly at me, standing behind the queen, then at Dunheved, who sat on a stool to Isabella's right.

'Your grace.' He paused. 'Your grace, some great force lurks out on the moorlands. I also believe Flemish pirates are off the coast. In a word, we are cut off. I am fearful.'

'About what, sir?'

'Whoever the enemy are,' he replied, 'we can withstand an assault.'

'Then what is your fear?'

'Treachery, your grace.'

'You mean treason!' Dunheved snapped.

'Reverend Brother, last night I sent out one of my best guides—'

'But I thought you'd stopped that?' Dunheved interrupted, visibly agitated.

'No, Brother. The guide did not go to seek what was outside.'

'But the enemy within?' I added.

'Mistress, you have the truth. He reported that he'd glimpsed signals being sent out from this castle.'

'Signals?' Isabella asked.

'Simple but stark,' the Castellan replied. 'A lantern horn displayed high on the walls, opening and shutting, clear flashes of light to someone waiting and watching. These were shown at one place, then another. It would be impossible to discover who was responsible.' He licked his lips. 'I would defend this castle to the death. I can certainly vouch for the loyalty of myself and my men, but not for everyone here. If there is treachery, your Grace, this is all I can offer.' He rose, grunting at his creaking knees. 'If it please your grace to follow me . . .'

We had no choice. We left the Prior's Lodgings. In the courtyard below, Demontaigu was talking to the squires of the queen's household, young men barely out of their schooling as pages. The Castellan whispered a few words to Isabella, who ordered me to instruct Demontaigu and the squires to follow us. We continued along the line of the walls, past towers, across courtyards, into another mist-hung bailey and up to the iron-studded door of Duckett's Tower. Gaveston's Aquilae and their retainers were lodged in the storeys above. Because the weather was chill, all doors were firmly closed and windows shuttered. However, the Castellan did not lead us up that narrow spiral staircase, soon to become an assassin's path. Instead he pulled at a wooden trap door in the floor, took a cresset torch from its sconce and led us down steep stone steps.

An icy blast stung our faces as, heads bowed, we walked down a needle-thin passageway, its thick chalky walls pressing in from either side. Every so often the Castellan would pause to light cresset torches of the thickest pitch driven into makeshift gaps. The flames of these firebrands danced like fiery imps in the icy blackness of the tunnel. At times the path was so steep we found it hard to keep our footing. Demontaigu and the squires quietly cursed, while Dunheved began the litany of the saints, the words *Miserere nobis* ringing out like a challenge through the darkness. We reached more steps and down we went. Isabella did not object, one hand resting on my arm, the other on Dunheved's. She walked determinedly, as if memorising every step. The cold grew more intense. The sound of the sea was like an approaching drum beat. The darkness began to lift. Shafts of light penetrated the gloom. Down more rough-cut steps then out on to pebble-covered, salt-soaked sand, a small cove sheltered by the cliffs. We braved the slating sea wind, walked out and looked around. On either side, chalk-white cliffs soared up to the castle nestling on its crag high above us. In front of us, beached and ready, were three longboats, and out in the cove a war-cog riding at anchor, stout-bellied, with a high fighting stern and long bow strip. The cog's great sail was reefed. On board I could glimpse the crew moving about.

'Your grace.' The Castellan gestured across the sand. 'It's an answer to a prayer. The cog came in early this morning. If treachery occurs, the master of *The Wyvern* has strict instructions to wait for you. Who gave him these I do not know, but she is well provisioned and will ride at anchor until you leave.' He spread his hands. 'I can say no more.' He led us back into the castle.

The Castellan truly believed the real enemy was within and that any relief could only be the approach of a sizeable royal army; his appraisal of the situation was casual, as if he saw it as part of his duty, a sign of the times. Civil war had broken out, so why should his castle not have enemies lurking within? It certainly did! The following morning we were woken by the clanging of the tocsin and strident calls of *'Aux armes! Aux armes!'* I told my mistress to remain where she was. I summoned Demontaigu and the queen's household squires, all harnessed and ready for battle. We left the Prior's Lodgings and hurried into the great bailey, where the Castellan and his officers were in heated conversation with Rosselin, who was gesturing back towards Duckett's Tower. The Castellan seemed confused, shouting questions at Rosselin, who could not answer except by pointing back to the tower under his guard. I joined them, tugging at Rosselin's sleeve. He turned wild-eyed, blinked, then nodded in recognition.

'Gone!' he muttered.

'Who's gone?'

Dunheved, swathed in his great cloak, joined us.

'Kennington and two of his retainers! They have vanished! They were on watch, on guard vigil! They took the last quarter before daybreak.' Rosselin rubbed his face. 'They have gone!'

The Castellan told his officers to impose order as more people, half dressed, faces sleep-filled, thronged into the bailey. We followed Rosselin through that mist-strewn, ghostly castle to Duckett's Tower. Nicholas Middleton, another of the Aquilae, met us in the doorway at the top of the steps, a look of utter consternation on his unshaven, bleary face.

'Nowhere,' he murmured, fingers jumping about the medallions and crosses pinned to his jerkin. 'Nowhere at all.'

Chapter 4

Douglas was to come secretly there with
his chosen coven and kidnap the Queen.

Dunheved and I followed the Castellan and the others up
the narrow, winding spiral staircase, a breath-catching climb.
The freezing cold from the stone chilled our sweat. A heavy
oaken door at the top led on to the pebble-strewn oval
fighting platform. The wind buffeted us, stinging our eyes.
I had the sensation of standing just below heavy clouds,
whilst the raucous call of sea birds was almost drowned by
the surf crashing against the rocks below. I moved cautiously,
staring around. The high crenellated rim of the tower was

sure protection against any accidental fall. It was at least two yards high, whilst the gap between the battlements was spanned by iron bars. I walked across and looked over the edge at the sickening drop to the rocks below, where the angry black sea surged in a froth of white foam. Any speech was whipped away by the wind. I followed Rosselin's direction and saw a small table with a capped jug and leather tankards. There were three in all, as well as a wooden platter covered by an iron pot. Beneath the table were stored extra cloaks. The lidded braziers next to the table had gone out, and were filled to the top with feathery white ash. The lantern horns between these were also extinguished, their oil-soaked wicks burnt hard and black. It was futile to engage in any conversation. I walked around the summit of the tower. I could find nothing amiss, no sign of a silent intruder or secret assassin scaling the sheer walls and creeping through the dark. Dunheved followed me, murmuring a prayer. I examined the pebble-strewn floor but discovered no stain or mark, although I realised that the wind and rain would constantly wash it, hence the pebbles scattered to provide a surer grip for guards and watchmen.

I studied the heavy door leading on to the tower top. On the inside it had a latch as well as a hook and clasp to keep it secure. I gestured at Dunheved to bring the jug and tankards inside the stairwell, a welcome relief from the noisy, blustering wind. Rosselin led me down to his own chamber on the floor below, a spacious but bleak circular room with little comfort except for the fiery-hot braziers. The Castellan dismissed his guard, as I did mine. For a while Rosselin and Dunheved warmed themselves over the brazier whilst I inspected the jug, tankards and platter. The ale, or what was left of it, smelt rather stale; the bread and cheese were hard but untainted. I wiped my hands at the lavarium.

'Master Rosselin,' I asked, 'what did happen here?' I paused at the footsteps outside, and without knocking, Henry Beaumont walked in.

'The alarm was raised!' he barked.

'Because,' I hastened to reply in an attempt to forestall the Castellan's blunt tongue, 'Master Robert Kennington and two of his men are missing.'

'Deserted!'

'Never,' Rosselin snarled. 'Sir Henry, with all due respect, why are you here?'

'Like the rest of you, I'm worried.' Beaumont walked forward threateningly.

'We all are,' I intervened quickly. 'You knew Kennington, my lord?'

'As you did Lanercost and Leygrave.' Rosselin refused to be cowed. 'They once served in your retinue, as did I for a very short while, Lord Henry.' I hid my own surprise, but of course Gaveston would choose his henchmen from noblemen at least openly loyal to the king. I gestured at Beaumont to warm himself at the brazier, an invitation he swiftly accepted.

'I think, gentlemen,' I spoke quickly, 'we should first discover what happened to Kennington and the others: three fighting men who disappeared from the top of this tower. I understand they were on guard with particular vigilance for the sea.'

The Castellan just nodded.

'Even though I'm a woman,' I smiled quickly, 'I know enough about the science of war to realise that no assailant could scale such walls in the dead of night with those treacherous seas plunging beneath them. Yes?'

They all agreed.

'And no intruder could attack from within.' Rosselin added. 'They'd be challenged. Kennington was a warrior; his two guards were veteran swordsmen.'

'I saw you inspect the ale and platter,' the Castellan said.

'Nothing,' I replied.

I caught Beaumont's contemptuous look. 'Sirs, can I remind you,' I added, 'that I'm here at the specific request of both their graces.'

'The food?' the Castellan asked.

'Kennington himself prepared that,' Rosselin replied. 'He took it out for the last watch, the last four hours before dawn. I thought there was nothing to worry about. I fell asleep after my own watch. I heard no alarm. I woke up and went to see that all was well. What I saw, you've now seen: deserted, empty, no trace of Kennington or his companions.'

'In a few hours the tide will begin to turn,' the Castellan declared. 'I'll order a search of the shore below.'

We all went back on to the top of the tower for one last thorough search, doing our best to ignore the buffeting winds and the roar of the sea. Once again I walked to the edge and peered over that heart-stopping drop. Kennington hadn't deserted, I was sure of that. To whom could he flee? An assassin had climbed on to the fighting platform, that place of vigil, and some great evil had fastened on Kennington and his companions, but who, what and how? The salt-soaked winds hurt my eyes and stung my cheekbones. I signalled that I wished to withdraw, and we gathered inside on the stairwell. I noticed the Castellan slip a large hook on the door through a clasp fastened on the lintel. I asked why, and he explained how these were secured on each door in every tower.

'The winds, you see.' He smiled. 'If a door comes off its latch, it can bang and eventually shatter.'

'Mischief-makers would like it,' I pointed out. 'They could lock someone in.'

'Yes and no.' The Castellan grimaced. 'My children, God bless them, used to do that, but anyone armed with a dagger can open the door from the inside by sliding the blade through the gap and lifting the hook.'

'Your children?' I queried.

'God took them,' he murmured sadly, 'like he did everything in my life. Mistress?' He blinked. 'You wish to inspect Kennington's chamber?'

I nodded.

'I'll go with you,' Rosselin demanded.

'No, sir, you will not.' I opened my wallet and took out the two seal casts: the king's and that of the queen. '*Negotium regis* – king's business,' I whispered. 'You agree, sir?'

The Castellan was only too willing to comply. I asked Dunheved and Demontaigu to search the rest of the tower. The Castellan led me down the steps, unhooked the clasp and swung open the door. Kennington's chamber was like that of a monk. A crucifix hung black and stark on the grey-white wall above the cot bed. I closed the door and searched his paltry possessions. I felt a profound unease. Kennington's belongings were sad; rather pathetic. Like Demontaigu, he'd collected mementos of his childhood: locks of hair, a battered toy horse with a mounted knight, a faded miniature diptych of Lazarus coming out of his tomb, scrolls of parchment: letters from his mother and sisters. It was sad to see the child behind the warrior, the glimpse of innocence before the glass darkened, the soul choking on the cares and ambitions of life. I sat on the cot bed and wondered what had happened to this squire. I knew so little about him and his companions. I tried to recall the rumours, the stories. How the Aquilae had become Gaveston's sworn henchmen, sealing indentures to be with him 'day and night, body and soul'. Some had whispered how they were all catamites, loving their master and each other. Gaveston used them as his minions, as his personal bodyguard. God knows what they plotted. Why had the favourite sent them to Tynemouth and not kept them with him? Ostensibly it was to defend the queen. Any other reason? And why had Lanercost been sent to Scotland? What had he been plotting? Why did the Beaumonts have such a deep interest in his mission?

As if an answer to these questions, a harsh knock on the door startled me, and without my reply, Rosselin sauntered into the room. He rubbed his arms against the cold, then took an extra cloak from a peg and offered it to me. When I refused, he wrapped it around himself. He expected me to challenge him, to ask him to leave, but I'd finished my search and wanted to question him. Rosselin picked up a stool and came across. I studied that ruddy, unshaven face, the blue eyes, red-rimmed and bleary. The sea wind had chapped his cheeks and his thick lips were salt-soaked.

'Master Rosselin, can you help resolve these mysteries?'

He shook his head, eyes cold and calculating. He seemed not to like me, to resent my presence, though he was still determined to remain cordial.

'I know why I'm here,' I began, 'but you, Master Rosselin, and the rest, shouldn't you be with Lord Gaveston?'

'No,' he retorted. 'We're here to guard the queen. Lord Gaveston has a personal regard for her grace. Who else can the king send? He lacks troops for himself. Her grace is important. Our presence, and that of the Noctales, will strengthen the garrison here.'

I could not dispute that; it made sense.

'And you,' I asked, 'you will live and die with Gaveston?'

'What else is there?' Rosselin's voice hinted at sheer desperation. He glanced away, boots shuffling on the paved floor, and when he looked back, both his face and his voice had softened. 'Mistress, we're all trapped: myself, the others and Gaveston.' He pulled the stool closer. 'We took blood oaths and devised perilous stratagems when the days were good. These have come shooting back like barbed arrows during this time of distress. We are committed. There's no going back. No turning to the left or to the right. I could tell you things, but I cannot; except that if Lord Gaveston goes down, so do we.'

'Why?' I asked. 'Why did Lanercost go to Scotland?'

Rosselin refused to answer.

'Why?' I persisted.

103

'Possibly,' Rosselin refused to meet my gaze, 'to seek sanctuary for my lord, if he decides to go into exile again.'

'Or help against the great earls?' I asked.

Again Rosselin refused to meet my gaze.

'Is that true? Is Gaveston plotting treason?'

'I don't know,' he replied. 'I truly don't.'

'My lord Gaveston was distressed by Lanercost's death?'

'Of course, you've heard the whispers. He and Lord Gaveston may have been lovers.'

'And what are you involved in now?'

'Too late.' Rosselin's voiced thrilled with the passion of sadness. From outside trailed the harsh calls of the sea birds above the muffled thunder of the waves smashing against the rocks.

'What do you mean, too late?'

'Just too late!'

'And you are here to guard the queen?'

'Yes. I can tell you little more, mistress. It's too late, too late. We are committed to our lord, even though the case against us presses hard. Too late for penance.' He sighed. 'Too late for contrition, too late for absolution.'

'So why have you visited me now?'

'You know Kennington hasn't deserted. He's dead. I've watched you, mistress. Flattery aside, you are honest. You have compassion. Apart from my lord and my comrades, I am alone. If I fall . . .' He opened his purse and took out two gold pieces. He insisted that I take them, pressing both into my hand. 'Light candles,' he pleaded, getting to his feet. 'Have a priest whisper absolution in my ear. Go to some chantry chapel, have masses for the dead sung for my soul. As for my body, make sure I am not treated like some dog's carcass but get honourable burial in consecrated ground.'

I offered the coins back, but he shook his head.

'Mistress, to whom else can I turn? I trust you.' He walked to the door.

'Master Rosselin?'

He turned.

'Who wants your life?'

'God does. I may die like a dog because I've lived like one that goes constantly back to its own vomit.' He bowed and slipped through the door.

I realised then the truth of what Isabella had said. The glass was darkening. Soon the light would be extinguished.

Kennington's corpse and those of his two companions were found later that day, floating in the furious flurry of the angry sea. I watched as they were brought back to Duckett's Tower. They had apparently fallen with cloaks, boots and war-belts on, though these had been caught, snagged and shredded by the waves and rocks. All three corpses were disgusting. Sodden and swollen with salt water, a mass of gruesome wounds, gashes and bruises, shattered by the fall and battered by the rock-pounding sea. It was almost impossible to determine anything except that they'd fallen sheer on to the rocks, to be swept away by the sea and then hurled back again by the turbulent tide: three cadavers proclaiming the true horror of violent death, be it murder or suicide. Dunheved administered the last rites. Rosselin and Middleton acted as chief mourners at the sombre requiem mass in the gloomy chapel, followed by swift interment in the Field of

Souls, Tynemouth's small but crowded cemetery. The news swept the castle, deepening our gloom and sense of isolation. A sinister premonition for the next chapter in the swirling, bloody mist of murder and mayhem engulfing our lives. What could be done? I was confronted with a tangled mystery. How had three veteran swordsmen, on guard, vigilant in the dark hours before dawn, been so brutally killed?

I retraced my steps through Duckett's Tower, only to discover nothing. Rosselin came to ask my opinion. He and Middleton were now men whose courage had been shredded. He also brought a small oilskin pouch found in Kennington's wallet, tied securely to his belt. It contained the same message, written in a neat, precise hand: *Aquilae Petri, fly not so bold, for Gaveston your master has been bought and sold*. The warning was stark, the conclusion obvious. Kennington and his colleagues had been murdered, but by whom and how? I could offer no reply, no solution. In all that turbulence, one small problem still nagged at me. It started as a query, a question, but the more I reflected, the more important it became. The war-cog *The Wyvern*, provisioned with full armament and riding at anchor in that narrow cove. Who had summoned it to Tynemouth? The king, Gaveston, Isabella? The Castellan could not help. He simply tapped the side of his nose and whispered how its master was under secret orders to wait until the danger had passed and only then sail away. I was about to thank him and leave when the Castellan plucked my sleeve and took me into a dark, narrow corner.

'Mistress, I must tell you this. We know marauders lurk out on the heathland. We have also discovered, through the master of *The Wyvern*, that Flemish privateers prowl the northern coast. Now, *The Wyvern* has sailed out simply to make sure all is well on board, no leaks, nothing wrong. They've encountered local fishing craft, whose crews have told a strange tale. Not only do the Flemings prowl, but a force of French war-cogs, fully armed and flying the royal standard, has also been glimpsed. Now why is that, eh? Why should Philip of France be meddling in these cold, misty waters?'

Again, I could not reply. I went to see my mistress. She'd hardly left the chamber, being concerned with her books, sleeping or sometimes just huddled in a cloak before a roaring fire, staring into the flames. I went down on my knees before her, placing my hands in her lap.

'Mathilde, *ma petite*.' Isabella's eyes crinkled in a smile. 'What is wrong?'

'Mistress, I ask you the same question. You shelter here like some anchorite in her cell. You very rarely leave except to catch a breath of air in the morning and evening. We used to talk; now you are silent.'

Isabella cupped my cheek with her hand.

'Mathilde, if I told you . . . No, no, I cannot.'

'Your grace,' I pleaded. '*The Wyvern*: who ordered it to be brought here?'

Isabella's face crinkled into a smile.

'Why, Mathilde, I did.'

'But mistress, what do you think will happen?'

'I don't know, Mathilde, but I have reflected on every possibility. If I cannot escape by land, then it's logical that I must go my sea. The master of *The Wyvern* is well known to me.

He is loyal. He will wait until I give the order, but more than that, I cannot and will not say.'

'And your father's war-cogs?' I could tell by Isabella's face that the Castellan had already told her the news.

'What my father does, what he plots, Mathilde, is a matter for him and those who shelter in his shadow. Do you know,' she leaned forward, 'how Kennington died?'

'Your grace, I know you too well to be distracted.'

Isabella threw her head back and laughed.

'In which case, Mathilde, all I can ask you to do is *vide atque tace* – watch and keep silent.'

The Beaumonts sought me out, inviting me and Dunheved to Henry's chamber, which was probably the best furnished in the castle. A log fire sparked in the oddly shaped mantled hearth. Beaumont and his kin were garbed in the most gorgeous livery. They had their own cooks, who'd bullied the servants of the castle kitchen. Good food was served along with wines full and rich-tasting. Candles and sconces glowed, their light shimmering in the silver and gold weaving of the tapestries hanging on the walls. The floor had been swept and scrubbed with sea water and sprinkled with crushed herbs. A warm, comfortable room in that cold, brooding castle. The Beaumonts, as I have said, could be charming. They certainly were that night, though their one and only purpose was to discover what was really happening, and who better to probe than the queen's confessor and the woman they contemptuously termed her shadow? A strange evening. The courses were served in that grand chamber decorated with shields and hangings, warmed by a fire, braziers and chafing dishes. The conversation moved from courtesies to the crisis. The Beaumonts eventually showed their hand, betraying the fears that gnawed at their ambition. They were powerful lords with extensive estates in Scotland. They were terrified that the king would reach some sort of understanding with Bruce and so lose them a great source of revenue.

'What sort of understanding?' Dunheved asked sharply.

'Help against the earls. Support for Gaveston in return for recognition of Bruce's claims,' Louis murmured.

His reply created silence. Lady Vesci stared up at the rafters. Louis became interested in his wine goblet. Henry sat flicking his fingers against the samite tablecloth. Dunheved's blunt question had taken them by surprise.

'And what if,' the Dominican paused, measuring his words carefully, 'Lord Gaveston was removed permanently?'

This time the silence was menacing.

'What do you mean?' Lady Vesci declared.

'What if the earls are successful?' The Dominican spread his hands before crossing himself quickly. 'I am not saying I wish such a fate on the king's own favourite, but it is a possibility. Lord Henry, what would happen then?'

Beaumont took a deep gulp of wine, staring at me over the rim of his goblet. Dunheved could ask such a question. He was a Dominican, a churchman, the king's own confessor. He could even say he was trying to probe, to find out the true hearts amongst the king's subjects. If Beaumont wasn't careful, his reply could be construed as treasonable.

'If Lord Gaveston,' Henry put his cup down, 'yes, if Lord Gaveston, God forbid, became the object of the earls' anger, then it might lead to civil war, but for what? No war can bring back the dead. There is the possibility that Gaveston's death – and I say God forbid – might bring about a long-term reconciliation. The king and his great earls might unite and, God willing, move across the northern march to defeat Bruce.'

'And the queen, God bless her?' Dunheved continued. 'What would she think if the king's favourite was no more?'

'I cannot speak for her grace,' Lady Vesci interrupted quickly. 'I am sure that she would be distraught, but there again, these things do happen.' Her voice trailed away.

'Mistress Mathilde?' Henry turned to me. 'What do you say?'

'Like your sister, my lord, I can only speak for myself, not for the queen or the king. I am not their confessor but I am deeply concerned by my mistress' plight. Here we are in this eagle's nest above the northern seas. Not far off shore, Fleming pirates prowl, whilst out on the heathland God knows what enemy lurks: the earls, a Scottish war party? I just pray that we leave here unscathed, that her grace rejoins her husband and we all remain safe and well.'

'Tell me . . .' Dunheved turned to me, his clever eyes narrowed as if the light from the candelabra were hurting them. 'Mathilde, why do you think the Aquilae are here?'

'To protect her grace.'

'I wonder?' Louis Beaumont spoke up.

'So do I,' Dunheved said.

'They have one important purpose.' Henry spoke, eager to show his loyalty. 'They have been dispatched here by Lord Gaveston to protect the queen. I am sure that is the reason.'

'As well as spy on her?' Dunheved asked sharply.

Beaumont just shrugged and raised his wine goblet to cover his face.

'And these murders.' Lady Vesci fluttered her fingers at me. 'I understand, so rumour has it, Mathilde, that the king gave you his secret seal to investigate them?'

I nursed my own thoughts about the deaths. Although I had no solution to the mysteries, I decided at least to share my conclusions and see what response they provoked.

'I think . . .' I paused, as if listening to wind beating like some angry sprite against the wooden shutters; living high above the ground, exposed to biting winds and lashing rain, that sound now seemed to dominate my life. I recalled songs from my childhood. How we used to gather around the winter fire and sing about the approach of summer. I so wanted to be away from that gloomy castle, out in some sun-filled meadow.

'Mathilde?' Henry smiled. 'Your thoughts?'

'As regards Lanercost,' I began, 'everyone in this chamber was at mass with Brother Stephen when the Aquilae fell from that tower. I do not know why he went up there or why he was unarmed, though it's clumsy to climb that ladder with a war-belt on. The same is true of Leygrave. Why did he return to a place where his close comrade had been so mysteriously killed, again unarmed? No one saw either of them go up. There is no evidence in that bell tower of any struggle. Leygrave definitely stood on the ledge from which he fell. But again, nothing else. Brother Eusebius, the bell-ringer? Or rather,' I smiled thinly, 'assistant to the bell-ringer. He may have seen something, hence his gruesome murder.'

'And Kennington?' Dunheved abruptly asked.

'Brother, I truly don't know. Three men patrolled the fighting platform of that tower; they were armed and vigilant. They feared the enemy without. They must also have known about the enemy within. Their food and drink was untainted. No alarm was raised, yet someone or something entered that tower and climbed those steps, passing Middleton and Rosselin's chambers. The attacker, or attackers, went on to that fighting platform and either killed those three and hurled them over the battlements, or . . .' My voice faltered.

'I have reflected on their disappearance,' Dunheved remarked, rocking gently backwards and forwards. 'My order provides members for the Holy Inquisition. Our tribunals investigate black magic and sorcery. Did that happen here? There were three watches over a period of twelve hours from six at night to six in the morning. The first four hours were Middleton's, the second Rosselin's and the third Kennington's. Mistress Mathilde, you scrutinised those tankards and the platter; those men were not drugged with some potion or powder. I could detect no bloodstain on the tower top. No sign of any struggle. I do wonder if some demon from the darkness swept across the top of that tower and hurled those men to destruction.'

Henry Beaumont laughed, shaking his head.

'My lord,' the Dominican refused to be cowed, 'can you provide a better explanation?'

For a brief while the conversation moved to matters spiritual: the influence of demons, the possibility of a witch or a sorcerer in the castle. Of course, no one really believed that, but it was a sombre evening. Dunheved's account of diabolical intervention was fascinating; whether it be true or not I could not say, but that was Brother Stephen, he could tell a good tale. Henry Beaumont, however, brought the conversation back to more pressing matters, tapping his hand against the table.

'Sooner or later,' he began, once he had our attention, 'and I should say sooner rather than later, we must leave this castle. We cannot stay here for ever. Eventually the Castellan will have to send out scouts to make contact with the king, or at least ensure the roads south are safe for the queen. Time will tell, but there again, another possibility is that Tynemouth might be attacked or betrayed. The Castellan has archers, men-at-arms and some elderly knights who have retired and live here at the king's grace and favour. However,' he paused for effect, 'I have heard how Alexander of Lisbon, who leads about three score and ten hardened veterans, baulks at being cooped up in the castle. He claims he holds no commission, no mandate, no writ to serve here. He is his own master, allowed to travel the length and breadth of this kingdom on matters affecting the Holy Father in Avignon and King Philip of France.'

'In other words,' I declared, 'Alexander of Lisbon finds the hen coop too tight and wishes to fly.'

'Yes, and there is little we can do to stop him. However, if he does leave, those who watch this castle will learn that our strength is much depleted.'

Now this news came as a surprise. I had kept well away from the gatehouse and bailey area, distancing myself from Alexander of Lisbon and his comitatus. I understood the

Portuguese mercenary's wish to leave – this was not his quarrel – but I wondered if there was anything else.

'What difference would it make?' Dunheved spoke up sharply. 'My lords, ladies,' he smiled, 'in my youth I served as a squire before I entered the novitiate. Let us look at the possibilities and apply logic. If this castle is attacked, we will all have to defend her grace, but can we count on Alexander of Lisbon? Lord Henry, you have it right: he's a mercenary. Lisbon receives his commission from the pope and King Philip to hunt Templars. Why should he risk his men for us? I suspect that if he can, he will slip away, go about his own business.'

I looked sharply at the Dominican. This was the first time he had portrayed any animosity towards Lisbon.

'In the end,' Dunheved spread his hands, 'it's best if he leaves. There is another possibility. Rumours are rife in this castle that there's a traitor within. Is Lisbon that traitor? He couldn't care if the castle stands or falls. He wishes to be gone. Let him leave and the devil go with him.'

Louis Beaumont agreed. I too was taken by the Dominican's logic. Alexander was a killer, a bully. I wondered if he had the courage to withstand an all-out assault on the castle walls.

Once the banquet was over, I thanked my hosts and left. Dunheved insisted on accompanying me back to the Prior's Lodgings. We walked slowly. Now and again Dunheved would pause, plucking at my arm, as we discussed what was best for the queen. I will concede this: looking back down the years at Tynemouth, Dunheved was genuinely, even passionately, concerned about my mistress. A cold-hearted man, nevertheless, at that moment in time, he saw her safety as a God-given task. We continued on to my mistress' chamber. I was surprised to find her still swathed in robes, sitting in her throne-like chair before the roaring fire, slippered feet resting on a footstool. Around the chamber lounged those young squires whom Isabella seemed to have taken a great liking to. On a stool nearby, Demontaigu, in the light of a lantern, was reading a story from King Arthur. Isabella seemed in good spirits. She asked Demontaigu to pause while Dunheved and I quickly reported what had happened at the dinner with the Beaumonts. She heard us out with a half-smile, her face looking even more beautiful in the firelight.

'The Beaumonts . . .' She leaned back in the chair and stared up at the black-raftered ceiling. 'They are so ambitious! They would do anything! I sometimes wonder who they work for.'

'Madam?' I enquired.

'Well, they have blood ties with every sovereign in Europe. I do wonder if the information and gossip they collect from the English court goes to my father, to the pope in Avignon, indeed to anyone who would buy it. They have a finger in every pie, yet what they say is true.' Isabella's smile faded. 'I cannot stay here much longer. If the roads south are dangerous, then perhaps it's time we left by sea.'

'Your grace,' Dunheved retorted, 'it is late spring. The seas are rough and dangers await there. I beg you to wait. The king, surely, will send messengers soon.'

'I wonder.' The queen stirred on her chair, gesturing at Demontaigu. 'Continue reading. It's good to hear how things

115

should be rather than how they are. You have a fine voice; read that passage again about the knight entering Arthur's court and challenging any of his paladins to a joust.' Isabella clasped her hands. 'Wouldn't it be good to be back at Sheen, Windsor or Westminster, to wait for the sun, be out in the fields, to watch night returning?' Her voice grew bitter. 'Instead we are like rabbits on the moorlands, scuttling away from the shadow of the hawk. Lord Henry Beaumont is correct. This must be brought to an end, but how and when I cannot say. Mathilde, you may stay if you wish; if not . . .'

I bowed and withdrew. I'd drunk quite deeply at the Beaumonts' feast, so I retired to bed early.

The next morning a loud rapping on the door aroused me. Demontaigu stood there fastening on his war-belt, a cloak about his shoulders.

'Come, Mathilde, come. There is a disturbance near the gatehouse. Rumour has it that Alexander of Lisbon and his Noctales are about to leave.'

'Let them go,' I replied. 'What use are they here?'

'Now, Mathilde, please!'

I closed the door and hastily dressed, putting on a pair of coarse leather boots and wrapping a cloak firmly about me. I explained to one of the queen's squires what I was doing and followed Demontaigu down across the mist-hung bailey to the barbican and the great gatehouse where Lisbon and his fellow demons waited in their black garb, standards fluttering, war-hounds barking. The bailey was crowded. Sumpter ponies had been led out with bags, chests and casks strapped to them. I stared·at these men, this legion of demons who, for the last four years, had hung like some

116

deadly miasma around the court. A coven of hideous malignity and malice, they'd dogged the steps of poor broken Templars, carrying out hideous murder and acting like the lords of hell. Now they were intent on leaving. The Castellan and his officers, serjeants of the bow and spear, were dismayed at being weakened by the departure of so many fighting men, especially when the danger lurking out on the misty moorlands had yet to be confronted. Alexander of Lisbon, one hand holding the reins of his sleek black destrier, was gesturing dismissively at the Castellan. Beside him a man-at-arms unfolded the black and gold banner of the Noctales, a sign that they were about to mount and leave. Demontaigu and I edged closer. Lisbon stepped to one side and waved forward a figure garbed in dry animal skins, hair and beard all tousled.

'This is my guide,' he yelled at the Castellan. 'Oswyth of Teesdale. He says the king and Lord Gaveston with a sizeable host are not far. He'll lead us by moorland paths to meet them.'

I gazed at Oswyth: that large head, the tangled hair and beard, those fierce eyes, cheekbones brushed raw by the wind. I listened to him chatter in the local patois, one word swiftly running into the other, which a clerk of the stables had to translate for both the Castellan and Lisbon. Oswyth, a mere churl, gave an accurate description of the royal party: the blue, gold and scarlet banners, the snarling leopards. The king and Gaveston, a host of Welsh archers swarming about them, were now marching north. I believed it myself. The news had to be true; a peasant could not invent such detail. Demontaigu squeezed my wrist.

'Look upon his face, Mathilde,' he whispered. 'Do so carefully.'

Oswyth had all the mannerisms of a ploughman trying to impress his betters. He betrayed country ways, constantly moving, stamping his feet, scratching and muttering to himself. Now and again he'd step forward and chatter to the clerk of the stables. Only when he moved did I become more curious. I stared hard. Despite the tousled hair and beard, I recognised someone I knew. I gazed in horror! I did know Oswyth! No northern peasant or unlettered ploughman, he was Ausel the Irishman, the consummate mummer and mimic, God's justice incarnate, His anger in flesh against Lisbon and his followers of Baal! Ausel had come to lead Alexander of Lisbon not to the king but to hell! I opened my mouth. I wanted to shout a warning. Even though I hated the Noctales, it is hard to watch men prepare so willingly and yet so unwittingly, for a violent death. Demontaigu gripped my wrist tighter, whispering that I should remain silent. I could only stare, marvelling at the Irishman's cunning at posing as a peasant. A high-ranking Templar could provide detailed descriptions of the king, Gaveston and the royal cortège, but not a local unlettered peasant. What better way of convincing Lisbon? He certainly had. The Noctales were determined to leave and the Castellan could only protest.

'God have mercy on them all,' Demontaigu whispered. 'There is nothing I can or want to do to stop it.'

The bells of the castle chapel clanged, summoning us to the Jesus mass, as the Noctales, banners and pennants unfurled, a long line of mounted men with their sumpter ponies and barking war-dogs, clattered through the yawning gate to meet their nemesis on that fog-bound moorland. To elude death is not easy. Try as we might, we soul-bearers must allow our souls to travel on when the Lord demands it. Lisbon and his devils were about to meet their God. The early-morning air held the taste of death. My mind began to play tricks, as if I could already hear the shrieks, the clatter of swords, the hiss of arrows and the slicing, sickening thud of the war-axe. Lisbon was hastening to hell; his slaughter bed was being prepared.

All I could do on my return was to whisper to the queen, who crossed herself in a moment of prayer. Demontaigu and I then attended mass. I did not take the sacrament. I could not. I was torn by guilt, though there was nothing I could do. Alexander of Lisbon would have simply scoffed at my warnings, whilst if I had betrayed Ausel, the Templar would have gone to a hideous death.

After mass, Demontaigu and I sat on the ale-bench in the castle buttery, breaking our fast and waiting for news. It arrived late that afternoon: a survivor of Lisbon's group, still harnessed and all bloodied, his entire body a gaping wound, came hammering on a postern gate more dead than alive. He was helped into the castle's infirmary and I was summoned. The survivor was a Parisian by birth, young in years but now openly fêted by death. He had a mortal wound to the stomach, so there was little I could do except give him comfort and relief. He greedily drank the opiate, then babbled about playing in green fields, his mother and a young woman called Claricia. Eventually he broke from his drug-smeared dreams and, in haunting but lucid whispers, told me what had happened. How the Noctales had gone up into the fog, deep on to the moorlands, where water hags and demon wraiths swirled: a lonely, forbidding place. How many of his companions had become uneasy and began to curse Lisbon, but their leader remained insistent. The die was cast. An hour out from the castle, their guide led them into a trap as fast and as hard as any snare.

'Who?' demanded the Castellan, whom I'd immediately sent for.

'Templars.'

'Nonsense!' the Castellan snapped.

'Then ghosts,' the man pleaded. 'Out of hell, bent on vengeance. I tell you, I heard their battle cry, "Beauseant!" I glimpsed their piebald standard. They were ready and waiting like the wolf. A hail of hissing arrows, deadly sleet pouring through the mist, then they closed, spear thrusting and battle axe whirling. Our dogs and many of the horses took the brunt of the first assault.'

'How many were your attackers?'

'Their name must be legion. Alexander of Lisbon did his best. We dismounted, forming a spear hedge, but they cut through with axe, sword and mace. We became split into small groups, each man fighting for himself. The circle I was in broke. I remember receiving a burning cut here,' his hand fell to his stomach, 'then I fled. Behind me hideous screams and yells. It was easy to find my way back. I simply followed our tracks. I heard pursuers but a war-horn wailed; they must have wanted one of us to survive to tell the story.' The young man arched in pain.

I glanced at the Castellan, who shrugged. I forced a wine

cup between the dying man's lips. Demontaigu came just before dawn. He gave the Noctale what spiritual comfort he could. Afterwards we reported to the queen, who'd risen early and was already warming herself by a weak fire.

'My father,' Isabella never bothered to lift her face, but stared into the flames, 'my father in Paris will be furious! Alexander of Lisbon and the Noctales were his men. It all began in blood,' she whispered, 'and it will end in blood.'

Demontaigu and I withdrew to a small window embrasure outside in the narrow corridor. We sat on the thin cushions. Demontaigu leaned forward.

'There was nothing we could do, Mathilde. Alexander of Lisbon has received justice.'

'But what does it mean?' I asked.

'I would wager,' Demontaigu chose his words carefully, 'that Ausel and the others went into Scotland. They made their peace with Bruce, received his help then moved south. The journey would be easy; the pursuit of the king by the earls has brought everything to a halt. Sheriffs, bailiffs, the mayors of towns and cities are reluctant to move. The countryside is wild and desolate. It would be difficult to track even a sizeable war band. Ausel decided to act. Apart from the young man I shrived, I doubt if any of the Noctales survived. I must see the Castellan.' Demontaigu rose to his feet. 'If Ausel is here, then Bruce's forces can't be far behind.'

I insisted on accompanying him. The Castellan, that wily veteran, had already reached the same conclusion. He was still dismissive of stories about the Templars, but Demontaigu argued with him quietly. The Castellan listened, nodding his head. Just after daybreak he sent out scouts to follow the tracks of Alexander of Lisbon and the Noctales. These scouts, either because of their cunning or because they were allowed to, managed to return. The story they brought back was chilling. They'd reached the battle site, a place of broken spears, shattered daggers, a saddle cut and gashed, the odd item of clothing, but every corpse of both man and beast had been removed. Alexander of Lisbon and his Noctales had simply disappeared, extinguished, wiped off the face of God's earth. The scouts brought other news, of peasants in hiding who told them fearful stories about a Scottish war host plunging deep into the shire, following the valleys, carrying out savage raids against villages and local farmsteads. The Castellan needed no further encouragement. The castle was put on a war footing. A message was sent to the queen that she must be prepared to leave at a moment's notice, as well as the warning that the Castellan had not yet discovered if treachery still lurked within. We soon discovered it did.

Chapter 5

They had resolved to carry off the
Queen of England.

Two days after the massacre of Alexander of Lisbon and the
Noctales, the tocsin boomed out just as dawn broke. An
officer of the garrison came rushing into the queen's quarters, declaring that a postern gate had been found unlocked.

'God be thanked,' he added, 'it gave us a little time. Both
lock and latch had been smashed. The alarm was raised,
but shortly afterwards the sally port was attacked.' Even
from behind thick walls we could hear the growing clamour
of battle.

'It wasn't secured in time?' Isabella, already cloaked, was directing members of her household out into the bailey.

'No, your grace! A serjeant and a few soldiers were trying to do that. They were surprised and killed. The Scots now have a force in the castle. They are trying to reach the main gate . . .' The man babbled on even as we prepared to leave. Demontaigu, the queen's squires and other members of her household were all harnessed and armoured. Most of Isabella's chests and coffers had already been taken down to the cove outside Duckett's Tower. The rest was merely baggage, which was now sent ahead. Once ready, with Demontaigu and the squires as our escort, we left the Prior's Lodgings. A thick sea mist hid what was happening on the far side of the castle, where the garrison was desperately fighting to contain and drive out the invading force. The chilling sound of battle – screams, yells and the clash of weapons – carried across. Somewhere a fire burnt, its flames yellowing through the mist. Black smoke plumed up and billowed out. At the time we were in no real danger. The queen was well guarded.

We reached Duckett's Tower to find that Rosselin and Middleton had already fled down the tunnel. We followed swiftly out into the brisk, cold sea air. *The Wyvern* was ready for sea, its bowsprit turned, the large sail half unfurled, a royal standard floating from the high stern. Boats and wherries were bobbing on the waves between shore and ship. The tide was still out. We left the shelter of the cliffs, hurrying down to the waterline to meet the incoming wherries, powerful boats manned by six oarsmen. The first came in oars up, keel crunching the pebble-thick sand. Men leapt out to assist the queen and others. Demontaigu, Dunheved and I were waiting for the second wherry when one of the squires shouted a warning, pointing further down the beach. Now the cliffs stretched out sheer white, and the receding tide had exposed a broad path of sand littered with seaweed, rocks and pools. The sea haze was thinning. I glimpsed a glint of silver, a flash of colour. The terror of battle gripped my breath. Others were now shouting in alarm. The Scots had sent a force down some cliff path and out along the shoreline. Mere chance; the spin of fortune's wheel had saved the queen from entrapment either here or in the passageway of Duckett's Tower.

The squires screamed at the incoming boats to hurry. I glanced across the sea. The wherry carrying Isabella was safe, but the others seemed to take an age to beach. One of the queen's ladies – God forgive me, I forget her name – who'd been left behind with us sank down on to the wet sand, sobbing hysterically. I glanced along the water's edge. The Scottish party were closing, the light glinting on shield, hauberk, helmet and drawn sword. They paused. A group of crossbowmen dressed in black leather sped forward, knelt, aimed and loosened their bolts. They misjudged the distance and the volley fell short. Demontaigu, sword raised, organised our own force, strengthened by others now pouring out of the cave beneath Duckett's Tower. A line of archers, household men and squires, soldiers from the castle, anyone who carried an arbalest or longbow, was swiftly assembled. The Scots lunged forward, in their haste knocking aside their own archers. Demontaigu gave the order to loose. A volley of arrows and bolts brought down the front rank of the attackers and a host of those behind. Our second volley was sparser; only the longbowmen had the time to notch and loose again. Then the Scots clashed with us. A bloody, furious melee of whirling steel and strange battle cries. The hideous shock of men gripped in a deadly, vicious hand-to-hand struggle spread both along the beach and down to the water-line. Nevertheless, the attackers were held. The wherries were waiting in the shallows. Demontaigu and the squires pushed us out into the bubbling surf. We were grabbed, flung and bundled aboard. Our defenders also began to retreat deep into the water, archers going first so they could use their bows, shooting over our heads at the Scots wading through the swirling tide like dogs going for the kill. The racing surf became frothed with blood. The screams and yells of the attackers grew more furious. The Castellan, God bless him, had sent other men through Duckett's Tower. They now burst out of the cave, attacking the rear of the Scottish force. Our boats became dangerously overburdened. Wounded and dying sprawled, blood pumping out of grue-some wounds. The queen's lady-in-waiting had taken a crossbow bolt deep in her chest and was struggling in a welter of blood and pitiful, choking sounds. The oarsmen prepared. The captains of the boats were screaming to pull away.

At last we were free, rising and falling on the surging waves of the powerful tide. The boats were awash with a bloody swirl. Corpses floated on the water. The Scots, real-ising pursuit was futile, now turned to face the danger behind them. Already a few were breaking, retreating back along the shoreline. The wherries and boats drove on, braving the swell, almost crashing into the side of *The Wyvern*. We clambered up rope ladders, men shouting and pulling us over the side. We were shown little sympathy, lying on the deck where we were thrown. Water skins were passed around and I, clothes sodden, spent the rest of the morning tending to the wounded and dying. The master of *The Wyvern* was not concerned with us, more determined to break free of the coast, alarmed by beacon lights flashing from the clifftops, wary of the Flemish privateers prowling those waters. By midday I and the ship's leeches had done what we could for the wounded, Demontaigu and Dunheved assisting. Middleton and Rosselin came up but I shooed them away. Demontaigu remained cold and resolute. I thanked him for what he'd done. Dunheved certainly impressed me. He was calm, patient and watchful. Nevertheless, I could feel the fury curdling within him. We all entertained suspicions about what had happened, but now was not the time for discussion.

Once we had finished, Dunheved supervised the swift burial of the dead, committing their bodies to the deep and their souls to God. In the late afternoon the ship's crew assembled with their passengers to witness Dunheved, under an awning stretched out from the cabin, celebrate a dramatic mass for those killed. An eerie experience. *The Wyvern*, its sail full-bellied by a brisk north wind, surged through the waters under a strengthening sun. In a powerful, ringing voice Dunheved proclaimed the oraisons for the departed as well as leading us in a hymn of thanksgiving for our deliverance. I felt unsteady, as if I was in a dream. The rolling ship, its pungent smells, the creak and groan of timber and cordage. Above us a sheer blue sky, the sun washing the deck. Such a contrast to the fog-bound, craggy heights of Tynemouth.

In the early evening, the queen, unscathed and calm, left her cabin and met us under the same awning beneath which Dunheved had celebrated mass. She was ivory-faced, her hair tied tightly around her head, over which she pulled the deep cowl of her cloak. She publicly thanked the master of *The Wyvern*, her squires, Demontaigu and others of her household. She distributed precious stones as tokens of her appreciation, then sat in the captain's small, throne-like chair as Dunheved listed the dead.

'We lost eight in all. A lady-in-waiting, one of the squires and six of the queen's household.' The Dominican added that at least twice that number from the castle garrison had perished in our escape.

Isabella just sat, her face like that of a carved statue, hard eyes unblinking as she stared out across the sea. At Dunheved's question, she answered that she was well, but then returned to her reverie, those blue eyes, sapphire hard. Afterwards she shared a jug of hippocras and a platter of sweetmeats with us. Rosselin and Middleton, who'd been busy attending to matters below deck, joined us. They looked shamefaced. I'd glimpsed them during the day going up and down the deck as well as at Dunheved's mass. In truth, they confessed, they'd been as surprised and shocked by the furious battle on the beach as had *The Wyvern*'s master, a shaven-headed, cheery-faced seaman from the port of Hull. He declared how Rosselin and Middleton had wanted to go back to help them, but he had warned them that was futile.

Nevertheless, the master had the sense to realise that something treacherous had happened: Isabella, Queen of England, had almost been captured by a Scottish raiding party.

Dunheved and I remained with the queen till late in the evening. She insisted on reciting the Vespers of that day. Afterwards we tried to engage her in conversation, but she simply shook her head, raising a finger to her lips.

'Not now,' she murmured, 'not now, Mathilde, Brother Stephen. We must simply sit, wait and watch.'

We had no choice. *The Wyvern* had been turned into an infirmary as well as a ship prepared for battle. Its master was determined on one thing alone: to bring the queen out of hostile waters to a safe port. After a good night's sailing, he met Isabella and declared that by sunset we would slip into the port of Whitby on the Yorkshire coast.

'It's a mere fishing village, but high on the cliffs stands a famous convent.' He smiled. 'I am sure the lady abbess will be welcoming and give you good housing.'

True to his word, late that afternoon *The Wyvern* slipped safely into the cove of Whitby. The queen insisted on immediate disembarkation. Boats took her and her household to the beach, a messenger being sent to alert the abbess of St Hilda's. After a short while, a group of nuns in their dark blue habits, escorted by retainers from the abbey, whose majestic buildings we'd glimpsed from the sea, came down to conduct the queen up to lodgings being hastily prepared for her. A busy, exhausting time. I'd been so immersed in the dangers we'd escaped, I didn't have time to reflect on anything. Only now did I realise how tired, frayed, dirty and dishevelled I must have looked.

For the next three days we rested and relaxed in spacious and very comfortable quarters provided for us at the abbey. A strange time, an island of peace between the horrors of leaving Tynemouth and the storm gathering around the throne of England. Days passed. Messengers left on the fastest mounts from the abbey stables. Squires and retainers were dispatched to the master of *The Wyvern*, which dipped its sails three times in honour of the Trinity and sailed out of Whitby. It returned a few days later, its master hurrying up to take secret council with the queen.

I was certainly pleased to be away from Tynemouth. St Hilda's Abbey proved to be a fine resting place where Isabella could relax in beautiful surroundings, be it rich, oak-panelled chambers or luxuriant gardens and shady cloisters, especially as the weather had changed, one sun-filled day following the other. I became busy in the infirmary, assisting with the wounded, or helping in the dispensary filling pots and jars with various remedies. Demontaigu begged leave to be excused on his own secret business, as did the Aquilae Petri, who hired horses and thundered out to discover the whereabouts of their master. People came and went. Rumour was rife. Stories gathered as plentiful as fleas in a dog's fur, but Isabella never showed her hand. She truly was schooled in the harsh, bloody conflicts of court. As a child she had been abused by her three brothers, and she'd acquired the patience of a waiting cat. She had a mind that teemed, yet openly she smiled and acted so graciously. She still seemed a little distant from me, as if absorbed in some secret problem she could not share. I tended to her. She allowed me to examine her and I was relieved to find that she and the child she carried had come through safe and unscathed. Isabella was that rare flower, elegantly beautiful and lissom but in fact hard and tough as the finest armour in the land. She was, both body and soul, in good spirit. True, her belly was much swollen and she suffered quietly the usual pains, aches and discomfort of being *enceinte*, but such petty problems did not concern her. She sat in her chamber dictating letters, closeted herself with Dunheved, walked out to meet the abbess and the good sisters or acted the bountiful seigneur in the grand refectory of the abbey. All this was a device, a shield carried before her, not only to protect her but behind which she could plot her own devious path. The queen was spinning her own web, watching and waiting.

Isabella would discuss little except to question me about Tynemouth, the Noctales, Lanercost's death, my suspicions and what I saw and heard. She would only talk when she was ready, and on the last day of April, she decided she was. We met, Dunheved and myself, in the queen's personal chamber, an octagonal room lavishly furnished with gleaming oak stools, a writing desk, a lavarium and high leather-backed chairs placed before the mantled hearth shaped in the form of a hood. Above this hung a brilliantly hued tapestry telling the miraculous story of Caedmon, a local cowherd who'd learnt to write the most elegant poetry. On either side of this, paintings picked out in red, gold and black described scenes from the life of St Hilda and other great saints of the northern shires. The heavy door was barred and locked. Its ox-blood-coloured leather drape had been rolled down, whilst the black and white lozenge-shaped

131

tiles on the floor had been covered with thick rugs, as if the queen wanted to deaden all sound both within and without. The small oriel windows, gilded and painted with religious devices, coloured the light of the setting sun. Certainly a place for secrets and hushed council.

Isabella looked resplendent in a tawny-coloured gown of the costliest taffeta beneath a sleeveless coat of blue and gold. Silver slippers, laced with the softest lamb's wool, were on her feet, a gauze veil over her hair, which hung down luxurious and thick. When we gathered, I noticed that a jewel-studded casket in which the queen kept her *secretae litterae* – secret letters – lay open, its lid thrown back. I recognised a letter, very recent, the vellum was still a fresh cream colour, carrying the purple seal of Philip of France's secret chancery. I wondered when she'd received this and why she was being so enigmatic. For a while we clustered around the fire, the candles and oil lamps dancing shadows around the walls. Outside a growing silence as the sisters gathered in their chapel for meditation. The queen abruptly brought the courtesies to an end.

'What do we have?' Isabella's voice crackled with anger. 'By God's good grace and no one else's, we are now free of Tynemouth, well away from Scottish marauders and Flemish pirates. No, no, I am not ungrateful.' She pinched my wrist. 'Demontaigu and my squires did good service, but it should never have happened.' Again she pinched my wrist. 'Mathilde, the king and Gaveston now bathe in a pool dirtied by their own making. The Noctales have met with God's justice, but the deaths of Lanercost, Leygrave and Kennington remain unresolved. More importantly, what did happen in Duckett's Tower? Were Kennington and his guards removed as part of a plot against me?'

Isabella and Dunheved shared a glance, as if savouring some secret. I curbed my temper.

'Plotting against your grace?' I asked innocently. Isabella had kept me out of her secret council, so what could I say? The queen just smiled, tapped my wrist and leaned closer.

'Of course a plot against me! If the good Lord hadn't intervened, those Scots would have forced the main gate of Duckett's Tower. Someone alerted them, not only to my presence but as to how I might escape, hence that furious assault on the beach.'

Again I bit my tongue. Isabella was talking as if reciting a speech, not so much searching for the truth as for what I might think.

'Does your grace have news of Tynemouth?' I asked.

'Good news,' Isabella replied. 'The Castellan managed to hold the attackers and drive them back. The garrison made a good account of themselves. My fair cousins the Beaumonts survived unscathed and, I believe, will join us soon.'

'God be thanked,' Dunheved murmured. 'But I ask your grace, can your noble cousins be . . .' He paused.

'Trusted?' Isabella queried. 'Brother Stephen, apart from the people in this chamber, I trust no one!'

'And the treachery at Tynemouth?' I asked.

'In his letter,' Isabella replied, 'the Castellan apologised but admitted that a traitor would find it easy in that fogbound castle to slip along the narrow runnels, damage a postern door and leave it vulnerable to those beyond.'

'But who could communicate such a design to the Scots?

The castle was besieged. No one could leave. Messengers were few and far between.'

'The Templar Ausel could slip in and out unscathed,' Isabella replied. 'Why not someone else? Duckett's Tower was our escape. The traitor could also have used it to alert the Scots. And,' she added bitterly, 'let us not forget those signals flashed from the castle walls.'

'True,' I murmured. 'A Scottish force could have been brought into Duckett's Tower, but it would have been dangerous. The tide can sweep in and cut off any escape, whilst once in the tower, the Scots would have had to clear it and then fight their way across to the Prior's Lodgings. They might never have reached that and would certainly have been slaughtered in any retreat. The Castellan would have ensured that. Yes,' I reasoned, 'the Scots needed to bring you out of the castle, hence their attack. St Michael and all his angels be my witness, it was hideous treachery, but why? By whom?' I glanced at Dunheved, who simply crossed himself and murmured his own prayer of thanksgiving.

'By whom?' I repeated and turned to the queen. She did not answer. 'Did you fear such treachery, your grace? If so, why shelter at Tynemouth?'

'What other choice did we have, Mathilde? Better than wandering lonely heathlands on the northern march. A secure fortress high on the cliffs overlooking the sea was safer than some deserted farmstead.'

I nodded in agreement.

'And *The Wyvern*? Who ordered it to take station off Tynemouth?'

'My husband, at my insistence.'

'Why?'

'Mathilde, I was fearful. I still am.'

'About what?'

Isabella put her head down, rubbing her brow with her long white fingers. 'I don't really know. If I did, I could confront the danger.'

'And your saintly father?' I added with mock sweetness.

Isabella laughed girlishly behind her hand.

'Why, Mathilde?'

'Your grace,' I retorted, 'mischief bubbles in England. Your father could no more resist stirring it than a bird could flying.'

'True, true.' Isabella leaned back in her chair and glanced swiftly out of the corner of her eye at Dunheved, sitting on her left.

The psalmist says that the human heart is devious, and so it is: that one glance portrayed a secret alliance between the queen and the enigmatic Dominican. Yet at the time, what could I make of that? Dunheved was the guardian of her soul, the keeper of her secrets. Certainly my mood was tinged with jealousy. I thought I held that benefice, but time also has its own secrets, and only the passing of the years reveals the full truth. At the time I had no doubt that Isabella had been in contact with her father. I recalled the Castellan's remark about French war-cogs being off the coast. I wondered if the master of *The Wyvern* had taken secret missives to them and returned with their reply. Hence that letter, so recently come from France, bearing Philip's secret seal.

'And his grace the king?' I asked.

'Fleet as the deer,' Isabella remarked. 'Once again he's

eluded his pursuers. My husband, his grace,' she added sardonically, 'is approaching York. We are to meet him there.'

'And the earls?'

'Retreated south of the Trent but vowing to return.' Isabella shrugged. 'It costs great treasure to keep troops in the field.' She rose abruptly as a sign that our meeting was over. 'Mathilde,' she touched me lightly on the face, 'as in chess, *ma cherie*, the pieces might return to their places but the game is not yet over.'

No, it certainly wasn't! News came in like a blizzard of snow. Bruce's force under his war-leader Douglas had retreated. Tynemouth was safe and secure. The Beaumonts were hurrying south and royal officials were now hunting down various carts and sumpter ponies laden with the queen's household possessions. Most were saved. A few went missing, never to return. Thomas of Lancaster, the king's cousin and the leading earl, sent letters to Isabella making it clear that his quarrel was with Lord Gaveston and not with her or the king. A pretty letter full of pious insincerities, but at least, as Isabella drily remarked, Lancaster offered to return some of her baggage seized along with the king's at Novo Castro.

Demontaigu also returned, slipping into the abbey late one afternoon. I met him in St Aidan's rose garden, though he refused to talk there. Instead we left by the Antioch Gate, moving down the steep cliff path on to the rough cobbled streets of the little fishing hamlet. He seemed to know his way and took me into the Root of David, a merchant's tavern on the outskirts of the village, overlooking the craggy seashore. A pleasant enough place, I remember it well.

The tap room was divided by barriers to form little closets, each furnished with ale-benches either side of a table. The room smelt fragrantly of grilled fish and almonds and the food we ordered, venison broiled in wine, black pepper and cinnamon, was delicious, as was the ale brewed in the house at the back. Demontaigu washed his hands in herb-laced water and ate hungrily whilst listening intently to my news. Once I'd finished, he mopped his mouth with a napkin and moved the candle closer. His eyes were red-rimmed, his face tired and drawn. He pushed the candle a little nearer, searching my face as I did his.

'Mathilde, we have been now together for four years. We are reaching a path that is about to divide. I came to Isabella's household as a Templar in hiding. People now know who I really am. You must realise that I might flee, must flee at a moment's notice.'

I nodded.

'Even more so now.' He took a deep breath. 'The Templar order in England and Wales has been ruined, not one stone left upon another. As you know, those Templars who weren't taken up went into hiding. Philip's agents hunted us through France, Hainault, Flanders, even beyond the Rhine, but in Scotland we are safe. Bruce has created a haven, a sanctuary for us. Templars from England, Wales and Ireland have fled there, as well as others from France, Castile, Aragon, Italy and the Rhineland states. These are men, Mathilde, who've been persecuted for years. They've heard the most gruesome tales about what has happened to their brethren in the dungeons of the Louvre and elsewhere in Philip's kingdom. Men broken on the rack, bodies twisted, strung from scaffolds, burnt and scalded, limbs amputated, eyes gouged out, ears cut off.' He lowered his voice. 'But I am telling you what you know. The Templars have a blood feud not only with Philip and his ministers but with his family, and that includes our queen. Now the Templars have gathered in Scotland, their hearts full of anger, their ears crammed with hideous stories. They want vengeance.' Demontaigu paused. 'Bruce sent two forces south. The first was under James Douglas, a skilled and ruthless fighter—'

'And the other was under Estivet, leader of the Templars?' I suggested.

Demontaigu nodded in agreement.

'Estivet's force numbered about two to three hundred men, swollen by Scottish Templars and those in Bruce's own army sympathetic to our cause. They made swift march. No one opposed them, not out there on the moorlands, following secret paths with copses and woods to hide in. You could ride for a day and not meet anyone. Estivet and his host had one desire: to search out the Noctales, bring them to battle and utterly destroy them. We knew the Noctales were garrisoned at Tynemouth. Ausel volunteered to act the false guide and Alexander of Lisbon, a coward, rose to the bait.'

'They were massacred?' I asked.

'Every one of them, except the man who was allowed to escape, to take the grim tidings back to Tynemouth. Alexander of Lisbon and the Noctales were cut to pieces. No one was shown quarter, their corpses tossed into bogs and marshes, their harness, weapons, armour and horses taken for our use, never to be seen again. Amongst the

Templar host in Scotland there is great rejoicing. Philip of France of course will be furious.'

'Did the Templars play any role in the attack on the queen at Tynemouth?'

'No!' Demontaigu replied quickly. 'Ausel would not agree to that. I met him. He still lurks in England with an eye to any other mischief he might cause. He took the most sacred oath a Templar can, on the Cross and Face of Christ, that the Templars had nothing to do with the attack on the queen. However,' Demontaigu leaned across the table, his voice falling to a murmur, 'Mathilde, stories at the Scottish court talk of Gaveston having some control over the king. Other clacking tongues whisper that the attack on Tynemouth was to capture the queen and hold her hostage.'

'As a bargain counter with her husband?'

'Of course.'

'And the traitor?'

'No one really knows. The Beaumonts were mentioned.'

'Impossible!' I retorted. 'They are the queen's kinsmen; they'd be disgraced . . .'

'Listen, Mathilde, when it comes to treasure and lands, no one can be trusted. Some English lords with extensive estates in Scotland have joined Bruce's standard, so why shouldn't the Beaumonts?'

I stared down at the table. Was it possible? I wondered. The Beaumonts had been in Tynemouth and escaped unscathed. Was that part of their secret agreement with Bruce?

'You're sure?' I asked. 'To capture the queen, not to kill her?'

'To capture her. Think, Mathilde, what could happen. If Bruce held Isabella, Queen of England, Princess of France, what terms could he dictate? French help? Have Edward withdraw from Scotland and give up all claims?'

'Of course, of course,' I hastened to agree, 'but that is not the problem, Bertrand. The real mystery is who would do that. The Beaumonts have been mentioned, but who else would prosper?' I paused. 'The earls, perhaps? Edward would have to give up Gaveston in return. Perhaps Philip of France? He would love to see his son-in-law humiliated. If Isabella was captured, she would be treated honourably, perhaps even sent back to France. Philip would have not only her in his grasp but the future heir of the king of England. Edward would lose. He'd be a laughing stock. Gaveston would be more vulnerable than ever. People would see it as God's judgement on the king for his friendship with his catamite.' I sipped from my tankard of ale, possibilities teeming in my mind. Isabella was certainly a prize – both the queen and the future heir – yet who could be involved in such devious treason?

'Murky and misty,' I whispered. 'Someone definitely tried to betray the queen at Tynemouth. Is that why Kennington was flung from Duckett's Tower? Did he know or see something? Was his murder part of the preparation for that assault? The queen escaped by God's good favour. Another hour, the entire castle might have been taken and everyone in it captured.'

'One thing Ausel assured me.' Bertrand pushed away his tankard and collected his cloak. 'He again took the oath and swore that neither he nor, to the best to his knowledge, any of our brethren had anything to do with the deaths of Lanercost and the others.'

We were about to leave the tavern when I noticed a pilgrim armed with a staff, his cloak decorated with the conch shell of St James of Compostela, the palms of Outremer and the papal insignia of Rome. I recalled the Pilgrim from the Wastelands who had pestered the queen at York, his frenetic face stained with that strawberry mark, then the moment passed, at least for a while. On my return I did not inform Isabella about what Demontaigu had told me. We became busy gathering her household at Whitby. Moreover, what was the use? More questions about deep-tangled mysteries that only time and evidence could resolve.

The Beaumonts eventually arrived in a show of gorgeous livery. They portrayed themselves very much as the heroes of the hour, with a litany of praise about their valiant prowess during what they now called 'The Great Siege of Tynemouth'. To anyone stupid enough to listen, they described how Lord Henry had stood like ancient Horatius in the breach and single-handedly resisted the Scots. Lady Vesci, that armoured Minerva, used her cross-bolt to deadly effect, whilst Louis, like Moses of old, held his arms up in supplication to the Almighty. Oh, the Beaumonts were *sans pareil*! None were more given to double-dealing and mischief than that unholy trinity. They'd managed to reassemble their retinue, retrieve their baggage and journey south through that early summer like a triumphant Caesar entering Rome. 'A veritable stone wall' was how Henry trumpeted his defence of Tynemouth against the Scots. In truth they could provide little information about the treachery which had allowed

141

the Scots in or the mortal calamity that might have befallen the queen, who in turn could only welcome her 'sweet cousins' with open arms.

Once Isabella was ready, we travelled in glorious state to York. Outside Micklegate we were met by an escort of knight bannerets in their brilliant livery of blue, gold and scarlet with banners and pennants displaying the leopards of England. These escorted us into York. The city had put aside its trade to stage pageants and welcome their beautiful fairy-tale queen, now bearing the royal heir, who'd miraculously escaped the devilish plots and guile of the Bruce. The city conduits poured wine. Full oxen were roasted on enormous spits above roaring fires. At corners, before the gilt-gabled mansion of the city merchant-princes, speeches were made. Coloured cloths, standards and banners hung from windows. Trumpets sounded, horns brayed. The people cheered as Isabella, mounted on a milk-white palfrey, its harnessing all burnished and embroidered with gold stitching and silver medallions, processed along the streets and thoroughfares, scrupulously cleansed and sweetened for her progress. Spectacular pageants were enacted at various points along the approaches to the Ouse Bridge. The mayor and city aldermen, richly attired in their guild robes, presented the queen with a purse full of silver and a bowl of pure Venetian glass. Further along a group of maidens, garbed in snow-white drapery, their heads garlanded with spring flowers, enacted some scene from the city past before honouring her with a platter of pure gold studded with gems. Choristers from the nearby abbey church, clothed in dark red robes, sang *'Isabellae reginae, laus, honor et gloria'* – 'Praise, honour

and glory to Isabella the queen'. Another pageant, celebrating the life of Saintly Thurston, a hero of the city, was
enacted on the steps of St Michael's church, so it was midday
by the time we reached the gatehouse of the Franciscan
priory. Here, as was the custom, a horde of ragged beggars
waited to plead for alms. Isabella had given me a fat purse
of copper coins to distribute whilst she and her cortège swept
in to meet the king and Gaveston in the friary grounds. I
stayed, guarded by Demontaigu, to give the queen's pennies
to the poor. God be my witness, there were so many, with
their pitted skin, red-rimmed eyes and scrawny bodies
displaying hideous wounds and deformities. The fragrance
of the queen's cortège, of perfumed robes over oil-drenched
skins, as well as the gusts of incense could not hide the
rank, fetid smells of that legion of poor. Skeletal fingers,
curved like talons, stretched out to grasp the coins. I distributed these as fast and as fairly as I could. As a sea of gaunt
grey figures surrounded me, I glimpsed the Pilgrim from
the Wastelands, that distinctive mulberry stain on his
sunburnt face. He lunged forward, took a coin then thrust
a small scroll into my hand.

Once the alms were distributed and I was inside the gates,
I unrolled the greasy black scroll and read its strange
message: *Ego sum vox clamans in deserto – I'm a voice crying
in the desert. I beg you for the sake of the mistress you serve
that I see thee, or thy mistress. I shall wait for you every day
at Vespers bell near the Golgotha Gate.*

I handed this to Demontaigu; he read it and pulled a face.

'See him, Mathilde, as soon as you can. I shall be with
you.'

Of course I couldn't do so immediately. The king and Gaveston, garbed most royally in the costliest silks, velvet and ermine, awaited the queen in the great friary yard. I watched the mummery and court etiquette as both king and favourite welcomed Isabella and her entourage. The royal couple and their escorts mingled in a gorgeous collection of butterfly colours, watched by the gaping friars in their dark brown or grey robes. Speeches were delivered. Kisses and embraces exchanged. I glimpsed Rosselin and Middleton in the lavishly embroidered livery of their master, before glancing up at the looming church tower with its sinister history, the chimes of its great bells Peter and Paul booming out over the pageant below. I wondered again about the secrets the belfry held, before, along with the rest I was swirled away in the festivities that became the order of the day.

A royal banquet was held in the Prior's Lodgings. A blaze of lighted candles dazzled the heavy gold and silver platters, jugs, ewers and goblets. Cooks and servitors brought in delicious dishes – venison, beef, swan and lampreys – whilst the wine flowed as if from a never-ending fountain. Yet it was all shadow with no substance. Nothing had really changed, and the following morning, in the same chamber, a more sober king and favourite listed the stark realities confronting them. Edward, flush-faced after acting the toper the night before, began to describe what was happening. The king hadn't changed, but Gaveston certainly had: his beautiful face was pale, lined and haggard, and silver streaks glinted in that once dark, rich hair. The favourite looked thinner. He betrayed his agitation with nervous gestures, constantly fidgeting, and rubbing his stomach as if full of bitter bile. He'd lost that overweening arrogance, whilst the two Aquilae standing behind his chair also reflected their master's unease.

In truth, sentence of death had been passed against them. The great earls brooked no opposition. Gaveston was to surrender himself, face trial and suffer execution. The time for negotiation was over. The earls were massing their forces and sending out writs summoning levies; their outriders visited ports and harbours to block any escape by the royal favourite. No help would come from France; that door was firmly closed. The shire levies would not move. The sheriffs and bailiffs, uncertain about what was going to happen, simply turned away. Royal writs were not answered, whilst the commissioners of array could not raise troops or collect purveyance. Edward spoke haltingly to the same chamber council that had last met the day Leygrave was killed. He mumbled about Tynemouth, about the Scots having a traitor within the garrison. How he was so pleased to be reunited with his queen, for whose safety he had so strenu-ously prayed and worked. During his rambling speech Gaveston's mood altered, that furious Gascon temper manifesting itself, face muscles twitching in anger, gnawing his lips, fingers falling to the hilt of his long dagger. Isabella, on the other hand, remained serene, as if she just enjoyed a regal and stately progress through the kingdom.

Edward eventually reached his conclusion. Gaveston would, within a day, leave for Scarborough Castle. The king paused and asked who would accompany him. A profound silence eloquently answered his question. *Causa finita* – the cause is finished. So was Gaveston!

The royal favourite stared beseechingly around. I appreciated Gaveston's horrifying predicament. If he was locked up in Scarborough, apart from his now depleted Aquilae, he would be alone. Edward, growing even more distracted, rambled on about witnesses needing to be present lest mischief befall his 'sweet brother'.

Dunheved volunteered. Isabella looked at me and nodded imperceptibly. I reluctantly agreed, as did Henry Beaumont and his kin. Once the meeting had ended, I met my mistress, who thanked me.

'It's best, Mathilde.' She stroked my hair, then cupped my face in her hands. 'It's my way of showing my husband that I still believe all is not lost. You and Demontaigu must accompany Gaveston.'

'And?' I asked.

'Watch,' she replied.

I thought of Gaveston locked up in Scarborough Castle. 'And the king?'

'He cannot be in Scarborough,' Isabella replied wearily, 'not held fast, cut off from his kingdom. Edward must go south and try to raise support, seek loans from the London merchants. I . . .' She paused, turning slightly, a gesture that betrayed her own unease. I understood what was going to happen.

'Scarborough will be definitely besieged, won't it?' I asked. 'The king does not want himself, or you, at the behest of the earls.'

'And?' Isabella asked.

'Someone may have to treat with the earls. Someone who will be acceptable to them.' I smiled thinly. 'Like Stephen

Dunheved, the Dominican, and me, *domicella reginae camerae* – a lady of the queen's chamber – trusted and privy to royal business.'

'Yes, Mathilde.'

'And the Beaumonts,' I added bitterly, 'with a foot in either camp, as I am sure they have.'

'Yes,' Isabella murmured. 'Slippery as eels, twisting and turning, my sweet cousins constantly looking for their own advantage.'

'Could the Beaumonts have acted the traitor at Tynemouth?' I asked.

'Possibly. You told me about that cloth and button displaying their livery found near the trap door to the charnel house. The Beaumonts weave their own dark designs.'

'Why should they betray you to the Scots?'

'I don't know.' Isabella half smiled. 'Perhaps to impress Bruce, to attract his attention, to gain favour with him. The Beaumont estates in Scotland are prosperous: fertile crop fields, good meadowland, dense forests and streams rich with salmon.'

'And the Aquilae?' I asked. 'Could the Beaumonts be responsible for their deaths?'

'Mathilde, if he wanted to, Henry Beaumont could put Judas to shame. Yes, they gather around the throne. They fawn and flatter both the king and Gaveston, but in the end, the Beaumonts have only one cause: themselves.'

'But why should they kill the Aquilae?'

'To weaken Gaveston. To prepare him for death. Is that not the way of those who plot assassination? To first remove the guards?'

'*Quis custodiet custodes?*' I quoted Juvenal's famous jibe. 'Who shall guard the guards?'

'So true.' Isabella stepped closer. Her face, framed by a white wimple, looked truly beautiful, her skin translucent, those eyes a deeper blue, sensuous red lips slightly parted. 'I have closely studied my husband, Mathilde. I know his soul. He is lonely, vulnerable. His mother Eleanor died when he was still a child. The old king was too busy slaughtering the Scots or plotting against my father to care for him. There's a great emptiness in my husband's heart. I don't think I will ever fill it. Gaveston might. So why shouldn't the Beaumonts remove Gaveston? But first, as in chess, the pawns must be cleared, then the castles, bishops, kings and queens become even more vulnerable.'

'So,' I replied, 'the Aquilae are removed, slain one by one in a mocking way. The assassins creep closer to Gaveston. It could be the Beaumonts. They must view him as a nuisance, a gross distraction to their ambitions . . .'

'Better still,' Isabella pressed a finger against my lips, 'better still, Mathilde, if Gaveston goes, who will replace him in the king's affections? The Beaumonts? Is that what they dream of?' She paused. 'God knows,' she added drily, 'my sweet cousins couldn't really care except for whatever is good for them.' She looked away, lips moving soundlessly, then nodded at me and swept out of the chamber.

The preparations immediately ensued for Gaveston's departure for Scarborough. The king's clerks truly believed the earls had spies in York, even in the friary itself, and their main fear was that once Gaveston left, the Great Lords might send a comitatus to intercept him. Accordingly, where

148

possible, our preparations were hidden, hurried and secret. I did have words with Demontaigu about what the queen had told me. He immediately agreed with what she'd said.

'Everybody wants Gaveston to go,' he murmured.

'Except the king?'

'Except the king!' Demontaigu's voice was rich with sarcasm.

I stretched out and ran a finger around his lips. 'The king?' I queried. 'Has the king tired of Gaveston?'

'Think, Mathilde! For four years the Crown has been domin-ated by Gaveston. Has Edward, since the day of his father's death, been given one moment's peace? Has he been allowed to exercise true power? Look at what's happened to him, chased about his realm and threatened. At times he is no better than some felon before the shire court, put to the horn as an outlaw. Edward must be seething with anger, but he must also be exhausted. Now,' Demontaigu spread his hands, 'life has swept on. Four years a king, Edward faces problems in Scotland and France. At Westminster the Commons demand to meet him. The Lords Spiritual have their own list of grievances. They ask why the king doesn't settle and live on his own? His wife, a young, beautiful woman, is now *enceinte*, hopefully with a male child. I'm not saying his grace wills Gaveston evil. Edward may just want a little peace for himself.'

Long after Demontaigu left, his bleak description of the king remained with me.

Rosselin and Middleton also came to see me. I visited the priory's scriptorium, a gracious, elegant chamber, its fragrance so precious to me: pressed vellum, neatly scrubbed, ink, sandstone and calfskin bindings. I found it comforting to walk along the polished floor and peer over the shoulder of some brother as he copied a manuscript or decorated a book of hours with beautiful miniature pictures that shone like jewels. I glimpsed Dunheved standing near the unbound manuscripts, all filed neatly in their pigeonhole shelves. He explained how he was searching for a copy of Anselm's *Cur Deus Homo – Why God Became Man* – and returned to his scrutiny. I smiled to hide my own surprise, then felt guilty; after all, Dunheved belonged to an order famous for its learning in the schools of Oxford and Cambridge. He was more than just a preacher, and I idly wondered in what branch of the trivium or quadrivium he was interested. Lost in such thoughts, I left the scriptorium. Rosselin and Middleton were waiting for me in the small cloister beyond. They rose and blocked my path. Rosselin raised a hand, palm extended in a gesture of peace.

'Mathilde, we do not wish to alarm you, but the deaths of our comrades Lanercost, Leygrave and Kennington, have they been forgotten?'

'Has your master forgotten them?' I retorted.

'His mind is all a muddle,' Rosselin declared.

'He is faced with a sea of cares.' Middleton's boyish face under his shaven pate was anxious and concerned. A set of Ave beads hung round his neck; he fingered these as if for protection.

'So your master is not concerned,' I replied, 'but you are? Take great care, sirs, I have warned you. Whoever killed your comrades may also have singled you out for death.'

'We heed your warnings,' Middleton whispered, 'but

mistress, how can we truly protect ourselves when we do not know the enemy?'

'And neither do I, sir. If I did, I would tell you!'

'One thing we have found.' Rosselin stared around as if some eavesdropper might be lurking. 'One thing we have found,' he repeated, 'is that the day Leygrave was killed, a Franciscan, certainly a man garbed in the brown robes of the order, was seen slipping out through the Galilee Porch of the friary church.'

'But that could have been anyone,' I replied. 'This friary is full of brothers going about their business.'

'No, no.' Rosselin shook his head. 'The lay brother who was killed, Brother Eusebius? He told Father Prior that when he entered the church that morning to sound the Angelus, it was empty. Then he heard a sound, turned and glimpsed a figure, not walking like one of the brothers, but darting fleetingly like a shadow through the door of the Galilee Porch.'

Chapter 6

*A man appeared at Oxford who claimed
he was the old King's son.*

I asked both Aquilae if they could tell me more; both shook
their heads. I courteously thanked them for the information and promised to reflect on it. Yet what could I do? I
was as mystified and apprehensive as the rest. We were
about to leave the friary and journey to Scarborough, where,
I knew, violence would occur. Once the earls learnt that
Gaveston had locked himself in there, they would come
seeking him. Indeed, everybody accepted that, and a pall of
gloom settled over the court, the reality behind all the empty

pomp. Gaveston was hardly ever seen. Edward, however, remained precocious and fickle as always. He could drink, slur his words, have a tantrum, but at all times Edward of Caernarvon was changeable. He could weep at Vespers and be merry as a Yuletide fire by Compline.

I thought the king had forgotten both me and his commission to investigate Lanercost's death. I was wrong. On the same afternoon I met Rosselin and Middleton, I retired to my own chamber to study a manuscript loaned by the brothers from their extensive library. I think it was a copy of Peter the Spaniard's *Thesaurus Pauperum – A Treasury of the Poor*: a veritable *multum in parvo* – a little encyclopaedia of medicine. I was examining the strange symbols inscribed in the margin when a knock on the door aroused me from my studies. I hurried across, thinking it was Demontaigu, but Edward the king, cloaked and cowled, pushed his way into the chamber. He closed the door and leaned against it, pulled back his hood, sighed, then went and sat on a stool. He acted like a little boy, looking round, smiling to himself, tapping his feet and playing with a tassel on his cloak.

'Mathilde?'

'Yes, your grace.'

'On your oath, tell me what you have discovered.'

'About what, your grace?'

'Everything since Lanercost fell like a stone from that tower. Have your reflected on that, Mathilde? The Aquilae of Gaveston,' he forced a laugh, 'soaring like eagles ever so high. The highest they say any bird can reach. All brought low from towers, crashing like stones to their deaths.' He pointed a finger at me. 'You've thought of that?'

'It has occurred to me, your grace.'

'Then tell me what you know.'

I did so, describing everything as honestly as I could. The king heard me out, now and again interrupting me with the odd question, rubbing his face in his hands.

'A mystery,' he murmured, 'a true mystery.' He rose to his feet and walked to the door. 'Do not stop, Mathilde.' He paused, hand on the latch, and glanced over his shoulder. 'One day, when the sky is clearer, I will want to know the truth.' Then he left as the bells chimed for the brothers to leave their tasks for the next hour of their day.

At the time I thought the king's visit was part of some great design. In fact Edward was as confused as anyone. He'd lost control and the mystery only deepened his weakness. He'd told me to continue. I certainly did, not only because he'd ordered me. I had also taken my own sacred oath to protect his queen. Tynemouth had proved how vulnerable she had become on the shifting, treacherous sands of the time.

At Vespers bell Demontaigu and I approached the Golgotha Gate of the friary to meet the Pilgrim. A beautiful summer's evening, the perfume from the friary gardens mixing with the appetising smells of its bakeries and kitchens. A lay brother had set up a makeshift stall to serve soup, bread and a clutch of fruit for the beggars of the area. The poor swarmed around, wanderers, traders, tinkers and pilgrims, as well as a legion of beggars who waited for their first mouthful of the day. They had all gathered at the entrance to to Pig Sty Alley, a dark-mouthed runnel opposite the Golgotha Gate. A motley throng garbed in outlandish scraps of clothing: an old man with his pet ferret, two jesters in monkey-eared red hoods, some ladies of the night desperate for food, rogues, nightwalkers and counterfeit men constantly sharp-eyed for any advantage. I searched for the Pilgrim. I left Demontaigu and walked across to look down Pig Sty Alley, a long strip of a lane that ran under leaning, decaying houses. A place truly drenched in sin and wicked-ness, its open sewer gleaming in the middle, the dancing light of lintel lanterns illuminating the shadow-walkers flit-ting across the alley from one doorway to another. A gust of saltpetre strewn to cover the smells made me step back. I wondered where the Pilgrim could be. I rejoined Demontaigu just as a royal scurrier, his horse caked with mud, forced his way through to the gate. He dismounted, raising high the leather pouch embroidered with the royal arms. He shouted, demanding passage, as he pushed his way through the crowd.

'More trouble,' Demontaigu whispered. 'The king must leave here. Mathilde, we are wasting our time. The Pilgrim will not come . . .'

I glanced sharply at him. 'You have other urgent matters?'

'Ausel,' he replied. 'He's back in York on unfinished busi-ness, though God knows what that is!'

We waited a little longer but caught no sight of the Pilgrim. We made our way back through the Golgotha Gate. I became aware of a Franciscan just behind me, cowl pulled over his head, Ave beads hanging down, the whispering patter of *'Ave Maria gratia plena'* – 'Hail Mary full of grace' . . . We crossed the friary grounds, going through an apple orchard, the overhead branches rich with lacy white blossom, and entered a small rose garden. Demontaigu was talking about the need to leave at a moment's notice when I heard my name called. I turned. The Franciscan, still following us, pushed back his cowl as he quickened his step towards us. Demontaigu's hand fell to his dagger; the Franciscan lifted his hand.

'*Pax vobiscum, amici* – peace be to you, my friends.' He raised his head. The Pilgrim's face, strangely marked but now shaven, his tousled hair cropped close, tonsured like that of a friar, smiled at us.

'Why?' I asked. 'Why act like a nightwalker?'

The Pilgrim just shrugged. 'When you wander the wastelands, mistress, you have to be sure. Now, I offer no deceit, no trickery.' He stepped closer.

I abruptly remembered what Rosselin and Middleton had told me about a figure garbed like a Franciscan. Was it the Pilgrim? I studied the close-set eyes in that ascetic face. The Pilgrim was never still, tapping his chest, head turning now and again to ensure that we were alone.

'Why the subterfuge?' Demontaigu insisted. 'Why can't we sit here and discuss what you have to tell us?'

The Pilgrim grinned. I noticed how firm and white his teeth were: a man who took care of everything.

'What are you frightened of?' I spoke my mind.

The Pilgrim peered up at the sky, then back at me.

'Mistress, I simply want to make my confession. What I've learnt may be of use to you, then I'll feel I've discharged my duty and so leave.'

'And my friend's question?' I asked. 'Why can't we meet here?'

'This is a place of death,' the Pilgrim replied. 'Three men have been killed here, barbarously slain; a meadow of murder, mistress. Look, I am not wasting your time,' Again he peered up at the sky. 'The good brothers will celebrate Compline. After the bell rings, as a sign that it is completed, I will be with you. Meet me at the Pot of Fire, the tavern on Pig Sty Alley.'

'A Franciscan seen there?' Demontaigu asked.

'In this realm of tears,' the Pilgrim retorted, 'you never know who you might meet or where. After all, I never thought I would encounter a Templar in disguise so close to the King of England! Mistress, at the hour, yes?'

I had no choice but to agree. The Pilgrim turned and left. Demontaigu and I continued through the garden. I glimpsed Dunheved and raised a hand. He sketched a blessing in my direction and hurried on. We reached the great cloisters. Demontaigu was about to leave when a lay brother came up. Now, before I went to the Golgotha Gate, I'd sent a message to Father Prior asking if I could see him. The servitor hurriedly explained how in fact the prior had not attended Vespers and was now waiting for me in his chancery office.

Prior Anselm was kind and welcoming, a gaunt, severe-faced man, thin and dry-skinned. A sharp-eyed churchman, clearly fascinated by what was happening here in his own friary, a keen observer of the court and all its foibles. He ushered us in and made us comfortable on a settle before his chair. Beside him stood a stout lectern on which a book lay open. I was fascinated by the painting on the wall behind it. The prior followed my gaze, and smiled back at me.

'What do you see, Mistress Mathilde?'

'A beautiful vineyard,' I declared. 'Yes, I can make out the vines, the wine press, but the ground is littered with corpses.'

'The work of one of my predecessors.' The prior shrugged one shoulder in apology. 'He was fascinated by the story of Naboth – you know it? In the Old Testament, King Ahab wanted Naboth's vineyard, and when he wouldn't give it, Ahab's wife Jezebel plotted to kill Naboth. In return the prophet Elijah declared that both Ahab and Jezebel would die violent deaths and dogs would come to lick their blood.' The smile faded from the prior's face. 'Little changes, does it, mistress?'

I wondered if the prior was referring to Edward – and was he making a play on Isabella's name by his reference to the pagan queen Jezebel?

He narrowed his eyes. 'I read your thoughts. I make no comparisons, mistress. The painting was there long before I even attended this friary as a novice, but the stories from the Old Testament ring true. Where there's power there is always blood. The court has come here; his grace the king, the queen and all their entourage are most welcome.' He paused.

I noticed he had omitted Gaveston.

'However, be that as it may, three men have been killed here, one being a member of this community. You sent a message asking to see me. I suspect you've heard the stories about what Eusebius claimed to have seen?'

I respected his honesty and frankness. He offered us some wine, but I refused.

'Father Prior, please, what did Eusebius say to you?'

158

The prior rubbed his brow, then stared around.

'Eusebius could be fey-witted, a madcap. Like a magpie he loved to collect things. Some of our community used to laugh at him, but now and again he would surprise us all by his keen observations. On the day Leygrave fell to his death, Brother Eusebius went into our church long before the Angelus bell was rung. He liked to go there because it was quiet. The community should all be at their work. Consequently he was surprised when he glimpsed one of our brothers, or so he thought, a figure dressed in a brown robe, slipping like a shadow through the Galilee Porch and out of the church. He reported that to me.'

'Anything else?' I asked.

'Yes, on that same day, after Compline, I met Eusebius when the brothers were relaxing in the cloisters. Eusebius had been shocked by the two deaths. There'd been whispers that he blamed himself, and of course, he was always full of stories about the belfry being haunted. I approached him and asked how his day had gone. He was more agitated than usual and made a very strange remark. You've heard the jibe, how someone can be as madcap as a bat?'

'Yes!'

'Eusebius was faltering in his speech,' the prior scratched his hand, 'and turned away, then came back with a remark that intrigued me: "Father Prior," he asked, "can a bat be more cunning than a dog?" I asked him what the riddle meant. Eusebius seemed to recollect himself. You know how he was; you met him, mistress. He just shook his head, muttered something about his duties and hurried away.'

'So Eusebius saw someone in church dressed as a friar

or disguised as one,' I asked, 'when no Franciscan should have been in that church? And what provoked his suspicions was the haste in which he left?'

The prior nodded.

'And that strange remark about the bat and the dog, but there's more?'

'Yes, yes, there is.' He paused, cocking his head, listening to the sounds of his friary. 'I was concerned about Eusebius. Our seraphic founder Francis told us that the leader of our community must be like a mother and look after all members as if they were children in a family. I was also concerned about the church. How had those young men fallen to their deaths? Had they committed suicide or had they been murdered? I wondered if I should write to the bishop and ask for the church to be hallowed and reconsecrated. Canon law has certain regulations regarding such matters. If blood is spilt in God's holy place, then it must be cleansed.'

'Do you suspect it was murder?' Demontaigu asked.

'I think it was.' The prior crossed himself. 'But I will leave that until the court moves. Once this friary is settled and returned to its peace, I shall deal with such matters.'

'But that evening, Father?'

'Yes, mistress, that evening I became anxious about the church, about Eusebius, so I decided to meet him. Darkness had fallen. I went into the church; the sacristan had yet to lock the doors. I entered the bell tower. Eusebius was there, kneeling on the ground, a knife in his hand, carving something on the wall. I crouched down beside him. "Brother Eusebius," I asked, "what are you doing?" He wouldn't reply. I could see he'd been crying and had grown very agitated.

I picked up the lantern and peered at the wall. What seemed
to be a bird had been carved, and next to it some wild
animal.'

'A dog?' I asked.

'No, I asked Eusebius that. He shook his head and said
it was a wolf. I tried to soothe him. I prised the knife out
of his fingers, persuading him to join the other brothers,
adding how it was late and the sacristan must lock the
church. We went out in the evening air. Eusebius grew
calmer. I invited him here to share a goblet of wine to soothe
his rumours, tire his mind and prepare him for sleep. He
thanked me but refused. I bade him good night, then he
called my name. 'Father Prior,' he said, 'perhaps you'll hear
my confession?' 'Now?' I asked. Eusebius just shook his head.
'No, Father, but you should shrive me sometime and listen
to my sins,' then he was gone. The following day he was
murdered in the charnel house.'

'And now?' I asked. 'What do you think?'

'Eusebius wanted to be shrived. He wanted to sit in the
mercy seat and receive absolution because he knew what
had truly happened in our church. I suspect Lanercost and
Leygrave were murdered. How, and by whom, I don't know;
that is a matter for the king and, if rumour is correct, for
you, mistress. You are the queen's physician, yes?'

I nodded.

'You advise her?'

'I do my best, Father Prior.'

'Well,' he sighed, 'we all have our duties. Once the court
leaves, I will have that tower exorcised, blessed and sancti-
fied.' He paused, collecting his thoughts. 'I have reflected,

fasted and prayed. What did Eusebius mean about the bat and the dog, and what about those carvings? Inspect them, mistress. You'll find them on the wall of the bell tower. A man torn by guilt and doubt always expresses himself somehow.'

'And you think that Eusebius, in his own pathetic way, was trying to confess his sins through that carving?'

'Yes, I do. It gave him a little peace, but eventually he would have come to me.' The prior eased himself out of his chair, thrusting his hands up the sleeves of his robe. 'Mistress,' he smiled, 'I shall not be displeased to see both king and court leave. Anyway, Vespers must be over. Why not see what Eusebius carved? Perhaps it might mean something more to you.'

Demontaigu and I thanked him and we left, his blessing ringing in our ears. When we reached the church, the swirl of incense still hung thick. The brothers had filed out; only the sacristan and his assistants were still busy in the sanctuary, extinguishing candles and preparing the high altar for the Jesus mass the following morning. I borrowed a lantern and returned to the bell tower. As usual it was cold, rather musty and dingy. I recalled Eusebius' story about the young novice Theodore, and wondered if his ghost had been joined by that of Eusebius. I stared around, and glimpsed the dust on the floor and the carvings on the plaster just to the right of Eusebius' bed. I handed the lantern to Demontaigu and crouched down. Both carvings were rough and hurried, as if done by a child; one looked like that of a bird, great wings extended, with claw-like feet.

'A bat,' Demontaigu whispered, 'or an eagle?' He was thinking of Gaveston.

I moved the lantern. The second carving was larger, crude yet vigorous. It had a long body, a curling tail, four stout legs and a great-jawed mastiff head.

'Dog or wolf,' I murmured.

'Perhaps it's not a wolf,' Demontaigu declared. 'Eusebius was not skilled. Was he trying to depict a leopard? Something he'd seen in the royal coat of arms?'

I stared hard at those carvings, memorising the detail. I can still recall them even now, many, many years later. That cold, musty tower, the light dying outside, faint sounds from the nave, and those rough etchings, the confession of a poor soul who, unbeknown to himself, had also been marked down for bloody death. It might be many a day before I returned to York, and I wanted to study every detail.

'Mathilde,' Demontaigu plucked at my sleeve, 'the hour is passing. If you wish to meet the Pilgrim at the Pot of Fire . . .'

I had seen what I had to. At the time it made no sense at all. We returned to our lodgings. Demontaigu went to collect his war-belt. I changed, putting on a pair of stout boots and a heavier cloak and cowl. I also secured my dagger in its secret sheath on the belt around my waist. Once satisfied, I hurried to the queen's quarters, but a lady-in-waiting told me that her grace was sleeping and I was not needed. A short while later, Demontaigu and I left through the Golgotha Gate, the cries of the lay brother who acted as night porter telling us to be careful. We crossed the thoroughfare into the stygian gloom of Pig Sty Alley, surely one of hell's thoroughfares. It was like slipping from one world to another. Demontaigu drew his sword and dagger. The glint of naked steel forced the nightwalkers back into the gloom of the dark-filled narrow entrances to runnels or shabby houses. Yells and shouts echoed eerily. Now and again a light gleamed in a window above us. Sounds came out of the darkness: a beggar's whine, a lady of the night shouting for custom, the clinking of coins, the bark of a dog. All around us was a brooding menace, as if the night held malevolent creatures just waiting for our one slip or mistake. The smell was so foul I had to cover both my mouth and nose, and I was relieved to glimpse the glow of an open doorway, the creaking sign above it proclaiming it to be the Pot of Fire.

Inside, I was surprised. I had expected some evil hovel, dank and dirty, but the Pot of Fire was clean, the floor well swept, the rushes sweet and brushed with herbs. The smell was not too good, as the tap room was illuminated by great fat tallow candles standing in dishes or spiked on spigots. Mine host, a huge pot-bellied man with a bloodstained apron around his waist, apparently kept strict order; in one hand he clutched a heavy tankard, in the other a cudgel, while more of his bully-boys clustered round the door or sat at tables. He looked us up and down.

'From the court,' he declared in a thick accent. 'I've been expecting you.' He led us around the counter, deeper into the tap room, which was shaped like an 'L'. At the far end, in an enclosed corner, the Pilgrim from the Wastelands was waiting for us on a stool behind a table. We took our seats. Demontaigu, as a courtesy, ordered tankards of ale, adding that he wanted the best in clean pots.

'What else?' Mine host laughed and lumbered away.

The Pilgrim was still dressed like a Franciscan, his cowl pushed back. He seemed more relaxed. He'd chosen his seat wisely, close to a window as well, where he could keep a sharp eye on whoever entered the tavern. The tap room was fairly quiet. There was laughter, shouts and the occasional scream, and ladies of the night wandered in and out, but the real noise came from below. The Pilgrim explained that a cock fight was taking place in the cellar. After this, two champion ferrets would compete to see how many rats they could kill before the candle flame sank from one ring to another. We chattered about the Pot of Fire, the Pilgrim regaling us with anecdotes while the ale was served. He paused at a roar of triumph from the cellar below. I glanced away through the unshuttered window. Ribbons of moonlight cut across the tavern garden, a ghostly place. I recalled what the prior had said about Eusebius and his need to confess. Was the same true of this stranger? The Pilgrim stretched across and tapped my hand.

'Mistress, are you well, do you feel safe?'

'No,' I retorted, 'why should I? I sit with someone who calls himself the Pilgrim from the Wastelands, who also pretends to be a friar, a man with no name. Someone who can slip in and out of that friary as easily as a cat. A place where three men have been barbarously murdered.'

'I agree, the friary has become a field of blood. I must be prudent, and so should you.'

I studied this cunning man even as I regretted my own mistake of ignoring him earlier. I'd been so swept up with the affairs of the court, I had forgotten how the king's residence at the friary would attract the attention of others beyond the pale. I gestured at his garb.

'Have you stolen that?'

'I was loaned it.' The Pilgrim pushed aside his tankard, resting his elbows on the table. 'Mistress, no lies, no artifice. You met with Eusebius; so did I. A collector of trifles, that bell-ringer: a coin, a pilgrim badge, some marks of favour . . .'

I recalled Eusebius' collection of baubles in the charnel house.

'And so you paid him, and he supplied you with robe and sandals?'

'Of course.'

'But you a poor pilgrim?'

'Mistress, that is part of my story.'

'But you could enter and leave the friary whenever you wanted?'

The Pilgrim just shrugged.

'You could be an assassin.'

The Pilgrim smiled and sat back. 'I never climbed that tower,' he murmured. 'I have, mistress, a horror of heights.'

'But you talked to Eusebius?' Demontaigu asked.

'Oh yes, I met him in the charnel house; he took me there. He showed me his collection. He also boasted how his wits were not as dull as others thought.'

'He may have known the assassin,' I whispered.

'I agree,' the Pilgrim replied. 'You've visited the charnel house, mistress?'

'Yes.'

'After Lanercost's death, I went down there to meet Eusebius. On the one hand he could act the fool, the madcap, the jester, yet on the other he could make the most tart observations about his own community or the court. He talked for a while about nothing being what it appeared to be. He knew a little Latin; he could recite the Pater Noster and the Salve Regina. Then he asked me about light and darkness.'

'Light and darkness?' I queried.

'I was mystified as well, but of course Eusebius lived in the church's liturgy. He was particularly struck by the ceremonies of Holy Week. I eventually realised he was talking about Tenebrae, the ceremony on Maundy Thursday, that part of the Last Supper when Judas leaves to betray Christ, and the phrase from scripture, *tenebrae facta.*'

'And darkness fell,' I translated.

'Yes, yes. Eusebius was talking about light and darkness. He wanted me to write the Latin words for them. I scrawled them on a scrap of parchment, but he didn't want that. He pointed at the plastered white wall and gave me a piece of charcoal. I inscribed the words *lux et tenebrae* – light and darkness. For a while Eusebius just sat and stared at it, then he murmured, "Yes, that is what it is: black and white, light and darkness."'

'Did he talk about the Beaumonts?'

'He called them grand lords. He relished the fact that he'd found one of their buttons on a piece of cloth, caught snarled on a thorn in the rose garden. It was part of his collection.'

I held my hand up and stared out at the moon-dappled garden. The shape I'd glimpsed in the charnel house had taken that button from Eusebius' tray and left it deliberately near the trap door, a ploy to mislead.

'Mistress?'

I glanced back at the Pilgrim. 'Did you have any doings with Lanercost or Leygrave?'

'No, no, I did not, but they came here . . .'

'To the Pot of Fire?' Demontaigu queried.

'Oh yes, why not? Well away from the court. Mine host told me how they came here deep in their cups. He stayed well away from them. After all, they could be dangerous: two powerful courtiers armed with sword and dagger.'

'But he tried to eavesdrop?' I asked.

'Of course. A tavern master makes that his business. He listens to confidences and passes them on, but Lanercost and Leygrave talked quickly in Norman French. Mine host said both men were extremely angry, yet sad. As they drank, they grew angrier. He caught the words 'betrayal' and 'treason' but nothing else. They drank deep and left with their arms around each other.' The Pilgrim pulled a face. 'Mistress, I tell you truth.'

'So why did you want to see me?'

The Pilgrim sipped at his tankard, placed it on the table, then glanced out of the window and back at me.

'I call myself the Pilgrim from the Wastelands. I was born Walter of Rievaulx. I am from these parts. My father, his father and his father before him were tenants of the great abbey at Rievaulx. Now God decided that I should be born with this.' He touched the strange birthmark on his face. 'From the moment I was born I was singled out to be alone. I did not want to be mocked. The Benedictines of Rievaulx kindly took me into their house and trained me. I became the abbey's best falconer, a hawker, a huntsman. There is not a bird of prey I do not know or cannot recognise. I know their habits, foibles, weaknesses and ailments. What they must eat. How they must be sheltered, protected and groomed. Before my twentieth summer I was already a master falconer, and my reputation spread, not only as a huntsman but as a retainer who could be trusted. Now this was in the old king's days. Four years before he died, Edward visited Rievaulx. The old king was passionate about venery; he had a particular love for falcons and hawks. I was introduced to him, and took him out for a hunt along the marshes. After we returned to the abbey, the king insisted I become a royal falconer. The abbot daren't refuse, whilst I was very ambitious.' The Pilgrim smiled. 'Oh, I know the stories about the old king. He could be hard and resolute, cruel and vicious at times, but give him a hawk or a falcon and he was as gentle as a dove. He also liked me. We would talk like father and son. I was put in charge of the royal mews at the new Queen's Cross, close to Westminster Palace. The old king pronounced himself very pleased. I was responsible for the royal falcons and hawks. If one fell ill, I would, if necessary, send for a physician, even make a wax cast of the bird and have a royal messenger place it before St Thomas à Becket's shrine in Canterbury. The king was a hard taskmaster. Anyone who abused or proved negligent towards a hawk, he would beat with his belt or whatever came to hand, but to me he was as gentle as a mother. Sometimes when he visited the mews we'd sit on the ale-bench and share a jug of wine. I was in paradise. Never once did the old king make reference to my face. He simply described me as the best of servants.

'I thought things would always remain like that, until the early spring of the year the old king died.' The Pilgrim paused. 'I'd been summoned to Westminster, to the Painted Chamber, at the heart of the royal quarters in the old palace. I had to kick my heels for a while until Edward invited me in. He'd bought a new manuscript from France on the training of hawks and peregrines, and insisted on reading sections of this out loud, asking for my opinion. I recall the day so well: light streaming in through the painted window glass. The chamber was littered with the king's armour, belts, shoes and boots. Manuscripts strewed the table. The old king was happy, as if by talking to me he forgot his own cares and troubles. A chamberlain entered saying that the Prince of Wales and Lord Gaveston waited to see him. The king was reluctant. I knew about the rift between father and son. The old king fiercely resented Gaveston's presence and, more importantly, his own son's deep affection for a lowly Gascon. Nevertheless he summoned both son and favourite into the chamber. Courtesies were exchanged. The king then asked his son why he wished to see him. Both prince and Gaveston glanced at me as if I shouldn't be there, but the king was losing his temper: his right eye was beginning to droop, his face was flushed, his hands were trembling slightly. He was growing old and weak. The campaigns in Scotland had taken their toll. Gaveston stood near the door; the Prince of Wales sat on a cushioned settle before his father. I had no choice but to stay; the king would not dismiss me. The prince talked about his affection for Gaveston, how he was a noble lord, his sweet brother. The king just nodded, but the anger in his eyes showed how much he hated Gaveston. The prince then made the most surprising request. He asked that Gaveston be given the Duchy of Cornwall or the counties of Ponthieu and Montreuil in France.'

'What?' Demontaigu exclaimed.

'Yes, the prince repeated the request: the Duchy of Cornwall or the counties of Ponthieu and Montreuil. The king sprang to his feet, fists clenched, glaring down at his son. He muttered something under his breath, then he attacked the prince. Grabbing him by the hair, he dragged him off the settle and across the chamber. Then he banged his head against the wall, threw him to the ground and started to kick him. The prince yelled and screamed. The king said nothing; just an old, greying man kicking and beating his son. Gaveston remained by the door as if carved out of marble, a look of utter terror on his face. The king paused, hands on his knees, gasping for breath, then he roared at his son: "You whoreson bastard upstart! If I had another heir I would give all to him. You want to concede lands! You who have never acquired one yard of extra territory! To give away honours to someone like that – you whoreson!" By now the prince had crawled away on hands and knees. He turned to face his father. He was frightened and bruised but still defiant. "How dare you!" he screamed back. "How dare you call me whoreson and bring great shame on my mother, your wife?"'

The Pilgrim paused, staring around. He wetted his lips with another drink of ale. 'Now, you know, Eleanor of Castile was the one and only great love of the old king's life. When this incident happened she'd been in her grave some fifteen years. The old king heard his son out, then moved across, finger jabbing the air. "You," he said, "you believe you are a prince? By God's right I say this to you. I look at you. I recall the stories that you are a changeling. Have you

171

heard them? Have you ever heard the stories?" The prince just gazed bleakly back. "You with your baseborn servants and friends, your love of digging and rowing and thatching a house! Do you know what they say?" The king crouched down, his face only inches from that of his son. "They say that as a child my son was attacked by a sow. The nurse in charge changed my true son for you, the by-blow of some peasant! God's teeth, I used to dismiss that as a rumour, but now I wonder. If that nurse was alive I would get the truth, but as for you and your so-called brother, you get nothing! Do you understand? Nothing! Get out!"' The Pilgrim paused once more.

The way he spoke conveyed the truthfulness of what he claimed. I knew enough about the old king to recognise his rage, but this was the first time I had ever heard such a story. Indeed, there had been rumours at the French court how king and son often clashed, even came to blows, but nothing like this.

'Gaveston and Edward left,' the Pilgrim continued. 'The king turned to me, his face red, lips flecked with foam. He just glared at me as if seeing me for the first time, then gestured with his hand that I should get out. I fled. At first I thought nothing would come of it. The king became busy preparing for his great expedition against the Scots. The council met. Letters banishing Gaveston were drawn up. Now, mistress, I had been in London for some time. I wore the royal livery. I carried a sword and dagger, and never once was I accosted. However, in the two months following that terrible confrontation in the Painted Chamber, I was attacked no fewer than three times in and around

Westminster by men cowled and masked. The only reason I escaped was that I was fleet of foot and most adept in the use of dagger and sword. Now at the mews I occasionally slept in the small hay store. Oh, I had my own comfortable chamber, but to keep an eye on the king's birds, I would often settle there for the night.'

'And it caught fire?' Demontaigu asked.

'You have the truth. A fire that had started both front and back at the same time. Again I escaped. I realised I had witnessed something I shouldn't have but I didn't know who was responsible for the attacks on me. The king, the prince, Gaveston or someone else? The old king remained cordial and courteous enough, though a coldness had grown up between us. Now I had been joined in London by my brother Reginald. He married well, the daughter of a local merchant, and they had a child. Reginald was a merry fellow. He liked nothing better than a jig or a bawdy story. One night around the Feast of the Birth of John the Baptist, Reginald left for a tavern in Thieving Lane near the gatehouse at Westminster. The weather had turned harsh. A cold wind was blowing rain in from the river. He took my cloak and beaverskin hat. Later that evening, bailiffs came to the mews carrying a stretcher on which Reginald's corpse was sprawled. My brother never reached the tavern. He'd been found stabbed at least four times in a nearby alleyway. You can imagine my distress, my panic, my fear, my anger. Ursula, Reginald's wife, was distraught. I could do little to help. I decided to flee. I went into hiding in Southwark. One day I crossed the river and wandered into St Paul's, where the tittle-tattlers and the gossip collectors gather. Proclamations are pinned on the great cross in the churchyard. I was studying these carefully when I recognised one against myself: Walter of Rievaulx. According to the proclamation I was a thief, a felon and an outlaw. Three times I had been summoned to court, though I did not know that, and when I had not appeared, I'd been put to the horn, declared *utlegatum* – beyond the law – a wolf's-head whom anyone could kill on sight.'

'And your crime?' I asked.

'I was accused of stealing from the royal mews.' He shrugged. 'Of course it was a lie, but what could I do? If I was taken alive I would hang at the Elms in Smithfield. More likely I'd either be killed outright or perish of some mysterious ailment in Newgate. The proclamation was signed by the mayor and sheriffs of London. Now I'd taken with me all the wealth I could gather. I had one friend, Ursula's father, a wool-smith. I went secretly to him. He believed my innocence. I gave him everything I had to pay him as well as to help Ursula. He secured me forged documents, licences and passes. I journeyed down to Dover, crossed the Narrow Seas and travelled to Paris. For a while I stayed there, working. My skills as a falconer meant I never starved; they provided food, clothing and a roof against the rain and wind. I listened to the stories from England about how the old king had swept north with fire and sword to avenge himself on the Bruce. I also recognised that my life in England was over. I had begun to travel and I wanted to continue. I felt guilty at Reginald's death, at Ursula becoming a widow, her son fatherless. I believed I should do reparation. I travelled south to Compostela, then to Rome, where I secured passage to Outremer. I have visited Jerusalem. I have worshipped in the place where Christ was crucified and His body lay awaiting the Resurrection. I went on to the great desert beyond Jordan. I saw many things, mistress, then I came home. By the time I landed at Dover the old king was dead, his son was crowned and Gaveston had returned to become Earl of Cornwall, the king's own brother and favourite. I hoped I'd been forgotten. My name had been obliterated, my appearance had changed, except for this.' He pointed at the mark on his cheek. 'Moreover, I had disappeared. Whoever had tried to kill me might take comfort that I'd fled, perhaps died abroad. I kept away from my old haunts. This is the first time I've returned to this shire since I joined the old king at Westminster.'

'Who do you think was responsible?' I asked. 'For the attacks?'

'God and his saints know: the old king, the prince, Gaveston, all three? What I have realised is that I should never, ever have been in that chamber. If that was just a scurrilous story, why should someone wish to kill me because I'd learn it? Go through York or London, visit the taverns and alehouses and you'll hear many a ribald story about the great ones of the land, the lords of the soil.'

'And did you ever,' Demontaigu asked, 'try to discover if there was any truth in that story?'

'I wandered the highways and byways. I visited royal castles the prince might have stayed at as a child. I heard of an incident, but nothing substantial. As I say, if chatter and gossip were worth a piece of gold, I'd be a very rich man.'

'So why did you come to York?' I asked. 'Why are you telling us this?'

'Because you, mistress, must tell the queen.'

'Why?'

The Pilgrim stared out across the garden. I followed his gaze. It was a gloomy place lit by pale moonlight. Somewhere a dog yelped. Nearby a relic seller was provoking raucous laughter by offering the most tawdry items as sacred pieces. A slattern, baited by a drunken customer, screamed abuse. Mine host roared for calm. Darkness had truly fallen. More oil lamps and candles had been lit and the Pot of Fire bubbled with shadows.

'You're here for revenge?' Demontaigu asked.

'No, sir, I'm here for justice. I was innocent. I was in a chamber where the king wanted me to be. Simply because of what I saw and heard, my life has been destroyed. My brother was foully murdered, his wife left a widow, her son fatherless. If it was a petty matter, why such loss? So yes, I am here for justice.'

'You think Edward and Gaveston are responsible for the havoc caused?'

'I have tramped this road and that, shivered out in the desert, gone to sleep in dark, dank woods. I have sheltered in cow byres and pigsties. One day I shall die. I wish to tell someone else, someone in authority, someone with power, what caused this dramatic change in my life. I reflect on Gaveston's control over the king. Does he bait him with this? Taunt him? Blackmail him? And these murders,' he took a deep breath, 'the deaths of the Aquilae? Did they know the secret their master holds? Is that why they are being killed?

Ah well.' He pushed away his tankard. 'Mistress, it's time to be gone. I never stay long in one place, but in the end, yes, I came here for justice, perhaps revenge. I have told this story to no other person except one.'

'Who?' I asked.

'A priest under the seal of confession: a Franciscan at Grey Friars in London. I went there to be shrived before I travelled to York. Even when I arrived here I dared not visit my father's house or the abbey, just in case . . .'

'Your confessor?' I insisted.

'He asked me to take an oath under the seal of confession that what I told was the truth. He replied that as my penance I should return and tell someone I trusted, someone in authority, what I know. I arrived in York, I listened to Brother Eusebius. I watched the court and the friary. You, mistress, have a reputation for honesty. Her grace the queen is innocent of any crime; shouldn't she know the secret that has destroyed me and those I love?'

'Where to now?' Demontaigu asked.

'I shall return to London.' The Pilgrim rose abruptly. 'Come,' he gestured, 'Pig Sty Alley at such a late hour is not a safe place.'

Demontaigu called mine host and settled for what we had drunk. We left, back into Pig Sty Alley. So many years have passed, yet I cannot forget walking through that filthy runnel, that tangle of shadows, the strange shapes of the nightwalkers, the swirling smells, the eerie cries that rang out like ghost song. Rats teemed, greyish in the poor light, cats hunted, dogs howled. The full moon had broken free from the clouds, washing the alleyway with silver light. We hastened by doorways and entrances, dark holes holding God knows what terrors and horrors. Demontaigu drew both sword and dagger, whilst the Pilgrim wielded a stout cudgel. I heard a sound and whirled round. Despite the gloomy murk, I glimpsed a shape, cowled and cloaked, last seen at 'The Road to Damascus' after we returned from the moors. I recognised that figure, the outlaw Furnival, and I wondered if Ausel was not far behind. We walked on. The Pilgrim was humming a song, Demontaigu reciting a Templar prayer about the face of God smiling benevolently at us. No one impeded us, no one stopped us, and at last we were free. Across the thoroughfare rose the walls of the friary, and through the dark we could glimpse pinpricks of light from the belfry as well as the curfew lamps set at windows and doorways. The corner of Pig Sty Alley was illuminated by fierce fires burning merrily in great casks. Sconce torches had been pushed into niches on the wall, their flames whipped by the wind. I stared up at the sky. I'd learnt so much that night, and yet what sense did it make? Nevertheless, I sensed that harvest time was close; the wickedness sown was coming to fruition.

We crossed the deserted thoroughfare. The occasional dog nosed the ground; a cat whipped across in a dark blur. The Pilgrim walked slightly in front of us. I heard a sound to my left just near the Golgotha Gate. A click, a snap that should have alarmed me, but I was tired. The whir of the cross-bolt was like an angry wasp. The Pilgrim screamed and staggered back, the feathered quarrel embedded deep in his chest. He waved his hands as if he could fend off the blow, his face contorted with pain, and fell to the ground as another cross-bolt whistled through the air above us. I screamed at Demontaigu not to go forward. I ran even as the Pilgrim turned on his side, fingers going to the feathered quarrel that had cut off his life. I put an arm beneath his shoulder and tried to lift him. Blood was already bubbling out of his mouth, heels drumming on the ground. He stared at me beseechingly.

'A priest,' he whispered. 'A priest.'

'Mathilde, Mathilde.' Demontaigu gently pushed me away. 'Listen, I'm a priest, a Templar priest. I have my faculties. I will hear your confession, I will shrive you.'

I edged away on all fours, staring into the darkness, wondering if the assassin was still there. Again a cross-bolt cut the air, then a voice called out, clear, with a slight lilt. Ausel!

'Mathilde, Bertrand, what ails you?'

I was aware of a shadow moving across the thoroughfare. Demontaigu, God bless him, even though he was exposed to danger, knelt by the fallen man, whispering to him, raising his hand in blessing as he gave absolution. The Pilgrim, on the verge of death, moved restlessly in his pain. I heard gasps and sighs as the blood gurgled at the back of his throat, then he shook once and lay still. Demontaigu crossed himself and rose. A shape detached itself from the darkness, speeding silently across like some soft-footed felon slipping through the dark. I glimpsed the glint of steel. Demontaigu, however, aware that danger might still lurk, pulled the Pilgrim's corpse out of the pool of light into a dark corner of Pig Sty Alley. He crouched down, going through the dead man's pockets and wallet, but all he found were medals and coins. I sensed the danger had passed. A shadow waited just beyond the light.

'Ausel,' I called, 'is that you?'

The Irishman stepped forward. He was much changed since the last time I'd seen him. Now his head was completely shaven, and his face had a stark, skull-like appearance. There was no hair on his mouth or chin; his eyes were gleaming and his mouth was pulled in a thin, bloodless line. He came and crouched next to us as if he had been our companion the entire evening.

'Was it you?' I accused. 'Ausel?'

He turned, eyes half closed. 'For the love of God, Mathilde, why should I kill this man? Sure, I was with you. I left before you and I was waiting here.'

'And the assassin?' I asked.

'I don't know,' Ausel replied. 'I journeyed south to meet Demontaigu. I followed you down Pig Sty Alley and into the Pot of Fire. You did not see me,' he smiled, 'but I saw you.'

'I glimpsed the outlaw Furnival,' I whispered. 'I did wonder. Ausel, why are you here?'

'To meet my good brother.'

I gestured down at the Pilgrim. 'There is nothing we can do for him; his soul is for God, his body for the ground. Ausel, I have known you for four years. Swear to me that you had nothing to do with the attempt at Tynemouth to capture the queen.'

'On the book of the Gospels! Summon Michael, the provost of heaven, and all his angels, the bailiffs of the divine gate, and I will swear. I knew nothing. We did nothing. Our sole aim was the total destruction of Alexander of Lisbon and the Noctales, but out of friendship, I'll tell you this. We are now members of Bruce's court and his power has grown. If Edward does not act soon, the English crown will lose Scotland and all it possesses there. You must walk prudently, Mathilde. The Beaumonts . . . well, I think you know their nature. They look only after themselves.' He edged closer, his face harsh and severe. 'Rumours run in the Scottish camp about all forms of treachery, like a swarm of writhing snakes, at the English court. No doubt Edward of England petitioned Bruce for help, but other stories swirl like foul smoke: that it did not matter if the queen was captured.' He paused, staring at me, his face ghostly in the poor light.

'Or killed?' I whispered.

Ausel nodded.

'But would Bruce be party to that? He is a noble. He was once a member of the English court himself, a knight.'

'Mathilde, across the northern march the king's father laid waste with fire and sword. He killed Bruce's brothers. He took Bruce's women and put them in cages, then hanged them from castle walls. Bruce has changed. This is war to the death. Bruce had scruples, but if he drew the line at murder, it wasn't because of any chivalrous feelings but due to the power of France. Bruce sits and watches. He and his churchmen pray that Gaveston will never be sent into exile. They hope civil war will flare here so Bruce can come into his own. Most of Scotland is lost. Further unrest in England would make Bruce king.' He pointed down at the Pilgrim. 'I don't know who he is or why he is important to you at this late hour of night. I told you I followed you from the tavern. I went ahead. I was waiting in the shadows of the friary wall; I saw you emerge into the light. This man was struck, but where the bowman was, God only knows.'

'And what now?'

Ausel stretched out a hand. 'Heaven knows, Mathilde. I do not think I shall look upon your face again. This is my last expedition into England. I will have words with Master Demontaigu tomorrow morning, then I will rejoin my brothers.'

I clasped his outstretched hand. Ausel was a killer, but he was also a man of his word. I believed he had nothing to do with the death of the Pilgrim. He melted into the darkness. Demontaigu and I went across to the Golgotha Gate and knocked on the postern door. A short while later, a group of bleary-eyed lay brothers came out with a stretcher. They placed the Pilgrim's corpse upon it and took it to the death house. We followed them in. Demontaigu escorted me to my chamber and kissed me lightly on the head, pressing a finger against my lips.

'Not now, Mathilde, no talk. I must see Ausel and you must sleep.'

Chapter 7

The Lord King and Gaveston became
separated from each other, the
Gascon stayed at Scarborough . . .

In the event, I did sleep. I was so tired I just stretched out on my bed, wrapped a cloak around myself and fell into a deep slumber plagued by nightmare memories: of violence and intrigue, of walking down filthy alleyways, of standing in squares where torches burnt and corpses dangled from gallows. I was pleased to wake early. I stripped and washed. The queen had not risen, so I went to the Jesus mass and busied myself about my own affairs. Mid-morning a grim-faced prior celebrated a requiem mass for the Pilgrim; two other corpses of beggars found lying near the friary had also been brought in for the last rites. The mass was simple. No incense, no chanting, simply the sombre words of the requiem about the Day of Judgement, of being committed to the soil, of the souls of the departed being escorted into heaven by Michael and all his angels. Afterwards I followed the prior and the brothers out into God's Acre, where all three corpses, wrapped in shrouds, were committed to the earth. Once the prior had blessed the grave he beckoned me over. Putting a hand on my shoulder, he stared attentively at me.

'Mistress, I do not wish to give offence, but this is a house of the Franciscan brothers dedicated to peace, preaching and penance, not murder and horrid death during the dark hours of the night. I wish you well, Mathilde. Please give my loyal regards to your mistress, but I would be dishonest if I did not say I shall be glad when you're gone.'

I left the cemetery and immediately sought audience with Isabella in her chamber. The room was busy, thronged with ladies-in-waiting, squires and pages, porters preparing chests and casks. Isabella took one look at my face and dismissed her servants. She was swathed in a heavy robe, her face rather pale. I asked her if she was well but she just said it was morning sickness and that it would pass. I insisted on distilling her a herbal drink. She sat in her chair, fingers over a chafing dish. I crouched on a stool next to her, leaned close and told all that had happened, what the Pilgrim had reported and what Ausel had said. Only then did I fully realise how mature the queen had become.

How closely she imitated her formidable father, who, to quote one poet, 'was terrible to the sons of pride'. She never interrupted or questioned me. Once I'd finished, she stretched both hands over the chafing dish as if to draw strength and warmth from the sparkling charcoal.

'Mathilde, I thank you. I have heard such stories and rumours. Sometimes I wonder. I doubt if they are true; scurrilous, tattling tales. The real danger in such stories is not that they are true but that they can become so. My husband does nothing to prevent the seeds of such a tale taking root in men's hearts. Here we are in York, chased by the earls of England, scurrying to Tynemouth, seeking help from a Scottish rebel. Edward should be in Westminster, the throne of his ancestors, administering justice, governing his realm.' She paused at a knock on the door, and Dunheved walked in. Isabella did not dismiss him but summoned him over. She pointed to another stool, then turned to me.

'Mathilde, I must have words with Brother Stephen. I have also conferred with my husband. Tomorrow morning at the latest, you and the good brother here,' she smiled at the Dominican, 'will leave for Scarborough.'

I glanced at the queen's confessor, who sat, cowl slightly pushed back, hands up the sleeves of his robe. He was so serene and watchful. I did wonder again what role this wily Dominican played in the affairs of the court. But Isabella was impatient to talk to him, probably under the seal of confession, when she would tell him everything we had discussed. I bowed, curtsied and left the chamber.

By Angelus time the news of our imminent departure was well known throughout the friary. I packed my belongings.

The queen did not need me, so I bolted and locked my chamber door, went to my writing desk, took out a piece of vellum and decided to collect my own thoughts on what I'd learnt and observed. I'd hardly started this task when a loud rapping on the door made me groan. I thought it was a message from the queen, but it was Demontaigu. He'd bade farewell to Ausel and I sensed his grief at the ties between himself and his brethren being so dramatically loosened. He sat on a stool, chatting about old times, expressing his sadness, and I let him talk, but Demontaigu always had a clear perception of others, and eventually he paused, smiled and pointed to the piece of vellum.

'Are you drawing up your indictment, Mathilde? Look, rather than sit and bemoan like a beggar at the gate, I will help you. Now, last night, the Pilgrim . . . ?'

For a while we discussed what our mysterious visitor had told us.

'But his murder?' Demontaigu concluded, tapping his feet. 'Who should murder him?'

'The same people who tried before?' I asked. 'Perhaps the Pilgrim wasn't as forgotten as he thought.'

'In which case you are talking about either Gaveston or the king,' Demontaigu retorted, getting to his feet. 'I accept that the Pilgrim's face was distinctive, easily recognisable, but the king and his favourite are caught up in their own swirl of affairs. Was it an accident?'

I asked him what he meant.

'A nightwalker,' Demontaigu replied, 'a felon, a footpad who was going to attack all three of us, but the presence of Ausel disturbed him so he fled.'

I was about to reply when there was another knock on the door. It was still off the latch and I was surprised when Dunheved swept into the room. The Dominican's face was contorted in anger. He was restless and agitated. I asked him what was wrong; he just shook his head, crossed himself and continued his pacing around the room. Now and again he'd pause to stare at the crucifix or one of the coloured paintings hanging on the wall. Now, I am used to artifices, subtlety and deceit, but I sensed the Dominican's rage was genuine. He'd come directly from the queen, who must have told him what I had learnt the night before. At last he paused, chest heaving, and crossed himself again: '*Mea culpa, mea culpa!*' he declared, striking his breast. 'My fault, my fault, Mathilde.'

I gestured at a stool. He sat down with a sigh of relief. Then he glanced quickly at Demontaigu, rose, locked the door and barred it. He returned to the stool, put his arms across his chest and stared up at me.

'I have come from the queen, Mathilde. She has told me the truth about that bloody mayhem at Tynemouth. She could have been killed; that was the mischief plotted.'

'Or so our informant would have us believe,' I replied.

Dunheved rubbed his face and pointed at the vellum lying on my desk.

'What do we have here, Mathilde, what do we have? Please.' He gestured at the writing desk. 'Let us all collect our thoughts. Here, before we move to Scarborough, become locked up in its fastness.'

I was a little surprised but I agreed. I felt confused by the presence of both Demontaigu and especially Dunheved, but there again, the Dominican's logic was flawless. We would soon be separated from the queen, confined in a fortress against people who might wish us the greatest of evil and mischief.

'So, Mathilde, what shall we do? How shall it be done? Tomorrow we leave here for Scarborough. I go grievingly. Why? Because her grace the queen will not be accompanying us. She is moving to Howden and will take shelter there.' Dunheved pointed at me. 'Mathilde, if you are a physician of the body, I am one of the soul. What are the symptoms here, what questions must we ask?'

I picked up my quill and began to write quickly in that secret cipher I was slowly mastering.

'Three of Gaveston's Aquilae,' I spoke my thoughts aloud, 'have been mysteriously murdered. All three fell from a great height, a macabre, ironic death. Was it a play on their title, the humiliation of soaring eagles? We know it was murder because of that taunting verse: *Aquilae of Gaveston, fly not so bold, for Gaveston your master has been both bought and sold*. However, God only knows why Lanercost went into that lonely bell tower. How was he overcome and hurled from such a great height? He took off his war-belt, leaving it for Brother Eusebius later to steal, so he must have met someone he trusted, but who?'

Dunheved murmured in agreement. Demontaigu sat tense. I returned to my writing.

'Secondly, Leygrave. Despite being wary and cautious after his close comrade's death, he fell in the same way from the same place. He too took off his war-belt. More mysteriously still, he actually climbed on to the ledge, but why? Who else was there?'

'You are sure of that?' Dunheved asked. 'You saw the imprint of his boots?'

'Yes, yes,' I replied absent-mindedly.

'Is it possible,' Demontaigu asked, 'that both men were in the tower with someone they trusted, and were simply pushed from behind and fell over the ledge?'

'No.' I shook my head. 'We've been there. The ledge is broad. I could understand if they were standing on the edge of a precipice. In the belfry, however, if they were shoved, they would simply grasp the ledge and turn around; they would fight, resist, raise the alarm. There is not much room in that tower. A struggle would mean one person, sooner or later, hitting one of those bells. Yet both Leygrave and Lanercost fell without a sound. No disturbance was heard, no mark of conflict found.'

'Yet you claim Brother Eusebius saw something?' Demontaigu asked

'Oh, I don't think it's a claim.' I turned and glanced at them both. 'Eusebius did see something. He was a magpie; he liked silver pieces. He was waiting for his moment to confront the killer himself and secure a reward. He also revelled in his knowledge. Eusebius loved to portray himself as a fool, then try and prove that he was as sharp-witted as the next man. He made some drawings in the bell tower, rough etchings carved on the wall, but what are they? An eagle, a bat? A dog, a wolf or the royal leopard of England? And his remark to the prior that a bat could be as cunning as a dog? Or those two words he had the Pilgrim scrawl on the white-plastered charnel house – *lux et tenebrae* – light and darkness. What does all that mean? Whom did he see?

Who followed Eusebius down into the charnel house and staved in his skull?' I turned back to the piece of vellum and wrote down my questions. Behind me, Dunheved muttered a prayer to himself.

'Thirdly: Kennington and his two guards.'

'Now that's a great mystery,' Demontaigu broke in. 'Those men were armed and alert, watching the seas as well as Tynemouth itself. They knew a hostile force was lurking outside. I have wondered . . .' Demontaigu snapped his fingers and stared around. 'Duckett's Tower had a secret entrance. We know that. The queen used it to escape. Is it possible that someone came up that secret entranceway? Don't forget, it was the dead of night.'

'He'd have to pass other chambers,' Dunheved broke in. 'He might alert them.'

'No,' Demontaigu shook his head, 'not if he was moving stealthily.'

'True, true,' I murmured. 'Remember what the Castellan showed us. Outside each door there was a hook and a latch. As the assassin passed he could have secured each door, as well as the one to the tower top itself, to give him enough time if the alarm was raised.'

'But this is where my theory fails.' Demontaigu pulled a face. 'The assassin, and there must have been more than one, would go through that doorway, but Kennington and his two guards were there. They'd draw their swords and daggers and raise the alarm, yet no one heard a sound. Nevertheless, someone definitely went on to that tower, overcame those three warriors then hurled them to their deaths on the rocks below.'

I busily wrote this down. Behind me Dunheved and Demontaigu were discussing in hushed whispers what might have happened in Duckett's Tower.

'Fourthly,' I called out, looking over my shoulder at them, 'Tynemouth itself. Bruce was clearly informed about the queen: where her residence was and how vulnerable she would be if she tried to leave through that tunnel on to the beach. Now, such an entrance was not secret, which explains the timing of the assault. As the castle was attacked from the front, the Scots dispatched a war party on to the beach.'

'*Deus solus,*' Dunheved whispered, '*et Maria ancilla Trinitatis* – only God and Mary, the handmaid of the Trinity, saved her.'

Demontaigu murmured in agreement as I turned back to the vellum.

'Fifthly: the Pilgrim from the Wastelands. He arrives in York hungry for justice and revenge, bringing a scurrilous story about the king.'

'But was it scurrilous?' Demontaigu asked. 'If our noble lord was powerful and vigorous, such a tale would be dismissed as a ribald fable, tavern talk, but now all are prepared to believe anything about him.'

I didn't object.

'Sixthly: Ausel. He confirmed our suspicions about what happened at Tynemouth. He also made the heinous suggestion that the queen and the child she carried were not only to be captured and held hostage, but even killed . . .'

I was surprised by Dunheved's reaction, as if my words kindled the rage twisting silently within him. He sprang to

191

his feet, lips bared like a dog, eyes darting to the left and right.

'A filthy abomination,' he whispered. 'Whoever plotted that deserves the death of Simon the Magus.' He walked up and down the room, rubbing his hands, muttering in Latin to himself. I watched him curiously. Dunheved could act the calm priest but really he was a firebrand. He had that flame of fanaticism so common in his order; little wonder the Dominicans were used as the inquisitors of God, to root out heresy and schism.

'Calm yourself, Brother,' Demontaigu murmured. 'For the love of God, a clear mind and a sharp wit will resolve these mysteries, not rage.'

'But it's still treachery, Bertrand.' Dunheved sat down on his stool. 'Treason of the most vile kind. The innocent queen and her child seized by Scottish raiders, humiliated, violated perhaps . . .'

'But let us think coolly,' I declared. 'Let us argue the case like a question in the schools. Would Bruce have done that? How would he answer to the courts of Europe, to the Holy Father in Avignon and, more importantly, to Isabella's father Philip in Paris?'

'Oh, I am sure,' Demontaigu brusquely intervened, 'that he would make his excuses. An unforeseen accident. How he'd given strict instructions for this not to happen. The fortunes of war. Who would he really blame? His men attacking an English fortress, or Edward of England and Gaveston his catamite leaving a young queen, *enceinte*, in a lonely fortress on those brooding, bleak cliffs.'

I had to agree with Demontaigu's logic. In the final

conclusion Edward and Gaveston would have been held responsible by all. Dunheved noisily took a deep sigh to calm himself.

'What is the root of this source? Now look, mistress, I was in the rose garden when you and Demontaigu came to inform Lanercost. Rumours later swept the court of how a party of Templars had been massacred out on the moors. Lanercost's brother was one of these. Only after that massacre did these murderous mysteries begin.' Dunheved glanced out of the corner of his eye at Demontaigu.

'I know where you are leading, Dominican,' Demontaigu declared tersely, 'but I swear on the Gospels, even the sacrament itself: my brothers were not responsible for Lanercost, Leygrave or Kennington's deaths.'

'Who could it be?' Dunheved's voice held a hint of challenge. 'The murders began then. Mistress Mathilde, you and I were in church. I was celebrating mass when the alarm was raised about Lanercost. You and I were with the king's chamber council when Leygrave fell to his death. We were all with the queen in the Prior's Lodgings at Tynemouth . . .'

'One other item,' I declared. 'The Pilgrim told us about Lanercost and Leygrave going to the Pot of Fire in Pig Sty Alley; both Aquilae were aggrieved, deep in their cups. They talked of treachery and treason, which makes me ponder the conclusion: was Gaveston himself responsible for the deaths of those close retainers, and if so, why and how?'

Dunheved stared at the crucifix on the wall, whispering a prayer, before glancing sharply at me.

'Mistress Mathilde, is there anything else? Anything at all?'

I shook my head. Dunheved blew his lips out and got to his feet.

'Bertrand.' He sketched a blessing. 'Mistress Mathilde, I bid you adieu. We will meet again.' Then he left.

Early next morning, before the mist broke and the sun rose, I met Isabella alone in her private chamber. For a while she just clasped my hand, staring sadly, then she drew me close and embraced me, kissing me on both cheeks. She stood back, squeezing my hands.

'Take care, Mathilde.' She abruptly turned away as if she wanted to prevent herself from talking further. I curtsied and left.

Our journey across the sun-washed moorlands to Scarborough proved uneventful. A long cortège of riders and carts: Gaveston and his Aquilae, Middleton and Rosselin; the Beaumonts and their retainers; porters and liverymen, carters and other household officials. The king also dispatched the captain of his Welsh archers Ap Ythel, who threw a protective cordon of mounted archers around us. We heard rumours about the earls being close, though we sighted no hostile force. At night we stayed in a spacious tavern close to the old Roman road that runs from York to London; the following morning we caught the freshening sea breezes as we approached the coast. Scarborough was a port for fish and piracy as well as a harbour where the great wool ships could shelter in a storm. It reminded me of Tynemouth, though more appealing. The town lay in the lee of a hill overlooking the sea, and along the brow of that hill sprawled the towers, gatehouses and crenellated walls of the formidable fortress. A place of refuge, we were assured, where Gaveston and ourselves could shelter safely. If danger threatened on the landward side, there were galleys and cogs in the harbour waiting to take us aboard. The castle was perched on the rim of a hill that fell sheer on the land-ward side to the main part of the town, and on the seaward, to the mansions of the wealthy burgesses. The coastline and the sea were not so rugged and rough as at Tynemouth, whilst summer had arrived, creating a delightful scene with the sun bathing both land and sea in a golden hue.

The constable of the castle, Sir Simon Warde, was a bluff Yorkshireman, a veteran of the old king's wars. He'd been given strict instructions to provision the castle and be prepared to withstand a siege. Warde formally greeted us in the outer bailey, kneeling to kiss Gaveston's ring. Afterwards his marshals and chamberlains allocated us chambers. Scarborough Castle was a rambling place, the great barbican leading into a ward that in turn led deeper into other baileys or wards. At the heart of the castle stood the soaring donjon, Queen's Tower, which rose above Mossdale Hall, a two-storey wood and plaster building possessing chambers on the upper floor and a great dining hall or refectory below. Scarborough was a place of winding alleyways and narrow runnels, sheer grey walls, open yards; a veritable maze of chambers, storerooms and dungeons. Steps stretched up to fortified doors or down into inky blackness. Demontaigu and I were lodged in Queen's Tower. Gaveston took over Mossdale Hall, whilst his two Aquilae, Middleton and Rosselin, lodged near us. Demontaigu acted concerned. I asked him why. Once our baggage had been stored, he led me into the castle gardens, close to the Chapel of Our Lady, and swiftly summarised the weaknesses of Scarborough.

'There are only two wells,' he said, 'and these can be easily blocked off. The castle is rambling. Warde has some troops; we have Ap Ythel and his archers, Beaumont's retainers and Gaveston's Aquilae. To put it bluntly, Mathilde, I wonder if we have too few men to man the walls yet too many to feed if a siege really began to bite.'

Strange, certain scenes from my life, even though they occurred some fifty years ago, I can recall clear and distinct. Scarborough Castle, however, despite visiting it since the summer of 1312, I find difficult to describe. Gaveston arrived there like some great lord, acting the general, deploying his troops, but within days the gossip amongst the garrison was that Gaveston and the king had committed a serious error. Scarborough had a port, but the problem was that between the castle and the harbour there was the fishing village, a small town in itself, with the mansions of merchants and wealthy fishermen. If a hostile force occupied that, Gaveston would have to fight his way through to the sea, and even there be exposed to a war-cog, commissioned by the earls, lurking off shore ready to hinder any escape. Ap Ythel confirmed Demontaigu's bleak perception. The castle could only be defended by a great host. Any besiegers would soon learn this and launch their attacks at various places, forcing the defenders to deploy their men thinly as well as be constantly moving them around.

Gaveston, however, behaved like the great seigneur of battles. He insisted on wearing the royal tabard of blue, red and gold with the lunging leopards of England, whilst the king's banners and pennants floated above the walls as if Edward himself sheltered there. Sir Simon Warde could be trusted. Scarborough was well provisioned and stocked with arms, but the garrison was a mixture of veteran men-at-arms, mercenaries hired by indenture and some local levies. I wandered the castle's narrow gulleys and alleyways, which snaked beneath the brooding mass of sheer walls, fortified towers and battlements. Even I, unused to the strategies of war, realised how meagre the garrison was compared to what they had to defend. Gaveston's shield-hedge, as he grandly called his war-band, was far too diverse: a few knights with their chainmailed squires; Ap Ythel's archers in their brown-green livery, braided leather jerkins and steel sallets; and Beaumont's retainers, jacketed men-at-arms with pot-like helmets and rounded shields. The constable's troop included some heavy armoured foot, a few horsemen, spear-holders and archers garbed in light cloth or scraps of leather. In itself the castle looked formidable, nestling on that long ridge, fortifications stretching up to the sky dominating the land on other side. From within, however, it was a sombre rat-run of alleyways and steep steps leading up to where the wind always buffeted or down to dark, deep-vaulted dungeons, storerooms and galleries.

My quarters were a square, solid chamber in Queen's Tower with nothing but a cross hanging on its dirty plastered walls. The bed was comfortable enough and a chest held my belongings, whilst Warde kindly arranged for a chancery table and writing stool to be moved in along with a lavarium and a parchment coffer for my writing materials. The floor was clean, the musty smell of dust and old plaster almost hidden by the smoke from the braziers and the crushed herb grains strewn on top. The door was stout and could be locked and bolted from within. The arrow-slit windows allowed in light and air and were easily sealed with wooden slats, whilst the narrow recess for the latrine had been thoroughly cleansed.

I made myself as comfortable as possible, but it was hardly a place to linger. Instead I spent a great deal of my time in and around the small Chapel of Our Lady, a miniature jewel of a church that stood in its own enclosed plot, an ornamental garden laid out with great care by some former castellan and his lady. A truly enchanting place with its neatly clipped square lawns, small herb banks and flower beds full of the first green shoots of summer. Trellises for climbing roses overlooked neatly trimmed bushes, and there was even a small carp pond surmounted by a fountain carved in the shape of a steeple. The chapel itself, approached along a pebbled path, was as simple as a barn, with a vaulted wooden roof, its timber beams turning golden brown with age. A decorative altar rail divided the sanctuary from the nave. The chapel had no transepts; its pillars and supports were built into the plastered wall, their capitals and corbels moulded in the shape of intertwined vine leaves then painted an eye-catching green. Near the door stood an ancient baptismal font, nothing more than a large bowl resting on a stout small pillar; over this brooded a wall painting of St Christopher bearing the Infant Christ. At the other end of the chapel the small stone altar stood on its own dais. Above the altar hung an exquisite silver pyx on a filigreed chain, beside which the sanctuary lamp, in its copper and glass holder, glowed a rich ruby red. The floor was tiled a strange black and yellow, reminding me of a chess board, but it was the paintings on the side walls that fascinated me. These were twelve miniature medallions, six on either side, describing the occupations of each month of the year, all executed in a vigorous style. The figures and occupations were picked out in vivid blues, greens and browns, be it the fattening of pigs in November or the killing of oxen in December. In the sanctuary lay a ladder, which I later learnt was used to clear the dirt from the arrow-loop windows covered with horn. The sacristy, which lay to the left of the sanctuary, was nothing more than a ward chamber. Paintings once decorated its walls, but these had long faded. It had a door leading out to the garden that was now rusted shut, locked and bolted. On the left of the sanctuary was a small lady shrine with a mercy chair and prie-dieu where the sacrament of confession could be celebrated.

I loved to sit in the garden or wander through the chapel: so peaceful, so ordinary and unpretentious, yet soon to be the haunt of murder. As for the rest of my time, I had left most of my potions and medicines with the queen's household, but the castle had a leech, a little old woman who constantly talked to herself, a veritable fountain of knowledge about what was best for an open wound, the disturbance of belly humours or rheums in the nose. Once I persuaded her that I was no threat, she chattered like a sparrow on a branch, especially about her own remedies, poultices and potions. In truth, such women are easily scoffed at, but she was very skilled and knowledgeable, particularly about mushrooms, so dangerous she said, that she'd never eaten one in her life. She was also a source of gossip about the castle. From her I learnt how Constable Warde believed Scarborough could not be defended against an army, whilst his levies openly grumbled about having to defend a Gascon upstart.

God forgive me, I forget that old woman's name, yet I learnt so much from her about medicines from local plants and the various spells and incantations used in their application. At first I wondered if she was a witch. On one occasion her lined face creased into a smile, and she grasped my arm and leaned closer.

'I watch your eyes, mistress, they are as clear as glass. You know, and I know, that no spell or incantation can cure anything. A prayer to the good Lord or His Blessed Mother is potent, but you see, mistress,' she winked, 'our patients don't know that! They think spells work. Have you noticed, mistress, how, if the mood of your patients grows benevolent, they are more easily cured?'

I certainly remember laughing at that. On another occasion she made a very strange remark, one that caught my attention. I had been full of questions; now she asked hers. One morning I went down for some dried moss mixed with curdled milk for a cut on my hand. I wanted it cleaned and kept free of pus; the old woman gladly obliged. We sat at the corner of the table, my sleeve pulled back. She carefully washed the wound and applied the mixture with the flat blade of a knife purified in the flame of a candle. I thanked her and offered to pay. She grasped my fingers and peered closely at me.

'Mistress,' she whispered, 'physic has its own mysteries,

but not as bewildering as the affairs of man. Why has his grace the king in all his wisdom sent Lord Gaveston to shelter here?'

'This castle is fortified,' I replied. 'There's the cove where ships may anchor. Lord Gaveston can withstand a siege. If he doesn't, he can always take ship and flee abroad.'

The old woman bowed her head, laughed softly to herself then glanced up.

'But how did they know that?'

'Mistress,' I pleaded, 'don't play riddles with me. What are you saying?'

'I have lived here for over seventy summers, and I can assure you, mistress, that never once has his grace the king ever visited here, and certainly not Lord Gaveston. So why should they come to a castle they've never visited? I go down to the town. Rumours mill as flies over a turd. The great earls are coming,' she gestured with her hand towards the window, 'and as for ships . . .' She laughed. 'Mistress, the cove down there is a haven for pirates, be they English or Fleming, from Hainault or France. Even if a ship came in, God knows whether it would be allowed to leave, and if it did, whether it would be safe.'

The leech had placed her finger on a problem that gnawed at my own heart. Why here? Why the castle of Scarborough? Demontaigu, for all his years as a warrior, was mystified, as was Lord Henry Beaumont, who could, and often did, provide a litany of countless places where Gaveston would have been safer. The old woman tapped the side of her nose and winked.

'Does his grace the king wish Lord Gaveston to be taken?'

She chewed the corner of her lip. 'God knows, mistress, I have said enough. Now, as for this cut . . .'

She wouldn't be questioned further, though what she said reflected the gossip of the kitchen, buttery and refectory. Dunheved, that great collector of gossip, wandering the castle talking to this person or that, offered his own solution.

'Perhaps it's not the castle,' he murmured, smiling. 'Perhaps it's the harbour. If Gaveston does flee to foreign parts, it will not be aboard a king's ship but a pirate vessel, someone who could slip in and out and take him safely away without attracting the attention of other ships.'

Yet in the end that was only one problem amongst many. For the rest, Gaveston insisted on holding his chamber councils, but these were mere chatter. We could only wait. The great earls threatened a siege, but Gaveston confidently informed us that his grace the king would raise levies and pin the enemy between his royal army and the castle walls. We had to be patient. Such was Gaveston's hope. He was living in a fool's world. No news came from either king or queen. To distract myself further, I worked in the castle's kitchens: busy, noisy places with ham, sausage, rope and game birds hanging from the rafters to be smoked and dried. The spit boys invariably needed help to collect and dry the bavins or bundles of hazelwood rods for the long ovens in the castle bakery. I always rose early to help in such ordinary tasks. I loved the misty coolness, the promise of a full sun, the light blue sky. The smells from the kitchen were mouth-watering, as Gaveston still insisted on delicacies for his table. Bakeries have always delighted me. The fragrance of freshly baked bread provoked bittersweet memories of those happy, innocent days in Paris when I raced along the Rue des Cordeliers on tasks for my uncle whilst the oven boys prepared their first batches for the day.

I would say my morning prayers in that delightful little garden and wait for the chaplain, a fussy grey-haired priest, to prepare the chapel for morning mass. Sometimes Dunheved and Demontaigu would join me, though usually the Dominican and my beloved Templar priest celebrated mass in their own chambers. On one occasion Dunheved remarked how little Gaveston fell to his prayers, and asked if it was true that his mother had been a witch. I simply smiled and said I did not know, voicing my own anxiety about Gaveston's foolery and the king's stupidity. Oh yes, I remember all those things: that homely chapel with its delicate paintings and its lovely garden; the morning tasks in the bakery and kitchen. I remember them because that was when and where the horrors began again.

It must have been about six days after our arrival in the castle. I was in the buttery chamber when Dunheved came hastening in, his black and white gown flapping in the strong morning breeze.

'Mistress Mathilde, I beg you, come to the chapel.' He was breathless, one hand against the wall, half bowed as he tried to catch his breath. Demontaigu, who'd been breaking his fast nearby, joined us as we hurried out of the bailey and along the pebble-packed path to the chapel. Rosselin and the Beaumonts were already there, clustered before the door. A distraught chaplain was tugging at the great iron ring. Demontaigu forced his way through.

'It shouldn't be locked, but it is securely,' the chaplain

wailed. He crouched down and peered through the keyhole. 'The key has been removed,' he spluttered.

'Did you lock it last night, Father?' Dunheved asked.

'No, I don't lock it – why should I? This castle is fortified; the chapel holds little of value except the sacred pyx, and who would steal that, eh?'

I walked around the side of the chapel overlooking the garden. The windows were really no more than arrow loops high in the wall, the horn that filled them long discoloured by the elements. I walked back.

'I'm concerned,' Rosselin declared. 'I cannot find Middleton. He used to come here after dawn; he was worried, prayerful!' I recalled the sacred medallions and badges Middleton had clasped on his jerkin.

'He has been so distracted.' Rosselin himself certainly appeared so, pacing backwards and forwards, now and again banging on the chapel door as if to rouse someone within.

'You think he might be inside?' Dunheved asked.

Rosselin just shrugged. Dark-faced Ap Ythel, chewing a piece of bread, sauntered over with a number of his archers. I appealed to him for help, and six of his companions were dispatched to fetch a great log from the wood yard to use as a battering ram. The chapel door began to buckle. Ap Ythel's archers shifted their aim from the lock on the left to the stout leather hinges on the right. The crashing brought others hurrying over to see what was happening. The archers continued their pounding. At last the leather hinges snapped and the door sprang loose, falling back so sharply that the lock tore away from its clasp. Inside was a ghastly scene. The beautiful chapel, with its exquisite silver pyx shimmering in the red glow of the sanctuary lamp, had been transformed into a place of hideous, brutal death. From a beam, twirling slightly at the end of a thick rough rope, hung the corpse of Nicholas Middleton. The medals and brooches pinned on his jerkin shimmered mockingly in the poor light. The makeshift scaffold, with the sanctuary ladder propped against the beam, was as brutal and stark as any crossroads gallows. A truly eerie sight. Middleton's corpse was all askew, booted feet hung toes down, his legs in their green hose slightly apart, hands dangling, his head lolling oddly as if his neck had been twisted like that of a barnyard fowl. One glance at that contorted bluish-red face, eyes half closed, swollen tongue pushed out, pronounced sentence of death.

I asked for the corpse not to be touched, then stared around, listing in my mind what I saw. The ladder against the rafters. The key to the chapel lying on the ground. The sacristy door half open. The mercy chair had been slightly moved. I walked up through the sanctuary and into the sacristy; inside was nothing but a dusty silence. The door to the garden beyond was still firmly bolted and locked, both top and bottom all rusted, secure and fast. I walked back into the sanctuary and studied that grisly scene. Ap Ythel's men now stood in the shattered doorway, driving back the curious. At my request the corpse was cut down and stretched out on the flagstones. Rosselin stood over it, pallid as a ghost. He was trembling, mouth opening and shutting, eyes blinking. I studied him carefully. Was he the killer? He knew Middleton came here, and yet sometimes you can look at a human being and sense his innermost soul. Rosselin was terrified, a broken man. A squire, used to the heat and hurl of battle, this ominous repetition of swift, mysterious death had broken his will.

A disturbance at the door made me turn. Gaveston, accompanied by the constable, swept into the chapel. He took one look at the corpse, groaned and, turning away, just stared at the ground. Eventually he straightened up, his face as pitiful as if he was looking upon his own death. I watched intently for any artifice or pretence. I had seen Gaveston in his glory days and the Gascon had certainly changed: the dark hair was silvery in places, the beautiful, smooth face furrowed, cheeks slightly hollow, eyes frenetic, as if his wits had begun to wander.

'How?' The question came as a croak. 'How?' he repeated.

'Only God knows,' Dunheved whispered.

'You!' Gaveston shouted, pointing a finger at me. 'You were commissioned to discover the cause of all this.' His eyes had that hunted look. I wondered if I should question him, but what was the use? He would lie. Gaveston was never one for revealing his innermost thoughts.

'Well?' he shouted.

'My lord,' I retorted, 'how can I, when we flee up and down this kingdom like robbers put to the horn?'

Gaveston raised a fist. Demontaigu's hand fell to his dagger. Ap Ythel hurried across and whispered into the Gascon's ear. Gaveston half listened before spinning on his heel and sweeping out of the church. I curbed my own anger, becoming busy with the corpse. Dunheved picked up the key and walked away, his sandalled feet tapping on the flagstones.

'No secret entrance here,' he called, 'no passageway.' He paused, shook his head and came back to ask Demontaigu to give the dead man the last rites. My beloved agreed, kneeling to one side of the corpse, myself on the other. The words of absolution were whispered whilst I scrutinised the corpse: his fingers, the palms of the hands and the head. I could not detect any contusion or bruise, nothing to suggest that Middleton, his sacred medals and badges still glistening in the light, had been murdered. I stared around. Dunheved was now at the porch door, pushing the key in and out of the broken lock.

'It would seem,' I whispered once Demontaigu had finished, 'that Middleton came here, moved that ladder and dispatched himself. The rope?' I called out to the chaplain.

'Oh,' the chaplain hurried over, 'there's rope kept in the chapel chest in the sacristy.' He spread his hands. 'Mistress, this is a castle; rope is easy to find . . .' His voice trailed away.

'So,' I gestured, 'Middleton came here early this morning.' My raised voice stilled the clamour as the rest gathered around, including the Beaumonts, who acted like spectators at a mummery.

'He brought in or collected some rope,' I continued, 'then locked the door, took the key out, moved that ladder, climbed up to secure the rope, fashioned a noose, tightened it around his neck and hanged himself.' I paused. Demontaigu, ignoring Rosselin's muttered objections, was now searching the dead man's clothing. He removed his right boot and shook out a small roll of vellum. He undid this, read it and passed it to me. The large scrawled letters proclaimed the usual message:

Aquilae Petri, fly not so bold, for Gaveston your master has been both bought and sold.

I read the words aloud. Rosselin moaned quietly like a child.

'Not suicide but murder,' Demontaigu whispered.

'So it is finished,' Ap Ythel murmured in his sing-song voice. '*Genethig* – little one.' He crouched down beside me. 'Gaveston is both bought and sold. He is ruined.'

'True, *fy cyfaielin*, my friend,' I whispered back. 'The only questions are when and how.'

I asked the chaplain to take care of the corpse. Demontaigu and Dunheved escorted Rosselin out into the garden. I knelt and inspected the corpse once more, as well as the ladder and rope. One of Ap Ythel's archers was sawing at the noose just above the knot. He cut this and handed it to me for scrutiny, then I examined the rest of the chapel. The horn-glazed windows were narrow and sound. The door from the sacristy to the garden was rusted fast, as if it hadn't been opened for years. The chaplain confirmed that there was no crypt or hidden entrance. Finally I inspected the door. The key had been fitted back into the ruined lock. I studied this and the rent hinges, then I glanced back down the small nave: nothing, no mark or sign of how Middleton had been murdered. Or had he, I wondered, received that taunting message about the Aquilae and decided to commit suicide? But would a man brimming with religious scruples and anxieties commit Judas' sin? On the other hand, if he, a young warrior, had been murdered, how?

I joined the rest in the chapel garden. We sat on a turf seat near a trellis covered by climbing roses. The morning was proving clear and crisp, the flower fragrances most pleasing and soothing. It was a place unsuited to the macabre death and secret malevolence we'd just witnessed. Rosselin was still stricken by what had happened. I questioned him closely; he could tell me little. Middleton had been frightened, determined like Rosselin to stay from any high place. He'd turned even more to religion, praying before a triptych of Christ's Passion in his chamber, worrying at any shadow. Rosselin sat, face cupped in his hands. He confessed how Middleton had discussed deserting Gaveston, but where could they go? Every man's hand now was turned against them. Rosselin was a squire, a soldier, but this silent, ominous war against him and the others had broken his will and sapped his courage. He talked hauntingly of murder tripping behind him like a bailiff waiting to pounce. About a host of shadows lurking at the top of darkened stairs or gathered in a coven, peering at him from some high place. I asked him what he meant. He retorted how he and Middleton felt they'd been pursued by the furies, by the ghosts of their dead comrades, by wraiths swirling in a black cloud around them. I could not decide if he was being honest or just babbling in fear. He talked of a scraping against his door in the dead of night. How he'd gone out into the stairwell and heard a whispering, as if a pack of hunting demons were plotting in the darkness below. I shivered as I listened. The dead do walk amongst us. Demons lurk in corners watching the affairs of men. Nothing draws them so fast as the feast of murder, a banquet of hot blood spilt in anger. I believe the preacher who said that Satan studies us most intently, lips curling with pleasure as he glimpses another son or daughter of Cain, the father of murder.

'Do you wish to confess?' Demontaigu asked. 'To be shriven?'

Rosselin gazed at him bleakly. 'Too late, too late,' he murmured, then he added those sombre words: 'With hell we have made a compact, with death an agreement.'

'And your master Gaveston?' Dunheved asked. 'Can he not help?'

Rosselin wasn't really listening.

'We flew so high,' he muttered, 'basking under his sun. Now we're blackened and shrivelled, falling like stones.'

'Please,' I begged, 'your four comrades are murdered. Can you not help us avenge them? Secure justice against their assassin?'

'I don't know,' he whispered. 'Yes, your sins do catch you out.' He straightened up. 'Who killed them?' He shook his head. 'How, why?' He shrugged. 'Punishment.'

'For what?'

'I choose,' he lifted a hand, 'you choose. Mathilde of Westminster,' he said my name slowly, 'watch your mistress! Subtle as a serpent she is.'

'Nonsense,' I retorted. 'Are you saying her grace had a hand in these deaths?'

'Subtle as a serpent!' Rosselin abruptly paused, as if realising for the first time who he was talking to. Then he rose quickly to his feet, mumbling about having to wait on Lord Gaveston, and strode hurriedly away. We watched him go.

'A man under sentence of death,' Demontaigu observed. 'I wonder if he will stay or flee.'

'Where?' Dunheved got to his feet. 'Where can any of them flee?'

'Perhaps at least we can find out what was in Middleton's mind.' Demontaigu opened his wallet and took out a small, thick key. 'I found this on Middleton's corpse; it must the key to his chamber.'

Chapter 8

The siege had begun, help from the
King frustrated, the Castle was without food.

The dead man's lodgings were on the second storey of the soaring keep, immediately beneath Rosselin's. The key fitted. We walked into that chamber, a chilling experience: everything had been left neat and tidy, as if Middleton was about to return. The bedclothes had been pulled up. Garments hung from wall pegs. A pair of boots and soft slippers lay pushed beneath a writing table holding a jug and pewter cups. Against the far wall the squire's chest and coffer were closed and clasped. Only the lighted candles flickering under their metal caps betrayed Middleton's agitation. The tapers had been placed on the table around a triptych of Christ's Passion, as well as on the floor beneath the rough yew crucifix on the wall, around which Middleton had woven his Ave beads. On the writing table, precisely arranged in the form of a cross, were a number of pewter badges venerating St Christopher, the patron saint of those who feared sudden, violent death. The small psalter lying beside these was well thumbed, especially the page with the litany to St Christopher. On the blank pages at the back Middleton had scrawled his own thoughts.

You have poured us a wine which has befuddled us.
My eyes are wasting with weeping.
The vision we were offered has been misleading and false.
Flight will not save the swift. The bowman will not stand his ground, the horseman is trapped.

'As he was,' I murmured, handing the psalter to Dunheved. 'Middleton was a soul torn by guilt and fear. He realised he was anointed for death.' Dunheved read the psalter, whilst Demontaigu and I searched Middleton's other possessions. We found nothing of interest.

'A man witless with fear,' Dunheved remarked, putting the psalter down. He turned to face the crucifix and crossed himself.

'Why, why was he killed like that?' Demontaigu sat on a stool, staring up at me. 'And the others? Why not a dagger slipping through the dark or an arrow loosed from the shadows?'

'Subtlety,' I replied, sitting down on the bed. 'Here we are locked in this gloomy castle. Middleton, who ostentatiously prayed for protection, was killed in that chapel. Now a place of blood, it is deconsecrated, its harmony and peace shattered. Mass cannot be celebrated there until a bishop reconsecrates it. An unlawful death in a holy place; now the garrison have no real place for mass. If it was murder, and I think it was, greater mysteries are fostered. How? According to the evidence there are only two entrances to that chapel: the sacristy door, but that's secured fast and sealed with age, and the main porch door. Yet that was locked from within. So,' I sighed, 'how did the assassin kill a nervous, wiry young man, stringing him up from that beam like a hunk of meat? Again, there's that taunting verse about eagles.'

'But Middleton was not hurled from the battlements.'

'No, but he was flung from that ladder with a noose around his neck,' I retorted. 'Don't forget, Middleton and Rosselin became very wary of heights, towers and battlements. Middleton stayed well away from such places.'

'So Middleton's death,' Dunheved asked 'was a subtle attack?'

'Oh yes! Such a mysterious death, and the despondency it provokes will seep like foul smoke through this castle,' I replied. 'Even here, Middleton's corpse loudly proclaims, the great Lord Gaveston is not safe. Even here, in this strong fortified place, death can strike like some hidden assassin, his bow strung and arrow notched. Middleton, for all his medals, badges and prayers, could not escape his fate. And what was that? To swing by his neck like some crow a farmer hoists on his fence to warn off other marauders.'

'But why Middleton?' Demontaigu broke in. 'The assassin is undoubtedly sly, devious and cunning.'

'And?' I asked.

'Never once,' Demontaigu lowered his voice, 'has Gaveston been attacked or threatened in any way – why not? Why kill his retainers but not the Great Lord?'

'As I said, to create unease.' I recalled Isabella's words about the assassin removing the guards first. 'Perhaps his time has yet to come.'

'Or could the assassin be Gaveston himself?' Dunheved whispered.

'Why?'

'God knows.' The Dominican's harsh, smooth face broke into a smile; try as he might, Dunheved found it difficult to hide his dislike of the royal favourite.

'Subtle but cunning,' I declared. 'What I said to Gaveston was true: he hastens here and he hastens there. A death occurs here, a death occurs there. Do we ever stay long enough to scrutinise the ground, to search for the symptoms? No, and it is true here. We have discovered nothing except that Middleton was terrified of sudden death, which unfortunately for him did close like a trap about him . . .'

There was little more to add. We left the chamber and went our different ways. I was still disturbed by Demontaigu's question. Why had the Aquilae been killed but Gaveston, so far, had not even suffered a scratch? Could he be the killer? But why? I returned to the chapel and stepped through the broken doorway. I examined the key and walked around the walls into the sanctuary and sacristy – nothing. I left the chapel and went up on to the battlements and stared longingly out. A heat haze now hung over the small town below and misted the far horizon. A breeze cooled the sweat on my face. Trumpets called, shouts and cries echoed up from the baileys. I leaned against the crenellations and wondered how this would end. Scarborough was a trap. Would we escape?

Later that same day Gaveston called one of his chamber councils: myself, Dunheved, Rosselin and the Beaumonts. The latter appeared in all their splendour, full of questions about Middleton's death and when the king would arrive. The more I watched and listened, the more I grew aware of why the Beaumonts had planted their standards so firmly alongside Gaveston's. They were fortune-hunters, gamblers. If Gaveston survived, he would be in their debt. If he went down, the king would remember their loyalty and perhaps they could fill Gaveston's place at court as well as in the king's heart. Just as importantly, they remained close to the king's chamber, where they could spy and eavesdrop on the royal council as well as keep a vigilant eye on their estates in Scotland. Nevertheless, the Beaumonts had finally realised which way the wind was blowing and had reached a conclusion. Gaveston was in dire peril and it was time for them be gone, at least for a while. Henry loudly questioned why they had to shelter here. What troops would the king bring? Such hot words made little impression. Gaveston slouched in his chair, a broken man, waving his hand, airily talking about the king sweeping up with masses of royal levies. He'd certainly drunk deep and loudly mourned

Middleton and the deaths of the other Aquilae, who had been so cruelly brought low. He yelled questions at me, then rose and walked down to Rosselin. He clapped his henchman on the shoulder, promising that one of Ap Ythel's archers would guard him day and night. In that dusty chamber, with the sun pouring through the lancet windows against the crumbling plaster and the faded colours of the battered shields fastened on the walls, the glass darkened even further. Gaveston returned to his chair, gabbling on about the past glories of his beloved Aquilae, then he dismissed us with a wave of his hand.

Later that day news arrived. Royal couriers, sweat-soaked and grey with dust, thundered through the gatehouse, swinging themselves out of the saddle, hands clutching the pouches of letters they brought. We waited a while; no mention was made of the king arriving, but the great earls were certainly on the march. Edward sheltered at York. The queen, much to my surprise, had separated herself from the king and was residing at the royal manor of Burstwick on the Humber peninsula. More curious still, a powerful French squadron of war-cogs had appeared, cruising off the mouth of the Humber, though with banners and pennants lowered in a sign of peace. The sorrows were gathering. Seeds were sown of a harvest that would come to crop year in and year out for decades to come, each with its own noxious fruit.

Our sense of foreboding deepened. Middleton's death, despite Gaveston's strictures, was whispered about as something ghastly, deeply malevolent, as if Satan, the provost of hell, had pitched camp in that grim fortress. Even during the day, when the sun shone in an angelic blue sky, our mood was always tinged by the fear of night and the descent into darkness. Once the daylight faded, strange sounds were heard throughout the castle. A sepulchral voice bellowed down hollow, vaulted passageways. Lights and fires were glimpsed where they should not have been. Strange groans and cries echoed along the empty stone corridors. One story fed upon another. A bat became a winged demon. A night bird's shriek the chant of a stricken soul; perhaps Middleton's, still earth-bound by his heavy chains of sin. Gaveston kept more and more to himself. Rosselin was rarely seen, and when he was, he was deep in his cups, his chamber constantly guarded by one of Ap Ythel's archers. On the few occasions I visited the Aquila, he would first pull back the grille high on the door and glare out at me. He would allow me in but could not help me with my questions. He was a broken man hiding in a filthy chamber.

Some days after Middleton's death, early in the morning, around Matins hour, we were all aroused by the clanging of the tocsin. I rose and peered through the window. A beacon fire had been lit along the battlements. Outside rose the call to arms. I dressed and hurried out, cloak about me, boots pulled over my bare feet. The warning bell high on its scaffold somewhere in the inner bailey had fallen silent, but men were still hurriedly strapping on harness and war-belt. Servants running beside them held torches; all were scrambling up the steep, dangerous steps to the castle walls. The clash of the portcullis, the winch of catapults being prepared cut through the cold night air, drowning the cries and shouts, the raucous barking of dogs and the frightened neighing of horses in the stables.

Demontaigu and I joined the others high on the windswept battlements. Guards were pointing out. Ap Ythel's archers were stringing their bows. Captains of the parapet shouted instructions. The night breeze carried the iron tang of water and oil being boiled on hastily prepared fires beneath. Ap Ythel, cursing loudly, roared at the others climbing the steps to stay below, to douse the fires and wait for his orders. Constable Warde came hurrying up. He and Ap Ythel conferred in hushed whispers. They leaned against the parapet wall, staring into the darkness, trying to establish what dangers threatened.

'Can you see anything?' Ap Ythel called. 'Anything at all?'

We peered out across the darkened town lit by pricks of light. The constable quietly cursed and shouted an order to his troops below. A postern door was loosened to the clatter of chains and the drawing of bolts.

'They are sending out scouts,' Demontaigu whispered.

The line of men along the parapet relaxed. Dunheved shouted my name from the bailey below but I could not catch his words. Gaveston, swathed in a cloak, came clumsily up the steps clutching a goblet of wine, loudly demanding to know what was wrong. The constable whispered furiously to him. Gaveston toasted the darkness with his cup and staggered back down. I followed. Dunheved came out of the darkness and clutched my arm.

'What is wrong, Mathilde? Beacon fires burning, tocsins sounding? I was trying to find out . . .'

'You know much as we do, Brother.' I gazed across the bailey; the wind was whipping the torch flames to a furious dance.

Accompanied by Dunheved, I asked a guard to take me into the inner bailey to show me the high wooden scaffold from which the great tocsin bells were hung. The man pulled a face but agreed. Once there, I climbed the steps on to the wooden dais. The rope for the bells still hung loose. I stared up and made out the yawning rims glinting in the light from my companion's torch. I had seen or heard nothing from the castle walls. I suspected the alarm was some madcap hoax, a suspicion the returning scouts confirmed. No force, friendly or hostile, had entered the town.

The constable immediately summoned everyone down into the large bailey and led them across into the refectory, where tired-faced servants served us fresh milk and strips of yesterday's bread. We gathered around the tables as Warde shouted questions no one could answer. The ringing of the tocsin, the lighting of the beacon fire and the rumours that had swept the fortress about the king approaching – or was it the earls? – could not be explained. The constable, red-faced with anger, stalked out. We and the rest drifted back to our own chambers.

The real cause for the alarm was revealed in all its horror the next morning. A servant hastened into the chapel garden to breathlessly inform me, Demontaigu and Dunheved that John Rosselin, God save his soul, squire to Lord Gaveston, had been found dead outside Queen's Tower. He took us across the bailey and around the donjon to the rocky incline that stretched about its base. Rosselin lay sprawled, gashed and saturated in his own blood, on the sharp cobbles. Gruesome bruises marked his face. The right side of his skull was completely staved in, like the wood of a broken cask. He was dressed in a soiled shirt, hose and boots, arms and legs grotesquely twisted. The dagger sheath on his warbelt was empty, the knife driven deep into his left side up under his ribs. The constable and Ap Ythel let me through. I turned the corpse over, peered at the blood-encrusted mask of Rosselin's face then felt his hands and neck.

'He's been dead some time,' I declared. I followed the constable's direction and stared up at the window high above us, even as I heard the dull thudding from the keep.

'He fell from his chamber window; he must have done,' the constable murmured.

'My men are trying to break down the door,' Ap Ythel explained.

Dunheved asked Demontaigu to look after the corpse whilst we went up into the keep. We reached the stairwell to Rosselin's chamber just as the door, locked from the inside, buckled and splintered. The men grasping the makeshift battering ram pounded it until it snapped loose of lock and hinge and crashed inwards. We clambered over it into the room. The large window, deep in its embrasure, was unshuttered. A desolate, untidy room, still reeking of Rosselin's sad spirit. The table was littered with cups and dirty platters. Scraps of parchments were strewn on the bed, its sweat-soiled linen sheets all twisted. A cloak lay on the floor. On a stool next to the bed was the key, a pair of beads, a brooch and two leather wrist guards.

'I'll collect everything,' Dunheved whispered. He picked up a wicker basket and crossed to the bed.

I stared around at the dirty plaster, the recess leaning into the latrine, the arrow loops in the wall. I crossed to the window embrasure and glimpsed the blood, dry and sticky, on the dark stone sill. I traced it back along the floor to the centre of the chamber, just where the cloak lay. The room had fallen silent except for Dunheved filling that basket, and the laboured breathing of the men who'd forced the door. A prickle of fear cooled my own sweat. The constable and Ap Ythel, who'd now joined us, were thinking what Dunheved was whispering about. The angel of death and all his minions from the meadows of hell had visited this chamber. Rosselin had certainly been murdered, his body picked up and hurled from that window, but why, by whom and how? Ap Ythel went out into the stairwell to talk to a comrade in the sing-song tongue of their own country. The constable checked the door and its shattered lock. It was futile to ask about secret entrances or someone climbing up the sheer face of that keep and forcing an entry through the window.

'Something evil,' the constable declared. 'Some malignancy fastened on Rosselin.' He went and sat down on the bed, his face all miserable. Warde was a seasoned veteran and I recognised his expression: a man who would do his duty but one who also realised when he could do no more.

'Our strength has been sapped from within,' the constable murmured. 'What happened here? Gaveston,' he checked himself, 'my lord Gaveston will want to know.'

'The tocsin,' I replied. 'This was the assassin's real purpose, but wasn't there a guard . . . ?'

'Goronwy Ap Rees,' the captain of the archers sang out as he came back into the room, 'one of my best men. He was on guard outside last night. He admits he was dozing. He

222

was aroused by the alarm, as was Rosselin, who came and lifted the door shutter. Ap Rees did not know what to do until a voice at the bottom of the stairs shouted that a royal army was approaching the castle and every man was needed on the battlements. Ap Rees left. He heard Rosselin yelling questions behind him but he concluded that if Gaveston's henchman wanted to know what was happening, he was free to join him.'

'So the keep was deserted?' I declared. 'The assassin must have rung that tocsin, lit the fire and come here. Somehow he persuaded Rosselin to open the door, then stabbed him, dragged his body across to that embrasure and hurled it from the window.' I paused. 'Swift as a cat pouncing on a mouse. Rosselin was befuddled, mawmsy with drink.'

'Yet whom would Rosselin admit?' Demontaigu asked.

'More importantly,' Warde declared, 'and word of this will spread through the castle, how did the assassin leave through a door locked from within?'

I couldn't answer. I crossed to the basket Dunheved had placed on the floor, took out the key and went to the battered door. The key fitted the lock, rusting and ancient though now all buckled

'I have found it.' Demontaigu's voice rang clear from the stairwell. He came into the chamber clutching a scrap of parchment and handed it to me. It bore the expected message: *Aquilae Petri, fly not so bold, for Gaveston your master has been both bought and sold.*

'Tucked under the cuff of his jerkin,' Demontaigu added.

'I had best tell my lord Gaveston.' The constable got to his feet and strode out. The rest followed.

Demontaigu sat on a stool, mopping his brow. Dunheved stood by the window with his back to us.

'We should go,' he declared, 'from this place of blood.'

'No, no,' I whispered. 'Let us first search Rosselin's possessions.'

We did so, but discovered nothing of significance. Demontaigu informed me that Rosselin's corpse had been taken to the castle death house.

'His soul has gone to God.' Dunheved was still staring out of the window. 'Mathilde, shouldn't we go?' He turned to face me. 'It's time we left here. There's nothing more we can do. This is a lost cause. What is the point in staying?'

I didn't answer. A few hours later we were given no choice but to remain. Early that afternoon the tocsin was sounded, booming out the truth. The earls had arrived! First their outriders, horses raising dust clouds beyond the town, then a stream of colour: pennants, banners and standards flapping in the sea breeze, a host of many hues: red, argent, blue, green, scarlet, white and black. The devices and insignia boldly proclaimed the power of England: gules, shields, bears and boars, wyverns and lions, greyhounds, crowns and swords. The earls' army camped beyond the town, a brilliant sea of shifting colours as pavilions, tents, bothies and horse lines were set up. The noise and smell of this great host wafted towards us, then, like a river breaking its banks, the enemy troops spilled out of the camp, threading through the narrow streets of the town and washing around the base of the castle and down to the port. I stood on the battlements with the rest. My heart sank. The earls had mustered a great host. This was the season for war. The lanes, tracks and roads were dry-hard, making easy passage for their foot, horses and carts, whilst the surrounding countryside was well stocked with provisions. They were quickly accepted by the townspeople. Order seemed good, discipline imposed. We even heard cheering as the citizens greeted the passing troops. If the earls wished to impress us, they certainly succeeded. Mail and armour flashed in the sunlight, the shimmering threat of what we were to expect. Worse was to come. Behind the troops, black and fearsome against the sky, trundled the terrible engines of war: trebuchets, slings, battering rams, mantlets, catapults and massive siege towers. The latter moved slowly, edging towards us like hideous monsters from the deepest pit. Once they reached the castle walls, the siege would be over.

The earls deployed their army, concentrating on the lower reaches of the castle. Against both our right and left flanks siege engines were set up. Behind these came the carts, rattling with stones, slingshots and barrels of tar, ready to be lit. By early evening we were encircled. Our lookouts on the coastal side brought even grimmer news: three cogs of war, high-sterned, well armed and thronged with fighting men, had slipped into the harbour, flying the pennants of the leading guilds of London. These would seal the port, cutting off help from the king's ships as well as any possible escape. The trap had snapped shut. The noose was tightening. The earls had brought Gaveston to the ring to dance, and dance he would. I recall that night vividly. The darkness fiercely lit by fire. The air polluted by the sickly burning smell of tar as the besiegers prepared in earnest.

The following morning, just after dawn, the earls sent

their defiance. An envoy carrying a leafy green bough, escorted by a priest holding a cross, and a herald with a trumpet and Pembroke's standard, rode to the edge of the narrow moat before the gatehouse of the castle. The strident blast of the trumpet brought us back to the walls. The ensuing ceremony was empty and pointless. The envoys demanded the immediate surrender of the castle and that Lord Gaveston give himself up into the power of 'the Community of the Realm'. The constable, on behalf of Gaveston, rejected the call, claiming he held the castle for the king. The envoy dropped his bough, turned his horse and galloped back with his escort. Two hours later the earls attacked. They concentrated on the lower stretches of the castle to both right and left, well aware of our difficulties, our inability to fortify and defend two places at the same time. The garrison was split. The constable had to hold even more men back in reserve lest these attacks were mere feints and the main assault might emerge elsewhere.

The succeeding days became a time of terror. The sky torched and seared with stones and other missiles coated with burning pitch. The air was riven by the screech of rope, the whir of wheels and the harsh crack as the engines of war launched a blizzard of fire. The earls tried to clear the battlements of our archers as the clumsy ox-hide-covered siege towers edged ever so slowly but threateningly towards us. The earls' strategy was simple and stark: to attack and overrun the low-lying flanks of the castle and push us back to the inner bailey and the bleak fastness of the keep. Everyone was mustered to arms. Even I had to crouch, clammy cold with fear, on the battlements with an arbalest and a quiver of bolts. Dunheved joined me, refusing to hide behind his cloth. He could often be seen edging along the parapet with what he called his 'miraculous wineskin' so he could provide both physical and spiritual comfort. The ominous whistle of missiles, the crack of rope, the crash of stones, the fiery bundles hurled against the wall or down into the bailey became commonplace. Great clouds of smoke plumed up above the castle, billowing out in a miasma of offensive stench. The assaults continued late into the evening, the machines of war singing out in their own horrid way a deadly Vespers to close the day.

Men were killed, heads and bodies smashed. Others were grievously wounded or badly burnt. I became busy in the infirmary, fortunate enough to be away from the heart-rending clatter of battle. Because of the heat, the dead were buried quickly, Rosselin and Middleton included, in a long gaping trench cut through that lovely garden. A broad, deep furrow for the dead that became crammed with the corpses of those killed in the murderous, fiery storm of missiles. I remembered my promise to Rosselin. I had him sheeted in a proper shroud, a wooden cross clasped between his dead fingers with an absolution pinned to his breast. I gave gold to the castle chaplain and he swore the most solemn oath to sing six chantry masses for the repose of Rosselin's soul and those of his comrades. The siege castles continued to edge their cumbersome way across the narrow moat and up to the flattest place before the walls. Already archers, packed in the various storeys, could loose dense clouds of longbow arrows. The constable retaliated with his own mangonels and slings; pots of fire, burning tar and boulders were hurled back, but the siege towers were draped in ox hide saturated in vinegar. Sallies and forays were attempted. Rumours that two of the earls had withdrawn their levies gave us little respite as the blazing fury returned. Our garrison began to weaken, due not so much to death and wounds but to the very reason for our resistance. Gaveston was now reduced to a drunken sot. No, he was not a coward; he was never that. He just accepted that salvation was not imminent. The king would not come. The raging battle became our lives. I could do little to resolve the murderous mysteries that had dogged our souls like lurchers on the scent. Such problems were overridden by the need to survive. Morning gave way to evening, and still the sky rained terrors.

The end came swiftly, unexpectedly, not from without but from the enemy within. One afternoon I was summoned from the infirmary to the inner bailey, where a crowd had gathered round the deep well, our main source of water. Women were screaming about the water being polluted. An archer volunteered to go down the foot holes in the walls of the well to investigate. He returned grim-faced, carrying a dead rat bloated with water. The bottom of the well, he reported, brimmed with such corpses. God knows how it was done. Were the rats poisoned and thrown into the well, or were they fed some noxious substance that gave them a raging thirst so that, true to their rapacious nature, they turned and twisted in the runnels beneath the castle searching for water. I was about to leave, to hurry to the other well in the outer bailey, when screams and shouts rose from the keep. Flames and smoke were licking at the half-windows just above ground. The great cellars of the keep, holding most of the castle's provisions, had been fired. Cavern after cavern, cellar after cellar, was ravaged by hungry flames, which destroyed the wooden lintels and doors, scarred the stone and reduced most of the stock to grey, shifting ash. No one could be accused, no evidence produced, except that the fire had been started quickly with some oil and a torch. Was it the assassin? I wondered. There again, it could have been any member of our garrison, tired, heart-sick and desperate for relief. Indeed, we were not so much concerned about who had done it but the effect. At a stroke the garrison had been gravely weakened, depleted of both food and water.

Gaveston's chamber council was in no mood to mollify the drunken, unshaven royal favourite when we met in the great hall of the keep later that evening.

'We must seek terms,' Warde declared defiantly. 'Our water and food stocks are no more. The enemy have tightened their noose around us. Talk of desertion amongst my men is common chatter. If the earls storm the castle they can, according to the usages and rules of war—'

'The usages and rules!' Gaveston screamed back. 'What are those?'

'Protection against being put to the sword if this castle is stormed and taken,' Warde shouted back.

'The king . . .' Gaveston yelled.

'His grace,' Warde retorted, 'has not come. He will not come. My lord, the castle is surrounded. The harbour sealed. Within three days those siege towers will reach our walls. I must now look after everyone here, including you. We must dispatch peace envoys . . .'

Our murmur of assent brought Gaveston to his senses. He blinked and gazed fearfully around.

'God have mercy.' Gaveston realised he was finished.

'We must follow a different path,' Dunheved insisted.

'Who?' he asked.

The sigh of relief that greeted his question was almost audible

'Who?' Gaveston repeated and his gaze held mine. 'Whom do we send?'

Henry Beaumont and his kin immediately pointed out that they too were the object of the earls' spite. Had they not also been included in the earls' ordinances and indictments against the court party? Gaveston just ignored them and continued to stare at me, pleadingly abject. He trusted me. He knew I would be honourable and not barter my life for his. God knows why he thought that. I was as tired and sick of him as anyone. Gaveston repeated his question. His chamber council stared bleakly back. The earls regarded everybody in the castle as their enemy. Nevertheless, the killing had to stop. This futile business brought to an end.

'I'll go.' I lifted a hand, knocking away Demontaigu's as he tried to restrain me.

'And so will I.' Dunheved smiled at me. 'A Dominican priest and a lady of the queen's personal chamber should be safe.'

'And the terms?' Gaveston tried to conceal the desperation in his voice.

'Your life, your honour,' I retorted. 'The earls have no power over any of us. We held a royal castle in the king's name.'

Gaveston sat in silence, nodding to himself, then, true to

his nature, fickle as ever, he abruptly changed, clapping his hands like a contented child.

'Tomorrow,' he declared, 'at Lauds time. Sir Simon, make the arrangements. We must send a herald as well.'

'I'll do that.' Demontaigu spoke up. 'I will be the herald. The earls can only offer you terms. My lord, it is a matter for the king and Parliament what happens to you, to us.'

Gaveston declared himself content and dismissed us.

Just after dawn the following day, I prepared to leave. It was a truly beautiful morning. The sun had risen in fiery splendour, its light glowing across the sea then sweeping in to bathe both castle and town in its golden warmth. Demontaigu, Dunheved and myself gathered in the bailey then left through the great gatehouse. Demontaigu rode on my right, bearing Gaveston's standard to which a rich green bough had been attached. Dunheved on my left held a crucifix lashed to a pole. I was no longer so fearful. At first light the constable had appeared above the gatehouse with a trumpeter to summon Pembroke's envoy to discuss a parlance about matters of mutual concern. The constable said he was prepared to dispatch emissaries. Pembroke's envoy, without even turning back to camp, quickly agreed. The earls also wanted to bring these matters to a close.

I had washed and changed into the best I could find: soft riding boots, a gown of dark murrey fringed with gold and a Lincoln-green cloak. I didn't truly know what to expect and tried to hide my nervousness as we clattered across the drawbridge to join Pembroke's envoy, who was also holding a green bough. He welcomed us courteously enough and we continued down into the winding lanes of the town. Despite the early hour, rumour as well as the noise of the heavy portcullis being raised had roused the citizens. Casement windows flew open, doors creaked back on their hinges, people shuffled out to peer at what the great ones had decided. A madcap, still mawmsy after drinking ale, danced out of the mouth of an alleyway chanting a verse from the psalms: 'For three times nay, four times thy crimes, punishment is decreed.' Pembroke's envoy drove him off.

We continued on. Dogs howled. Cats busy on the stinking midden heaps raced away, black shadows against the glowing light. On the corner of a crossroads a corpse dangled from a makeshift gibbet, head twisted, eyes bulging glassily at us. A piece of parchment pinned to the hanged man's tattered jerkin described him as a looter, powerful evidence that the earls were determined to keep order. Beside the gibbet a line of malefactors held tight in the stocks groaned and whined for relief. A town bailiff, in mockery of their pain, doused their heads with a bucket of horse piss then roared with laughter as the prisoners tried to shake the slop off themselves. Two beggar children, eyes wide, thin arms extended, watched us pass. Despite the glory of the morning, I caught a trace of the brutal cruelty of this life. Dunheved began to chant a psalm: 'I lift up my eyes to hills from which my Saviour cometh . . .' I quietly prayed that we'd be safe.

We reached a stretch of common land across which lay the sprawling camp of the earls' army, already roused and preparing for another day's bloodshed. We passed the siege machines and other engines of war and went in through the gate. The camp itself, probably at Pembroke's order, to impress us, was already bristling with menace. Archers and men-at-arms, hobelars and crossbowmen were dressed in their leather jerkins, chainmail coifs pulled back, helmets and sallets hanging from war-belts as their captains organised them for the first assault of the day. The camp reeked of all the filthy stench of battle: blood, dirt and fire smoke. A soft breeze carried a mixture of odours from the horse lines, latrines, smithies and cook pots. The enemy host was well organised, bothies and leather tents being pitched in neat rows. We passed along the main thoroughfare to a makeshift stockade housing the gloriously coloured pavilions of the earls; in front of these were planted their standards next to their armour and crested helmets displayed on wooden racks.

We were met by retainers, who helped us dismount and took away our horses. A stiff-backed chamberlain armed with his white wand of office led us to the centre tent, its folds neatly pulled back. Demontaigu gave up his standard and Dunheved his cross to the chamberlain; we were then ushered inside, where Pembroke, Hereford and Warwick waited for us behind a trestle table. Pembroke sat in the centre; on the table to his right lay his jewel-hilted sword, its wicked point turned towards us; on his left was a book of the Gospels, its reddish leather covering ornamented with Celtic designs done in miniature precious stones. We were invited to the three stools placed before the table. Aymer de Valence, Earl of Pembroke, did not stand on ceremony. He bowed courteously to all three of us, asked us to name ourselves, then, turning to his left, introduced Guy de Beauchamp, Earl of Warwick, and on his right Humphrey de Bohun, Earl of Hereford. He quickly added how the king's cousin, Thomas, the Earl of Lancaster, had withdrawn his levies to Pontefract but, Pembroke observed tersely, could always return.

From the very start, Pembroke was graciousness itself. He offered us ale, soft bread and freshly cooked meat. We tactfully accepted, and while servants brought in a platter and tankards I studied these three great earls. Of course I knew them, whilst they recognised me from court occasions, pageants, celebrations and banquets. I ate and drank sparingly, allowing Dunheved and Demontaigu, also known to our hosts, to go through the usual courtesies. The constable had lectured me on what to do and what to say, but in truth, I knew these nobles well. Some of them truly hated Gaveston with a passion beyond all understanding. Black-haired, swarthy, long-faced Pembroke, with his neatly clipped moustache and beard and deep-set eyes, I rather liked. Tall, angular and slightly stooped, Aymer de Valence, Earl of Pembroke, was the Crown's principal diplomat. A loyal captain of war, driven to this by the king's foolishness, he was nervous and eager to please, and our spirits lifted. Poor Aymer! He died on a latrine, poisoned, many years later on a diplomatic mission to France.

Humphrey de Bohun, Earl of Hereford, was also ill at ease. With a thatch of blond hair above a red-cheeked ploughboy's face, stout, fat Hereford was not the sharpest arrow in the quiver; a blusterer, with his fat cheeks, blue eyes and pouting lips. He followed where others went, even if it led to his own death. Years later, when poor Hereford tried to defend a bridge across the river Ure against Despencer, a pikeman got beneath and thrust his spear up into his bowels. Finally the dragon-slayer, Guy de Beauchamp, Earl of Warwick. A viper to the heart, he was a highly dangerous man, violent and malicious, who carried his head as if he'd been personally anointed by God Almighty to sit at the right hand of the power. Lean and sinewy as a ferret, constantly garbed in scarlet and gold, Warwick looked Italianate: his olive-skinned, high-cheekboned face gleamed with precious oil, his black hair was neatly cropped and sleek, his face freshly shaven. He had large, liquid dark eyes with a slight cast in the right one. He looked what he was – the devil at the feast. Rumour had it that he truly hated Gaveston, who had not only toppled him at the tournaments but mocked him with the nickname of 'the Black Dog of Arden'. Warwick never forgave or forgot the insult. He regarded Gaveston as a Gascon upstart, the son of a witch, a commoner not even worthy of holding Warwick's boots. On that morning he was friendly enough to me. He saw me as a retainer, *domicella* of the queen. He smiled crookedly at me and winked. I noticed that his left hand was bandaged. Apparently, so I learnt later, he had actually led the assault on Scarborough Castle, so eager was he to tear at Gaveston. Warwick had no dispute with us. He made that obvious; indeed, this emerged very swiftly at our meeting.

Once the servants had withdrawn and the tent flaps were closed, Pembroke came quickly to the point. The earls, he declared, the representatives of the *Communitas Regni*, the Community of the Realm, had no quarrel with anyone inside the castle except the lord Gaveston. We were free to come and go *ad libertatem* – with complete freedom.

Gaveston however, Pembroke continued remorselessly, had broken the ordinances issued against him the previous year. He must surrender himself to honourable custody and await the will of Parliament, to be summoned at Westminster. Dunheved fastened on the word 'honourable'. Pembroke explained that Gaveston should withdraw to a royal manor and await the king's pleasure. Face all earnest, he leaned across the table, informing us that Gaveston would be treated according to the dignity of an earl and be directly under Pembroke's protection. I was astonished at such generosity yet profoundly uneasy. On the one hand Pembroke and the rest wanted a swift resolution to this matter – that was understandable. They had spent great treasure deploying this army. More importantly, they had broken the king's peace. They were, in law, rebels and could be accused of treason. If Edward decided to seize the initiative, unfurl his banners and proclaim a state of war, the earls and all their followers, if apprehended in arms, could face summary justice and immediate execution. Pembroke earnestly wanted a solution to these legal and military difficulties. Nevertheless, I remained deeply suspicious. Hereford kept nodding solemnly as if he understood every word, which I doubted. Warwick just stared down at the table. Now and again he'd move his hand, fingers tapping; occasionally he'd glance up and catch my gaze with those dark, dead eyes.

Demontaigu, and subsequently Dunheved, spoke hotly, demanding that Gaveston be truly protected. Pembroke, who could have taken offence at his word being challenged, solemnly promised to go on the most sacred oath possible. He shouted for a servant; when the man came, Pembroke gave orders that a priest carrying the Blessed Sacrament be brought immediately to his pavilion. A short while later, accompanied by a thurifer, an acolyte carrying a capped candle and a small page noisily ringing a bell, the Blessed Sacrament was brought in with all ceremony and laid upon the table. Immediately we all knelt. The priest intoned a prayer, then Pembroke took the oath, one hand on the book of the Gospels, the other grasping the pyx like a priest at the consecration. He swore by life and limb, by his hope of salvation, that if the lord Gaveston surrendered himself into his protection, he would be safe and accorded all the dignity of an earl. I asked if my lords Hereford and Warwick would offer the same oath. Hereford seemed eager enough; Warwick just shrugged. Pembroke swiftly intervened. He pointed out that all the great earls had taken a solemn oath to each other, and what he swore they would stand by. The priest then picked up the Blessed Sacrament, covered it in a white silken cloth and solemnly processed out of the tent.

Cynical though I was, I had to be satisfied. These were honourable terms, and we promised Pembroke that by nightfall he would have Lord Gaveston's reply. Once the discussions were over, Pembroke grew even friendlier. He insisted that we toast each other with the best wine, which he'd brought specially for such an occasion. Of course courtesy demanded that we stay. The trestle table was withdrawn and for a while we exchanged pleasantries. Warwick sauntered over and commented on my gown: how fresh and sweet I looked after the rigours of the siege. I replied with some tart observation, Warwick threw his head back and laughed, rubbing his hand on my shoulder. I didn't flinch. Warwick was a dangerous man, but I could tell from his eyes that he meant no danger or threat to me.

'Little Mathilde,' he whispered and glanced across to where the other two earls were deep in conversation with Demontaigu and Dunheved. 'Little Mathilde, be assured, and tell your royal mistress this, we never did mean you any harm.' He leaned a little closer. 'We have heard of the deaths of the Aquilae, the eagles of Gaveston – what truth is there in that? That they were all murdered, dashed from a great height? Has Gaveston turned on his own?'

'My lord,' I whispered hoarsely, 'why should he do that?'

Warwick withdrew his hand. 'I shall tell you something, Mathilde, in confidence. I have known Gaveston many, many a year, since he was a lowly squire in the Prince of Wales' household.' He licked his lips. 'I have a reputation, mistress, and I deserve it, but no one understands the ruthlessness of Gaveston, remember that! He will betray anyone to protect himself.'

'Even his grace the king?' I whispered.

'Edward of Caernarvon is what he is, but even he doesn't understand Gaveston like I do. The reason why, Mistress Mathilde? Because we're the same kind. I recognise Gaveston for what he is. I beg you to be careful, and if . . .' Warwick paused to collect himself, then he put his hand on my shoulder and gently caressed it. 'Mathilde, what do you wish for your mistress?'

'Health and happiness, my lord, the same as you.'

'And so I do.' Warwick glanced quickly around. 'But I assure you, this realm will have no peace until Gaveston is gone.'

'You mean abroad, my lord?'

'I mean until he is no more. Remember that, Mathilde.' He tapped me on the shoulder, kissed me quickly on the brow and strode away.

We were escorted back to the castle and taken immediately to the keep, where Gaveston had called his chamber council. The discussion was brief but terse. The constable declared himself delighted by the terms and I recognised that Gaveston could no longer count on him. Demontaigu, Dunheved and I pressed Gaveston to accept. There was some hesitation on the royal favourite's part, but within the hour he too had taken the oath. Dunheved was dispatched back to the earls to inform them that early the following morning Gaveston would leave the castle.

I was pleased it was over. I was desperate to rejoin my mistress. Later in the evening, however, Dunheved visited me with the news that he and I, together with Demontaigu, were to be part of Gaveston's escort. The royal favourite argued that since we had witnessed Pembroke's oath and played a prominent part in the negotiations, it was only right and proper that we should accompany him. We had no choice but to agree. The Beaumonts, intrigued, also decided to join us.

The following morning Gaveston, face shaved, hair all coiffed, dressed resplendently in beautiful velvet robes of green, black and red, his horse carefully groomed, its harness polished, left the castle to the blare of trumpets and the cheers of the garrison. The fool thought he had won their support; little did he realise they were delighted that this bloody affray was finished.

Pembroke was waiting for us. He had promised that Gaveston be treated with all honour and grace, and this was observed. Our ride through Scarborough town was a triumphant procession, with people shouting and cheering from windows decorated with coloured cloths, whilst green boughs were strewn on the path before us. Maidens of the town had gone out and collected the petals of wild flowers to shower Gaveston. Priests from the churches processed out with cross, incense and holy water to bless and approve our passing. This time the town gibbet was bare and the stocks empty. The leading citizens presented Gaveston with a small gift, then we crossed that stretch of wasteland into the earls' camp. Hereford and Warwick were conspicuous by their absence, but Pembroke remained gracious, dressed in all his finery, silver chains around his neck, rings glittering on his fingers. He and Gaveston exchanged the *Osculum pacis*, the kiss of peace.

Oh, there was junketing and celebrating, mummery and music. The camp echoed with toasts and acclamations as well as the sound of rebec, viol and harp. Standards, pennants and coloured buntings floated in the breeze. Pembroke and Gaveston dined publicly at a trestle table set on a richly draped dais in full view of the camp. Servitors brought in freshly cooked dishes of venison, pork, beef and lamprey as well as jugs of the finest wine. Once the banquet was over, Pembroke and Gaveston again exchanged the kiss of peace, and the royal favourite loudly declared that he would go to Wallingford and reside there in peace until the will of the Community of the Realm be known. Pembroke in his turn proclaimed that he had taken a sacred oath: Lord Gaveston was directly under his protection and he would answer for him.

Afterwards, in the privacy of Pembroke's tent, Gaveston demanded, at my urging, that Pembroke leave for Wallingford with a very strong escort, whilst no one should be informed of our route south. Pembroke agreed, but insisted that his brother earls would respect his oath and that no harm would befall anyone.

Chapter 9

The said Earl should keep Gaveston unharmed.

The following morning we left the coast, journeying to the ancient Roman road that stretched south. A pleasant progress. The sun was strong, the roads dry. The fields on either side were rich in their greenery. By now it was the first week of June and the full bloom of summer was making itself felt. We left Scarborough on the sixth of June, the Feast of St Norbert. One of Pembroke's household priests chanted a psalm from the mass of that day, about Christ being our shepherd who would guide us safely through all perils and hazards. Perhaps we should have prayed more fervently. At first my suspicions were calmed somewhat. Pembroke was honest. He had taken the most solemn oath, and if he broke it, he would be condemned by both Church and Crown. Nevertheless, I felt everything was running too smoothly, too quickly. It was like walking across those water meadows outside Poitiers. Everything was green, soft and fertile, yet you had to watch your step. Take a wrong turn and you could find the green fields were a treacherous morass to suck you down and keep you trapped. Gaveston, now bereft of his Aquilae or any henchmen to advise him, was truly relaxed, believing he had secured a peace. I listened in horror as his relief gave way to boasting about what would happen when he was reunited with the king. Pembroke wisely ignored this. I wanted to send urgent messages to the queen, but Pembroke insisted no one could leave the column of march. I drew some comfort from the long lines of hobelars, men-at-arms and bowmen who accompanied us. Neither the constable nor Ap Ythel had been allowed to provide any escort. The Welsh captain of the royal archers had quietly assured me that once Gaveston had gone, he and his men would ride swiftly to the king. Ap Ythel was also deeply suspicious at the ease with which everything had been agreed.

'*Faux et semblant,*' he murmured. He clasped my hand, then embraced me close. 'For the love of God and His beautiful Mother,' he whispered in my ear, 'take care! Remember this. Do not let Pembroke become separated from you.' He kissed me firmly on the cheeks and stood back, one hand raised. 'Remember,' he repeated.

I did. I also recalled Isabella's words about assassins first withdrawing the guard before they struck their victim. Nevertheless, our journey out of Scarborough was happy, the atmosphere serene, as if we were a host of pilgrims journeying south to kiss the Lady stone at Walsingham or pray before the blessed bones of Becket in their gold and silver house at Canterbury. We met other travellers: moon people, gipsies in their gaily coloured wagons, merchants on horseback trotting south to do business in the wool towns. Tinkers, pedlars and traders with their sumpter ponies, baskets and panniers all crammed with trinkets and every item for sale under the sun, be it a horn or a pewter jug. Pilgrims of every variety thronged the road, lifelong wanderers in stained leather and linen jerkins, their hats boasting medals from shrines as far afield as St James of Compostela or the tomb of the Magi in Cologne. Relic sellers swarmed like fleas, badgering us with everything from the head of St Britaeus – God knows who he was – to a sandal-latch of the Blessed Virgin. A group of roisterers from a nearby village tried to tempt us to pause and watch them sing and dance to the raucous noise of bagpipes. Pembroke laughingly waved them aside. For the rest we journeyed on. I was just pleased to be free of the castle: the hurtling fire, the deadly whine of bow and arbalest, the screech of crashing boulders and pots of burning tar. The smell of hawthorn from the hedgerows, the fragrance of fields and meadows baking under a fierce sun and the call of labourers tending the soil whilst watching the harvest sprout were all blessed relief. The towers of village churches rose like welcome beacons against the blue sky. The noisy bustle of the hamlets we passed through was soothing to the soul.

Demontaigu, God bless him, remained suspicious. Late in the afternoon of the second day, as we approached the priory where we were to stay the night, he very skillfully left the column of march, claiming there was something wrong with his horse. Pembroke trusted him and raised no protest. An hour later Demontaigu rejoined us just before we entered the priory gates. He looked concerned: he had travelled back and met a group of pilgrims, dusty-faced, with worn clothes and battered boots; and yet, for men dedicated to praying before the shrine of St Osyth, they were extremely well armed. When Dunheved heard this, he just shrugged.

'What can we do?' he murmured. 'What can we do?'

I always believe God needs a helping hand. He depends on our wit and intelligence, and I was resolutely determined on resolving the mysteries surrounding us. Once in the priory I was given a small chamber close to the cloister, neat and tidy, with a window looking out on to the garden. A peaceful place. I relished it. I wanted to be alone, even from Demontaigu, just to collect my thoughts and reflect carefully on what I'd seen and heard. I took out my lists and scribblings from their panniers, but I could make little sense of them. Eventually I decided to concentrate on the two last deaths: that of Middleton in the church and Rosselin in his chamber. I drew a careful diagram of that beautiful lady chapel. Who had entered? What had happened? I did the same for Rosselin's chamber. I recalled my good uncle's advice about studying the symptoms of a disease.

'What begins with an ache can end as a pain,' he would advise. 'You must not hasten, but watch the final symptoms lest you make a mistake.'

Deep in my heart, now that all the Aquilae were dead, I believed there would be no more murders. I could make no sense of Lanercost, Leygrave or Kennington, but Middleton and Rosselin's deaths were different. They had both been killed in a locked chamber. The doors had been bolted. No one could have come through a window or some secret passageway. Those were final symptoms. But that's impossible, I reflected. Only an angel of light, or one from the valleys of hell, could pass through oaken wood or stone-fast walls. So, I reflected, the assassin must have left through the door, but how? I also recalled another piece of advice: to go back to the very beginning, to search for the prime cause. I scribbled the word 'Templar' on a piece of vellum and stared hard at it until I realised my mistake. Was the origin of these mysteries the massacre at Devil's Hollow? Yet those Templars had just come from Scotland, and so had Geoffrey Lanercost. Were the two connected? I brooded on this. My eyes grew heavy. I fell asleep at the table and woke in the early hours as the bell chimed for Matins.

During the journey the following day, I grew more relaxed. I sat easy on the gently palfrey provided and returned to those two mysterious murders in the lady chapel and that haunting chamber of Scarborough keep.

'Forgive me, God,' I whispered as I realised my error, yet what could I do? The siege and the fall of Gaveston had run a deep furrow through my soul, dulling my perceptions. Now, fresh and away from the horrors of the siege, I could concentrate more logically. I closed my eyes against the summer sun as if I was dozing. I recreated that small chapel: people milling about, the door of the sacristy with its sturdy key, the one to the church door lying on the floor. I recalled the details of Rosselin's chamber: his cloak lying on the floor, the trail of blood virtually from that to the windowsill. Suspicions spark their own fire. I returned to my first real mistake. Lanercost! He had come from Scotland, and his mysterious secret journey had preceded the massacre in which his brother had died. Then there was Demontaigu's question: why hadn't the assassin struck directly at Gaveston? Why had the murders continued when, to all intents and purposes, Gaveston was finished? Were those last two killings necessary? After all, Rosselin was nothing but a man of straw. What profit could be gained from his death unless there were other reasons: revenge, punishment, but for what?

The suspicions I had provoked began to hint at other possibilities. I reached a conclusion. The way ahead was like the corpse road to some sinister church: dark and full of menace, yet eventually it would lead me to my destination. Realisation of my mistakes provoked further anxiety and blighted my merry mood. I began to study my companions differently. I also sensed that the pleasant, summer-filled journey south was turning sour. Dunheved had fallen very quiet. Demontaigu was openly suspicious. The Beaumonts and their hangers-on, who'd kept to themselves during the entire cavalcade, began to object to the journey as well as to the increasing number of landless men, wanderers haunting the copses and thickets with their pikes and clubs, who now hung on the edge or rear of our column like hunting dogs waiting for a weakness. Any progress by Great Lords attracts those looking for quick and easy pickings.

Nevertheless, the Beaumonts were correct in their concerns, and I wondered if these hangers-on, like the pilgrims still trailing us, had some secret, nefarious purpose.

Pembroke simply dismissed our concerns, but the Beaumonts, those basilisks in human flesh, demanded to know where we were really going and how long it would take. In truth, they realised that they had made a mistake. In their eyes Gaveston was a prisoner and the future looked uncertain, so it was time for them to be gone. Sharp words were exchanged on the highway. The Beaumonts claimed they had been too long absent from their estates as well as the court. Eventually their protests brought the entire cavalcade to a halt. Henry Beaumont confronted Pembroke. Had not the earl himself, on solemn oath, promised that all within Scarborough were safe in life and limb – at liberty to go where they wished? Pembroke could only agree with this. He had no choice. The Beaumonts collected their retainers tightly around them and Henry insisted that they be allowed to withdraw immediately. They observed the courtesies: exchanged the kiss of peace with Gaveston, thanked Pembroke for his hospitality, tipped their heads towards me and Demontaigu and turned away, declaring roundly that they would go back to the crossroads and make their way to Lincoln. During the exchange, Pembroke declared that he would rest the night at Deddington in Oxfordshire, that Lady Pembroke was residing only twelve miles distant at Bampton, and perhaps they would like to go there? The Beaumonts would have none of it. They withdrew their escort, made their final salutations and rode off in a cloud of dust.

We continued on our way, slightly subdued. We rested for a while at two taverns, and just before the sunset rode into Deddington, a sleepy hamlet, no more than a long line of cottages with their vegetable gardens, dovecotes, beehives and pig pens stretched out along the main thoroughfare. Just before the crossroads stood a spacious tavern boasting the title of the Pilgrims' Final Rest. We passed this, watched by the cottars and their families, and made our way up the slight hill to the parish church of St Oswald, an ancient edifice built of dark grey ragstone with a black-tiled roof and a lofty bell tower that brooded over the great cemetery surrounding the church. A little further on was the rectory, a pleasant two-storey building with a red-slated roof, its smartly painted front door approached by a flight of steps. Both the rectory and its boundary wall, which circled a cobbled yard at the front and gardens at the side and rear, were of honey-coloured Cotswold stone, which gleamed gold in the dying rays of the sun. Pembroke's outriders had galloped ahead to warn the rector that Pembroke, who held the advowson to the church, intended to reside there. The stern-faced priest, his robes marked with candle grease, was waiting to welcome his patron. Of course the rectory was too small for everyone. Pembroke dispatched some of his retinue back to the Pilgrims' Final Rest; others camped in the churchyard and a few in the small pavilions of the rectory garden.

I was given an evil-smelling garret just beneath the eaves. Once I'd satisfied my hunger on the meagre platters the rector had laid out in the buttery, I decided to wander the garden to study its various herbs and plants. In fact, I wanted to be alone, well away from the rest, so that I could concentrate on unravelling the mysteries. Moreover, it was a beautiful evening and the rectory garden was rich in trees, apple, pear and black mulberry, which lay at the back approached through gorgeous chequerboard beds of beautiful flowers: primrose, colombi, purple iris and the like. I was immersed in studying these when chaos returned, slipping in like a thief in the night.

Truly scripture says, 'We know not the day nor the hour.' A rider claiming he'd been sent by the chamberlain of Pembroke's manor at Bampton came thundering into the yard, yelling that he had the most urgent news for the earl. Pembroke hurried down. The messenger, breathless after his ride, clutched his saddle horn and gasped out how the lady Pembroke had fallen grievously ill and was asking for him. Pembroke, God forgive him, was besotted with his wife. He never stayed to question, but immediately ordered his household squires to saddle their horses, sending one of them into the village to collect those who'd had been quartered at the tavern. Gaveston came down, offering to accompany the earl. Pembroke refused, claiming that his senior household knight, Sir William Ferrers, would be in charge.

Ferrers, God bless him, did not have the wit to realise what was happening. Jovial and trusting, he assured us that there would be nothing to fear and that we would soon be about our own business. Demontaigu, however, thought otherwise. He firmly believed that mischief was planned. He insisted the rectory gates be locked, and all doors bolted and sealed, but it was to no avail. Pembroke left, taking the greater part of his retinue; those left in the rectory were a mere handful, with a few camped in nearby fields. Sure enough, just before dawn we were aroused from our beds by the clatter of arms. I hastily dressed, went downstairs and peered through a casement window. The yard in front of the house thronged with men all wearing Warwick's livery. Demontaigu clattered down, saying there were more in the street outside. Gaveston, dressed in his nightgown, a robe about his shoulders, joined us in the small rectory hall, demanding something to eat and drink. The rector brought this even as the noise outside grew.

'What shall we do?' Gaveston yelled.

Ferrers began to arm, only to realise that any defence would be fruitless. The clatter of mail, the neigh of horses and the shouts of men from the yard rose sharply, followed by a pounding on the door. Gaveston, myself, Demontaigu, Dunheved and Ferrers clustered around the hall table just as Warwick's voice rang out like a funeral peal for all to hear.

'My lord Gaveston.' The words were rich with sarcasm. 'I think you know who I am. I am your Black Dog of Arden. Get up, traitor, you are taken!'

This was followed by a further pounding. Warwick's men then seized a bench from the garden and smashed it against the door. The rector wailed pitifully at Ferrers, begging him to open up. The noose had tightened. We were trapped. Those pilgrims behind us, those landless men so curious about us, had been Warwick's spies. Yet, there was also something a little more refined, skilful about this trap. How did Warwick know that Pembroke had left? Was the earl's wife grievously ill at Bampton? Had Pembroke broken his word? I doubted it. We had all been duped, Pembroke especially, and there was nothing more we could do.

'Open the door,' I whispered.

Gaveston rose, fingers to his lips.

'Open the door, my lord, there is no point in resistance,' I insisted. 'Warwick may well use that to kill you out of hand.'

'In God's name,' the rector wailed.

Ferrers did not wait any longer. He left the hall, shouting at a few of Pembroke's retainers clustered in the vestibule, their swords drawn, to open the door. Chains were released, locks turned and Warwick's men poured through the rectory. Warwick himself strode into the hall. We were ignored, totally unharmed. Indeed, Warwick pointed at us and shouted that we were not to be touched on pain of forfeiture of life and limb. Poor Gaveston was different. He was immediately seized and manhandled. Warwick pushed his way through the throng and punched him in the face, his gauntleted fist smashing Gaveston's nose and bruising his lips. The fallen favourite was dragged out into the cobbled yard and his cloak stripped off for him to be exposed to Warwick's troops, bare-legged, barefooted, dressed only in his nightgown. He was in a state of shock. He tried to speak, but no sound came. One of Warwick's retainers imitated him, much to the merriment of others. I hurried to kneel at Warwick's feet, to beg for mercy for this fallen lord brought so low so quickly. Demontaigu also tried to help, shouting at Warwick to remember Pembroke's oath. The earl's henchmen just pushed him aside, whilst Warwick, softly patting me on the head, helped me to rise.

One glance from those soul-dead eyes confirmed Gaveston's fate. No mercy was to be asked, as none would be given. The earl just nodded and gently pushed me away. Pembroke's retainers, to their credit, tried to remonstrate, their swords drawn, but Warwick had brought a host of men-at-arms and archers, and resistance was futile.

Gaveston was forced to stand in the centre of the yard. Some of Warwick's retainers pelted him with every piece of filth they could lay their hands on, whilst the rest bayed for his blood. Eventually Gaveston just sank to his knees. Warwick thrust a heavy crown of nettles and briars on to his head, then he was placed on a ribbed nag, facing its tail, fastened securely and led around the yard to the taunts and jeers of Warwick's men. Gaveston just slumped, head down. Warwick gestured at us.

'You may go,' he shouted. 'This peasant of Gascony, this witch's brat no longer needs you. Do you, sir?'

Gaveston raised his head, trying to see through the tangle hanging over his battered face. He searched the line of faces until he found mine, his bloodied lips mouthing my name. I stepped forward.

'My lord of Warwick, this does you no credit,' I declared. 'Remember Pembroke's oath. Remember too what his grace the king will make of this.'

Dunheved, Demontaigu and Sir William Ferrers supported my protest. Warwick stood, hands on hips. Then he pulled a face, raised a hand and stilled the clamour.

'It is best if you were gone,' he said. 'You, Mistress Mathilde, and your companions are free to go where you wish.'

'I shall stay with my lord Gaveston,' I replied. 'My companions also.'

Warwick just shrugged and turned away, muttering something about a wench and a priest being no threat. He didn't care whether we went or stayed. So began Gaveston's descent into hell. Warwick intended to move swiftly. The fallen favourite was roped and tied. He'd entered Deddington as a Great Lord; he left like a common felon, dressed only in a soiled nightshirt, a bramble-thorn crown on his head, feet and hands bound. In front of him walked one of Warwick's men, carrying Gaveston's once gloriously emblazoned tabard and shield, all besmirched and rent. Our captor was determined that no rescue attempt should be made; we would journey directly and swiftly to his own estates and the mighty fastness of Warwick Castle. Word would soon reach both Pembroke and the king, and Warwick was determined not to be trapped.

On our journey we were kept well away from Gaveston. Our entire cavalcade was ring-bound by Warwick's soldiers, armed men on horse and foot who swept the highways, thoroughfares and adjoining fields free of all travellers, the curious or anyone who approached even within bowshot. Gaveston was constantly abused. One night he was forced to sleep in a ditch, the next lowered into a pit and held fast by ropes. The favourite now accepted the inevitable. He recovered his dignity, refusing to beg for any mercy or the slightest concession. Once we reached Warwick, the earl had him taken off the nag and forced him to walk through the streets to the approaches of the castle. The townspeople had been summoned by heralds to witness the humiliation. Warwick tied a rope around Gaveston's waist and processed into the town with the hatless, barefooted royal favourite, staggering behind him. The earl was preceded by heralds, trumpeters and standard-bearers, whilst Gaveston's arms were worn by a beggar, specially hired, a madcap who imitated Gaveston's staggering walk, provoking the crowd to more laughter and jeers. The prisoner was pelted with dirt, horse manure and all kinds of filth. Horns were blown, bagpipes wailed. Finally, as a warning of what was to come, just before we left the crowd to climb the steep hill to the gatehouse of Warwick Castle, Gaveston was forced to stand between two forked gibbets either side of the thoroughfare. Each bore the gruesome cadaver of a hanged felon. He was made to acknowledge both corpses to the screech of bagpipes and roars of abuse. The procession then continued. Once inside the castle, Warwick consigned Gaveston to its dungeons, with the stinging remark that he who had called him a dog was now chained up for good. He provided myself, Demontaigu and Dunheved with three dusty chambers high in the keep; his message was stark enough: 'Stay if you wish, but you are certainly not my honoured guests.'

The following morning, after we'd attended Dunheved's mass in the small castle chapel, we were confronted outside by a group of Warwick's henchmen. They bore messages from their master. No one would be allowed to see the prisoner, and it was best if we left. The message was tinged with menace, a quiet threat. I seized the opportunity to persuade Demontaigu and Dunheved that Warwick would not hurt me; it was best if they left and immediately journeyed to York to inform both king and queen. At first

Dunheved demurred. Demontaigu was also concerned about my safety. I replied that if I was left alone and vulnerable, Warwick would take special precautions that I was not harmed; he would not wish to incur the queen's wrath. Dunheved agreed with me. The Dominican had changed since we'd left Scarborough Castle. He was more withdrawn, as if reflecting on something, always busy with his beads, lips mouthing silent prayers. He promised that he would first journey to a nearby Dominican house, where he could ask his good brothers there to keep a watchful eye on what happened at Warwick and so provide whatever help they could. Once his decision was made, he rose from where we were seated at the ale-table in the castle buttery. He clasped my hand, exchanged the kiss of peace, then left without a further word. I followed him to the door and watched as he hastened across the inner bailey towards the great keep.

'Bertrand,' I spoke over my shoulder, 'I want you to go, but I will write a letter.'

'To whom?'

'To you, my heart.' I turned and smiled. 'Please go to York. Once you are safely in that city, open the letter and do what I ask.'

By noon of that day, both Dunheved and Demontaigu had left. Once they'd gone, Warwick's chamberlain visited me and insisted that I move to what he called 'more comfortable quarters' in the castle guest chamber above the great hall. After that, I was left to my own devices. Food and drink were brought up to my room, whilst I was invited to go down to the communal refectory when the castle bell tolled at dawn, noon and just before dusk.

Warwick ignored me. Now that he had seized Gaveston, he was determined to bring as many of the earls as possible into his plan. They hastened to agree. Red-haired, white-faced Lancaster, Edward's own cousin, and the earls of Arundel, Hereford and Gloucester arrived like hawks to the feast. They and their households, a horde of armed retainers, clattered through the gatehouse into the bailey, to be greeted by Warwick himself. I mixed with the servants, helping where I could with cuts and scrapes, or offering advice. Once people know you are skilled in physic, they insist on regaling you with the state of their health: what is wrong with them and what can be done. From these I learnt that Warwick was determined to try Gaveston by due process of law, give him what could be called a fair trial, then condemn him to death for treason. To continue the semblance of law, he insisted that two justices holding commissions of oyer and terminer in the adjoining counties, Sir William Inge and Sir Henry Spigurnel, were to be included in his net, and persuaded them to move their court to Warwick Castle.

We had arrived on the twelfth of June; on the seventeenth, Warwick moved to terminate matters. He and the other great earls, accompanied by the two justices, sat in judgement in the great hall. Gaveston, his face shaved, hair all cropped like a felon, was prepared for trial. He was allowed to bathe, and was dressed in a simple tunic of dark blue, loaded with chains and brought to the hall, where his judges sat on a dais behind the high table. They came swiftly to sentence. No one, apart from a few clerks and guards, was allowed to attend or witness. Gaveston was not permitted to speak or plead, remaining gagged throughout his trial.

257

Thomas, Earl of Lancaster, was both judge and prosecutor. He accused Gaveston of a litany of heinous crimes: refusing to stay in exile, stealing and spoiling royal treasure, weakening the Crown, being the source of bad counsel to the king, refusing to obey the ordinances of the earls. The list of charges covered every breach Gaveston had made both in statute law and in the ordinances of the earls. The result was a foregone conclusion. He was summarily condemned to death. Sharp-featured Lancaster summed up the proceedings. He offered Gaveston one concession: because of his dignity as an earl, and more importantly, being brother-in-law to de Clare, Earl of Gloucester, he would not suffer the full rigour of the punishment for treason. Instead of being hanged, drawn and quartered, he would merely be decapitated. Sentence was to be carried out almost immediately. There was nothing I or anyone could do. Pembroke sent the most powerful protests, appealing to the University of Oxford to intervene or mediate. From the rumours sweeping the castle, Edward at York was almost beside himself, dispatching pitiful pleas to the earls, to Philip of France and Pope Clement V at Avignon, all to no avail. The earls were obdurate: Gaveston would die.

I tried to visit the prisoner, only to be turned away. I thought I would never see him again. Then, in the early hours of the nineteenth of June, a furious hammering at my door roused me. Warwick and his leading henchmen waited in the darkened gallery outside, faces lit by cresset torches. Warwick was calm, cold and courteous as ever. He sketched a bow, then gestured with his fingers.

'Come down, come now.' Again the gesture. 'The Gascon

upstart has asked for one friend and you are it. He wishes to speak to you.'

I hastily dressed and followed Warwick and his coterie down the stairs, not to the dungeons as I expected but over to the castle death house, a narrow whitewashed room adjoining the chapel. The sky was beginning to lighten. Despite being midsummer, the cool breeze made me shiver, and I wondered what would happen. The death house was heavily guarded. The unlocked door was pushed open and I was ushered in. Gaveston crouched by the far wall, the heavy chains on his wrists and ankles clasped fast to iron rings. He'd been given a crucifix, a jug of wine, a pewter goblet and a platter of bread, cheese and some dried fruit. The room was clean but stark, rather chilly in aspect and reeking of embalming fluids. Warwick respectfully pushed me over. Gaveston looked up. In the light of the evil-smelling tallow candle on a nearby table, the former royal favourite looked unrecognisable. The glossy black hair was all shaven, the once smooth olive-skinned face sallow and emaciated, his cheeks rather sunken. The purple-red bruises were fading, but his lips were still swollen and his right eye was half closed. Warwick picked up a stool and placed it opposite Gaveston.

'Your friend,' the earl declared. 'Gascon upstart.' Only then did Warwick's voice soften. 'I urge you,' he spoke slowly, evenly, emphasising each word, 'look to your soul! This will be your last day on earth.'

I sat down on the stool even as Gaveston lowered his head, shoulders shaking.

'No mercy,' Warwick whispered. 'None at all! His grace

259

the king cannot save you. A priest will come to shrive you. I urge you, look to your soul. Mistress Mathilde, do you wish something to drink, some food?'

I shook my head.

'So be it,' Warwick murmured and strode away leaving two of his men, mailed and harnessed for war, standing guard at the locked and bolted door.

From outside I could hear Warwick's shouts, his insistence that no one was to be let in or out without his express permission. I sat on the stool and stared pitifully. Gaveston cried for a little longer, then, in a clatter of chains, pulled himself up to lean against the wall. That once beautiful face looked ghastly, but he tried to smile.

'I asked for you, Mathilde.' He stretched out his hands. 'Hold my hand. I do not want to die alone.'

I moved the stool closer, grasping his hand. It was cold, as if already dead. I stared around that narrow, close place with its stained tables and strange, musty smells. Somewhere in the darkness a rat squeaked, and in the corner above, a fly caught in a tangled spider's web struggled in a noisy whir of wings. Gaveston followed my gaze.

'I'm truly trapped, Mathilde. The case presses hard against me.'

'You are, my lord, God save you. You must expect no pardon. What can I do for you?'

Gaveston took a deep breath, still clutching my hand like a frightened child. He gave me messages for friends at court, his love for his wife Margaret de Clare and their infant daughter, his profound contrition for all or any offences against them. He fought to control his voice.

'Tell my brother the king,' he whispered, 'that in death, as in life, I am, was and always shall be his sole comrade.' He paused to weep quietly, then he wiped his eyes on the back of his hand and mentioned other people. His voice eventually faltered. He asked me for a set of Ave beads. I gave him my own, which he clumsily put round his neck.

'And the Beaumonts?' I asked. 'You did not mention them!'

Gaveston smiled, recalling the glory of the handsome courtier who had first dazzled me some four years earlier.

'Give those sweet cousins my warmest wishes. Tell them I did not hurt their interests in Scotland, their precious estates.'

I grasped the opportunity. 'What mischief?' I asked, squeezing his hands. 'What mischief was planned in Scotland?'

Gaveston just shook his head.

'And my mistress, her grace the queen, you have not mentioned her.'

'More subtle than a serpent.' Gaveston echoed Rosselin's words. When I pressed him to explain, he would say no more.

'And the Aquilae, your squires, all dead. My lord, did you have a hand in that?'

'Of course. I let them fly high, only to fall like Lucifer – all of them, never to rise again.'

'But did you have a hand in their deaths?'

'Yes and no.' Again Gaveston refused to be drawn, saying that these were matters for the mercy seat and the shriving of a priest. He grew agitated and leaned forward in a rattle of chains. 'Mathilde, you'll stay with me? I mean to the end. I do not want to be alone. Please?'

I was about to refuse, to barter for what he might still be able to tell me.

'Please?' His grip grew tighter. 'Make sure my corpse is not treated like that of a crushed dog.'

I promised. Gaveston was still not reconciled to death. Now and again he would return to the king, wondering if royal forces were approaching Warwick Castle. I doused such false hopes; to encourage them would have been cruelty itself. Gaveston heard me out, eyes closed, then returned to his reminiscing, recalling past glories, until a harsh rattling at the door made him fall silent. A Dominican from the nearby priory was ushered in. Warwick's henchmen introduced him as Brother Alexander.

'I have come to shrive you, my lord.' Alexander was a stout, cheery-faced friar who refused to be cowed by either circumstance or surroundings.

I prised my hand loose from Gaveston, rose from the stool and offered it to the Dominican. He gently asked me to withdraw, as well as the others. He must have caught my suspicion, because he fished into his wallet and produced a warrant from the prior of his house, countersigned by the Earl of Warwick, giving him licence to shrive the prisoner. I studied this, handed it back and nodded in agreement. Gaveston just crouched, fingers to his lips, a look of stark recognition in his eyes. He was going to die, and no one would save him! I could not bear that stricken look. I gestured to Brother Alexander and walked to the door; the guards ushered me out, then locked and bolted it. I meant to return to my own chamber, but the captain of Warwick's guard made me stay.

'It's best, mistress. My lord says you must stay here until this business is finished.'

An hour must have passed before Brother Alexander knocked for the door to be opened. Outside he grasped me by the elbow and led me away towards the main gate to the bailey.

'Stay with him, mistress.' He peered at me through the gloom. 'Lord Gaveston has done such evil, plotted such malice.' He paused. 'I cannot tell you what is covered by the seal of the sacrament, but he said something strange. How you had saved him from the deepest sin.'

I could only stare back, as mystified as he was. I returned to Gaveston. He realised death was imminent and had fallen to his prayers, asking me to join him as he recited his Aves. A short while later they came for him: Welsh archers from Lancaster's retinue; tough, resolute men, faces bearded, their heads cowled, all stinking of leather and sweat. They strode into the death house, dragged Gaveston to his feet and unceremoniously pushed him out into the bailey, where the earls, led by Lancaster, were already horsed, hooded and cloaked against the early-morning cold. The hooves of their great destriers sparked the cobbles as if these beasts were aware of the bloody, grim business being planned. Lancaster and the rest looked like spectres from the halls of the dead, high in the saddle, black shadows against the brightening sky. Lancaster pushed his horse forward, his pinched, pale features peering from the deep cowl.

'Gascon,' his voice was filled with hate, 'come now, come now, your fate is decided.'

Gaveston ignored him. He stared up at the reddish glow lightening the sky. He fumbled with his chains and turned towards me.

'A witch once prophesied,' he hissed, 'that I would die at the waking hour.'

'Come,' Lancaster repeated.

The horsemen drew away. The guard of Welsh archers closed in around us and we left through the gatehouse, down the steep path, the trees and bushes on either side silent witness to what was happening. No retainers massed, preparing to throw filth; no jeering crowd. The earls had decided that if this was to be done it had to be done swiftly. We did not leave through the town but along a rutted alleyway snaking like a rabbit run under the overhanging houses. Signs creaked in the breeze. The rattle of horses' hooves carried like some sombre drumbeat. If anyone heard, no one dared show it. Windows remained blackened, shutters fast shut. No door opened. No tired voice asked what evil was being plotted at such an early hour. The occasional darting shadow made me jump as a cat fled for shelter. The mournful howls of a dog echoed through the harsh calls of crows disturbed from their plundering on the midden heaps. No beggar whined for alms. No one dared approach these great ones hurrying another to summary execution.

The smell of saltpetre and ordure grew less offensive as we reached the end of the alleyway and emerged on to a winding country lane. I was sweaty and breathless. Gaveston stumbled, only to be cruelly pulled up and hurried on.

Now free of the houses, I glanced around. In the strengthening light, I glimpsed a steep wooded hill. One of the
archers breathed the name 'Blacklow', and I gathered that
this was where Gaveston's soul would be dispatched to God.
We left the track-way, going through a half-open gate. The
horsemen reined in. Lancaster lifted a hand and pointed to
the line of trees.

'Take him – now!'

Gaveston was given no time to object. He was bundled
forward by three of the archers. I was breathless, tired and
eager for rest. Gaveston turned, face pallid as a ghost through
the murk.

'Mathilde,' he hissed, 'please!'

I followed the archers as they pushed their prisoner
forward in a clatter of chains. He turned once more to ensure
I followed. We entered the line of trees, a sombre, desolate
place. No bird sang. Nothing rustled in the undergrowth,
as if all God's creatures sensed what was being planned. I
glanced back. The earls still sat on their horses like a host
of demons, watching, silent, hungry for this man's death,
eager to see his hot blood splash.

'Far enough,' one of the archers breathlessly announced.
He dragged Gaveston to the ground. The prisoner crouched,
praying loudly, frantically trying to recall lines from the
Office for the Dead.

'Mistress?' The archer approached me. 'You need not stay
any longer.'

'I know Ap Ythel,' I whispered, 'captain of the king's
archers.'

'Ap Ythel.' The man seemed to forget why he was here.

'Now there's a great archer, a true soul.' He lapsed into Welsh.

I replied haltingly with the few words and phrases Ap Ythel had taught me.

'Mistress?' The archer whispered.

I opened my purse, took out three silver pieces and gave them to him.

'Let it be swift,' I said. 'Let him not see it.'

The archer pocketed the silver pieces and sauntered back to Gaveston. I glanced around. I can still recall it. That haunted wood. The sky brightening through the black outline of the trees. Ghostly figures. The archers in their hoods. The creak of leather. The glint of weapons. The pervasive stench of drenched rotting undergrowth, and those horsemen silent, sombre, waiting even as Gaveston gasped out his final Vespers.

'My lord,' the archer's voice sounded like the clap of doom, 'you must stand up.'

'So I must.' Gaveston struggled to his feet and tapped himself under the chin. 'Are you, sir, going to remove my head? I'm far too beautiful for that.'

'True, my lord.' The archer stretched out his hand. 'Let me clasp yours before you go.'

Gaveston did so. The archer moved swiftly, a blur of movement. He had secretly drawn his long stabbing dagger. Now he pulled Gaveston towards him as if to embrace him, and plunged the blade deep into his heart. Even I, who had begged for such a swift ending, was surprised. Gaveston stood, then crouched, falling back. The archer hurriedly caught him, withdrawing his dagger even as he lowered

Gaveston tenderly to the ground. I went and knelt beside the stricken man. Already his eyes were clouding in death; blood was bubbling through his nose and mouth. He turned slightly, coughing, and tried to mouth the word 'Edward'. His fingers fluttered; I grasped them. Gaveston stared hard at me, then he shuddered and fell back.

'He is dead!' the archer announced. 'Mistress, I beg you, walk away.' One of the other archers had produced a two-headed axe, which he'd kept in a sack. I stumbled away and stared at those horsemen, vengeful wraiths. I heard the archers whisper, followed by the rattle of chains. Gaveston's body was straightened out, his neck positioned on a fallen tree trunk.

'Now,' the archer murmured hoarsely.

I heard the rasp of leather, then a chilling thud. I took a deep breath and turned. Gaveston's body, slightly jerking, lay sprawled on the ground. A little distance away was the head, the eyes half closed, the lips of the blood-encrusted mouth slightly parted. The archer picked the head up between his two hands, careful of the blood spilling out. He carried it before him, stepped past me, out of the line of trees, and held it up so that the horsemen could see. One of these, probably Lancaster, raised his hand. The archer turned, took the severed head back and gently placed it beside the trunk of the body, now swimming in blood.

'Come, mistress.' The archer seized my arm. 'Come now, leave him here.'

'I cannot,' I whispered. I felt cold and frightened. I found it difficult to breathe; my stomach clenched. The archers talked to each other in Welsh. One produced a small wineskin, unstoppered it and forced it between my lips, making me take a gulp, then he stood back.

'Mistress,' he whispered, 'you cannot stay here, not in the shadows.'

'I have to,' I replied. 'I promised.'

The archers talked amongst themselves, shrugged and bade me farewell. They left the trees, walking leisurely back to the waiting horsemen. The earls and their retinue departed. I just crouched, watching them go, wiping the sweat from both brow and cheeks. I found it difficult to move; even more so to turn and look at the horror awaiting me. The darkness faded. The sun began to rise. I stretched out on the grass, turning on my side as if I was in bed like a child, trying to control my breathing. The woods remained silent. Eventually I felt composed enough. I rose and walked back to Gaveston's battered corpse. The blood was beginning to dry. The severed head had tipped slightly, the skin now turning a dullish grey. I moved it gently, trying not to look at those half-closed eyes. The skin was clammy cold. I had to repeat to myself that the essence of Gaveston, his soul, his spirit, had long gone to God. These were simply his mortal remains, to be treated with as much dignity as I could muster. I felt determined; I refused to be cowed by Lancaster's brutality.

I walked out of the wood and down to the road, where I begged for help. Eventually four shoemakers bringing their goods into Warwick agreed for a silver piece to help me. They stopped their cart, took off a ladder and followed me back into the wood. God bless them! They were sturdy men. They asked few questions, but simply put the corpse on the ladder, the head wrapped in a sack beside it, and loaded the remains on to their cart. I persuaded them to make the short journey to Warwick Castle, where I demanded entrance. Warwick himself came down, dressed in half-armour, a goblet of wine in his hand. He walked out, refusing to even glance at the grisly burden resting in the cart.

'Mistress Mathilde. You cannot stay here. You cannot bring him here. This business is finished.' He turned and walked back into the gatehouse even as I screamed abuse at him, begging him for the love of God and His Beloved Mother to show some pity for the dead.

'Mistress,' one of the shoemakers whispered, 'we have done what we can; it is best if we take him back from where he came.'

They turned the cart round despite my protest. We were about to leave, go back through that alleyway Gaveston had been marched along to execution, when I heard my name called. I turned. Brother Alexander, dressed in his black and white robes, stood at the corner of a street; behind him was a cart driven by lay brothers from his house. The Dominican walked over, his face all smiles.

'Mistress Mathilde, Mistress Mathilde.'

He helped me down from the shoemakers' cart, and for a while just stood holding my hands, lips moving as he quietly recited the requiem.

'My lord Gaveston's corpse.' He gestured at the cart. 'You have it there. Mistress, you've kept your promise. You fulfilled your vow. We will now take it.'

I could not object. What could I do? Brother Alexander called across to his colleagues. Gaveston's remains were transferred from the shoemakers to the Dominicans. The friar turned to me, lifted his hand, sketched a blessing in the air, then left. I watched the cart rattle away.

Brother Alexander was true to his word. The Dominicans, God bless them, took Gaveston's mortal remains to their house at Oxford. Here they were washed, embalmed and rubbed with balsam, the head stitched back with silver twine, and placed in an open casket. If I remember correctly, it was two years before the king finally agreed to the burial of the embalmed corpse of the man he loved 'beyond all others'.

Chapter 10

By God's soul, he acted like a fool!

I returned to Warwick Castle but was not allowed entry. A kindly chamberlain agreed to go to my chamber above the hall and brought down all my belongings. He even gave me a linen parcel of food and a small wineskin. I thanked him and took lodgings in a spacious tavern in the town. I used the gold and silver pieces stitched into a secret pocket on my belt to hire a well-furnished chamber. I also went out into the marketplace and bought some new clothes, for I felt dirty, soiled, polluted by what I'd seen. I returned to my chamber, stripped, washed, anointed my body and dressed.

271

Afterwards I took my old clothing in a bundle down to a beggar at the corner of an alleyway and thrust it into her hands. I stayed at the tavern three days, resting and eating. I gave the tavern master a coin to advise me who was staying there and where they were going. On the fourth day I met a group of wool merchants travelling to York; they kindly agreed that I could join their company.

Three days later I reached York and made my way to the Franciscan house. Father Prior made me welcome but assured me that the court, both king and queen, had now moved to the more grand furnishings of St Mary's Abbey, though I was most welcome to stay in their guest house. Master Bertrand Demontaigu had also visited but was now absent on business elsewhere. The prior added that he was surprised at Demontaigu's requests but had conceded to them in the hope that the mysterious deaths that had occurred in his friary church could be resolved. God bless those friars: they welcomed me as if I was their sister. I was given the most comfortable chamber and savoury food. The following morning Demontaigu returned.

We met in the same rose garden where Lanercost and all the other Aquilae had sprawled laughing and drinking when we brought the news about the massacre out on the moors. Now it seemed a lifetime away. The garden was silent, heavy with summer fragrance, a change from the stark bleakness of Scarborough, that horrid line of trees on Blacklow Hill, Gaveston's corpse saturated in its own blood, the severed head of a once splendid earl lying in the undergrowth like a piece of pork on a flesher's stall. I confided in Bertrand all the fears haunting my soul, the images and dreams, the phantasms and nightmares that plagued my mind. Bertrand sat on the turf seat beside me, clutching my hand, watching my face, very much like the confessor he was. Once I'd finished, he informed me of how the king was distraught at his favourite's death yet strangely unwilling to move against the assassins of his beloved brother Gaveston. Rumours, Demontaigu confided, were flying as thick and fast as feathers in a hen coop.

'God knows, Mathilde,' he declared, 'perhaps the king is secretly relieved that Gaveston is gone.'

Demontaigu then referred to other matters I'd asked him to investigate on his return to York. What he told me simply confirmed my own suspicions. He had visited the friary library and, much to the prior's surprise, had taken the 'man of straw', as he put it, dressed in clothes, up to that lonely haunted belfry. He laughingly described what had then ensued, and as if in gentle mockery of his words, the great bells began to toll the call to Vespers. Demontaigu waited until they'd stopped.

'You know the truth, Mathilde. Will you not tell me?'

'Soon.' I gently touched him on the cheek. 'Soon I will, when these things done in the dark have been brought to light. Eventually they will, but in the meantime, Bertrand, for your sake and that of my mistress, it is best if silence is observed. Gaveston's death has achieved little except to define where everyone stands. The pieces have moved on the chess board and they'll move again. A period of calm will ensue,' I murmured, 'until the furies gather once more. In the meantime, I follow my mistress' advice: *video atque taceo* – I watch and stay silent.'

Bertrand teased me for a while. He made me repeat the macabre details about Blacklow Hill. Perhaps he wanted to exorcise my soul as well as learn more about Gaveston and about the massacre of his Templar brethren out at Devil's Hollow.

'But that is not the root of this evil, is it, Mathilde?' he asked.

'No,' I replied. 'The malicious, murderous mischief plotted in Scotland is the cause of a great deal of what has happened since. The Beaumonts, God save them, were a mere irritation. They rightly suspected villainy was being planned but they thought it concerned their estates, that Edward was in some secret pact with Bruce to surrender all claims in Scotland. They were wrong. Gaveston was plotting greater villainy.'

'And now you know the truth?'

'Oh yes.' I let go of his hands. 'I wanted you back here and you have done what I asked.' I leaned forward and kissed him on the cheek. 'Trust me. I was no fair damsel in peril by land and sea. God knows, Warwick and the rest were courteous enough. They were just hawks who selected their quarry, Gaveston. They have made their kill. They are satisfied, at least for the moment. Our king is fickle. He will wait and watch, grieve and shout. He will hide his secret feelings because he will never let Gaveston's death rest. Eventually he will remember me and summon me to account, but I shall simply tell him what he wants to hear. Now, Bertrand, is the time of danger. I must, in some secret form, allow the truth to emerge, and you must leave. I have sent urgent messages to her grace to meet me – God knows when she will reply.'

In the end, Isabella, as I suspected, replied swiftly. Bertrand and I had kissed and parted. The good brothers were gathering in their incense-filled choir stalls when Isabella, with little ceremony or advance warning, accompanied only by her few trusted squires, slipped into the friary. She looked radiant, dressed in dark blue with a silver cord around her bulging stomach, a jewelled cross on a silver chain about her neck, her face almost hidden by a thick gauze veil. We met, kissed and exchanged the courtesies in the prior's parlour. Beside the queen stood Dunheved, his olive face a serene mask of contentment. He knew what had happened to Gaveston's corpse and openly praised my diligence as a great act of mercy. I just stared coldly back. Isabella caught my glance but chattered on merrily as if I had just been on a courtesy visit or shopping for her in the nearby market. Only when we three were alone in that rose garden, with the light beginning to fade, the perfume from the flowers thickening the air, did she drop all pretence. Her *Fideles*, as she called her household squires, those same young men who had resolutely defended her at Tynemouth, sealed all entrances to the garden. Isabella sat on a turf seat so her back could rest against the flower-covered trellis; she lovingly rubbed her stomach, caressing the child within.

'Gaveston is dead,' she declared. 'God give him true rest, but God be thanked.' There, in that short phrase, Isabella confessed the truth. She glanced out of the corner of her eye at me, then gently patted Dunheved, who sat silently beside her.

'Mathilde, *ma cherie*, my friend, you said in your note that you wished to have urgent words with me and Brother Stephen.'

'My daughter,' the Dominican smiled, 'you have much to say?'

I stared hard at that sanctimonious killer.

'Much to say,' I whispered, 'much to judge and much to condemn! Your grace,' I turned to the queen, who was still leaning back, her thick veil pulled away from her face so she could see me clearly. Never had she looked so glorious. *Regina Vivat! Regina Vincit! Regina Imperat!* – The Queen Lives! The Queen Conquers! The Queen Rules!' Isabella had come into her own.

'Mathilde,' she whispered, 'I wait.'

'When you came to England, your grace,' I began, 'you were a child, thirteen summers old but with a heart skilled in politic and subterfuge.'

Isabella laughed girlishly, covering her mouth with her bejewelled fingers, the silver froth of her cuff snow white against her golden skin.

'Your husband entertained a deep passion for his favourite. God only knows the truth about their relationship, but you, your grace, did not object. You bent before the storm lest you break, and so you waited. One crisis followed another. Your husband the king was baited and harassed, and so were you, yet you remained faithful, loyal and serene. Earlier this year, four years on from your marriage, you became pregnant, the bearer of an heir. The possibility that you could produce the only living grandson of both Edward I and Philip of France became a reality. Your husband was delighted. Through you, he had silenced all the taunts and jibes of those who mocked his manhood. He was a prince who had begotten an heir on his loving wife. The dynasty would continue. Gaveston, however, had always viewed you as a threat. Even more so now. What did the king call Gaveston? Brother, but also son. You were about to change that.'

Isabella wafted her face with her hand. 'Continue,' she demanded softly.

'By the spring of this year, Gaveston had emerged as a real threat to the Crown. Because of him, from the very first day of his succession, Edward had known no peace. Did the king, your husband, despite all his love for Gaveston, come to regard his favourite as increasingly irksome, especially when his love for you deepened and you became pregnant? Did Gaveston turn on the king, reminding him of those secret, malicious rumours about Edward being a changeling, the son of a peasant?'

'Nonsense,' Dunheved intervened. 'Such stories do no harm to the king. Gaveston would not dare—'

'Nonsense, Brother,' Isabella mockingly echoed. 'I must correct you. At this moment in time, such stories would do great damage to his grace. Gaveston would have done anything to save himself, to protect his position with the king. Four people knew the true Gaveston: the king, and we three. Mathilde, do continue.'

'Gaveston grew desperate. He had isolated the king. No help came from the earls, France or the papacy. Only the Beaumonts, for their own selfish reasons, planted their standards close to Gaveston's camp, but they could not be trusted. In the end, Gaveston was captured because he was defenceless. He was imprisoned and executed because he lacked any guard. More importantly, during the last months of his life he was reduced to treating with the likes of Alexander of Lisbon and his Noctales. Gaveston was desperate for troops. Lisbon could be useful, whilst it would also be a sop to both your father and the pope. In return the Portuguese would help – as long as there was no real threat. At Tynemouth that changed. The castle came under threat from both within and without. Lisbon left to meet his fate, but by then, the real damage had been done. Gaveston had given Lisbon secret information about a troop of Templars coming out of Scotland to York: specifically the day they would reach Devil's Hollow. Lisbon set his trap. He massacred those Templars then plotted to murder those who went out to meet them.'

'And Gaveston learnt that through Lanercost's brother, a Templar serjeant?' Isabella asked.

'Of course. Lanercost the Aquilae gave his master such information, never dreaming it would be used to kill his brother. We, of course, told Lanercost what had truly happened. Undoubtedly he confronted Gaveston, who was horrified, probably for the very selfish reason that he had alienated one of his closest followers. Matters might have stopped there. Lanercost was furious; he became inebriated. He confided in his close comrade Leygrave how he felt betrayed.' I pointed at Dunheved, who sat so placidly, hands tucked up the sleeves of his gown. 'He also confided in you, Brother Stephen. Mere chance, yet on the other hand, what better person? A Dominican friar, the king's own confessor, a man who could be trusted. The shrewd, ever-listening priest! Where did you meet him, Brother? Here in a lonely garden, a corner of the cloisters, with only the gargoyles, babewyns and stone-faced angels and saints as your silent witnesses?'

Dunheved removed his hands from his sleeves and threaded the tasselled end of the cord around his waist. For a heartbeat I wondered whether he'd ever used that to strangle a victim.

'You are an accomplished man, Brother Stephen. Demontaigu made enquiries about you here in the Dominican house in York. You are the brother of Lord Thomas Dunheved from the West Country, a former squire, a man once harnessed for war.' I paused. 'A scholar deeply interested in the peal of bells. You wrote *De Sonitu Tonitorum – Concerning the Peal of Bells*. Understandably you became a visitor to the belfry here. You befriended poor Brother Eusebius, whom you later murdered.'

Isabella sat up straight. She'd taken a set of coral Ave beads from the silken purse on her waist cord and was fingering the cross. Dunheved, God save him, stared at me as if relishing every word I uttered.

'Lanercost came to you,' I pointed to the Dominican, 'to confess, to confide, I don't know which. He gave vent to his anger and sadness. Gaveston had betrayed both him and his brother, so in revenge, Lanercost betrayed Gaveston. He would wax hot and lyrical about what he and the others had done for the favourite in Scotland.'

'Which was?' Isabella intervened sharply.

'A blasphemously murderous plot!'

'To which my husband was not party.'

'I don't think so, your grace. Lanercost was sent into Scotland ostensibly to seek help against the earls. Secretly, Gaveston and his Aquilae proposed thier own plot: the capture of Edward's queen, to be held to ransom or even,' I paused, 'killed.'

'Bruce, a prince?' Isabella murmured. 'Party to that?'

'Mistress, I have heard the same before, yet how many of Bruce's ladies, as well as those of his generals, Stuart, Murray and Randolph, have not been seized, violated or killed? Bruce himself may have baulked at it, but his commanders would not have. War by fire and sword rages in Scotland. What would they care? It could have happened, as it nearly did at Tynemouth: a stray arrow, an unknown swordsman. After all, one of your grace's ladies died in that bloody affray.'

My mistress simply tightened her lips and glanced away.

'Ostensibly,' I continued, 'Gaveston negotiated on behalf of the king. Secretly he and his coven were plotting the removal, perhaps even death, of his queen, Edward's wife.'

'Why?' Dunheved's voice was sharp and taunting.

'You know that, Brother, as I do. Gaveston was now truly jealous of her grace. He saw her and her child as supplanting him in Edward's affections. He fiercely resented the expected heir. Gaveston was a spoilt, pampered fop. He wanted to return to the old days when he and Edward were together, isolated from everyone.'

'And how was this to be done?' Isabella demanded.

'Why, your grace,' I replied, 'easy enough with the court vulnerable in the north and Bruce's forces ready to cross the border in lightning raids as they did at Tynemouth.

But I hurry on. Did Dunheved tell you, your grace, what he'd learnt from Lanercost?'

Isabella stared glassily back: no smile, no coquetry, just a hard, cold look. Beside the queen, Dunheved shifted rather nervously.

'You, Brother Stephen, were furious. Determined that these men who threatened her grace would pay for their treason. You relished that: judge and hangman. Your cause was certainly right. What Gaveston plotted was horrid murder and heinous treason.'

'To which my husband was not party,' Isabella repeated.

'My lady, no, I do not think so, and neither do you. Gaveston just wanted to rid himself of you and your child. You, Brother, decided not to strike directly at the favourite but to weaken him, as well as to punish him and his coven for their crimes. Lanercost was first. He had to be removed swiftly lest he had a change of heart and confessed to his master about what he'd said and to whom. Above all, punishment had to be carried out. Brother Stephen, you have a mordant sense of humour. You decided to bring Gaveston and his so-called eagles crashing to the ground. Just like Simon Magus, the magician who could fly, cast out of the sky by St Peter. You referred to that legend. What better place for it than the belfry of this friary, supervised by the witless Brother Eusebius, whom you had befriended? You could go up and inspect the great bells, the chimes of which you listened to. Do you remember, I was sitting here? You came over to discuss matters and made some passing remark about the chimes not being in accord, but that does not concern us now. You had decided the belfry was the ideal place for punishment: isolated, a sanctuary haunted only by someone you regarded as fey and witless.'

'And Lanercost would go up there?' Dunheved jibed.

'Of course! Why shouldn't he go with his father confessor, the friendly Dominican priest who only wanted to help? He trusted you so much he took his war-belt off to climb those steps.'

'I was celebrating mass when he fell.'

'I know that, Brother, I was also there, but you killed Lanercost much earlier that morning, just after Brother Eusebius had scuttled off to break his fast in the refectory or buttery. You and Lanercost went up to the bell tower, an ideal place where no one could see you or eavesdrop on a conversation. You struck him a killing blow to the back of his head that shattered his skull. By the time his corpse fell, bouncing off the brickwork and the roof of the nave to smash against the ground, it simply became one injury amongst many.'

'And how was that done,' Isabella asked, 'if Brother Stephen was celebrating mass?'

'The ledge of the belfry window overlooking the friary yard is broad, slightly sloping. It had been raining, so it would also be slippery. Lanercost's corpse was laid there, an easy enough task that cannot have been observed from below. Dunheved then left. Later the bells were tolled at the end of mass. Brother Eusebius told me to be careful when I climbed into the belfry. He explained how the belfry shuddered with the noise and the echo. That alone would make the corpse slide. More importantly, the thick rim of one of those great bells skims the ledge.' I used my hand to demonstrate. 'Sooner or later that bell, together with the sound and the shaking, would shift Lanercost's corpse along that slippery, sloping edge to fall in a hideous drop, hitting the roof of the nave before crashing on to the cobbled yard. I agree, you were with us when that happened. As you were when the same fate befell Leygrave.' I glanced quickly at the queen; she sat staring at the ground. Dunheved turned slightly away, face screwed up in concentration as he listened to me.

'Surely,' the Dominican turned back, joining his hands, 'Leygrave would be suspicious, especially after the death of his close comrade Lanercost?'

'Why should he be, Brother? Lanercost trusted you; so did Leygrave. Perhaps Leygrave knew all about the ghostly comfort you'd given his comrade. I cannot say how you sprang the trap. Did you tell Leygrave you wanted to see him privately – the same reason you gave Lanercost – in a place where the crowded court could not learn what was going on? Why should Leygrave suspect the holy-faced Dominican, so earnest in his help, so comforting in his words? An innocent invitation, a visit to the place where his comrade died, perhaps to search for something suspicious?' I studied that hard-hearted priest, who betrayed no shame or guilt, not even a blink or a wince. 'You lured Leygrave to that belfry. You killed him and arranged the corpse as you did Lanercost's. You made one mistake. To create the impression that Leygrave might have committed suicide, once you had killed him with a blow to the back of his head, you pulled off his boots and made a muddy imprint on that ledge. You then put the boots back on the corpse and left it as you did Lanercost's. At the next peal of bells the corpse would slip over silently like a bundle of cloth. That's how the fire boy described it: no scream, no yell, just dropping like a bird stunned on the wing.' I turned and gestured at that fateful tower rearing up against the evening sky. 'My good friend Demontaigu, much to the surprise of Father Prior and the brothers, took up a man of straw clothed and cloaked. He left it on that ledge.' I smiled thinly. 'Eventually, during a bell-tolling, it fell, confirming my suspicions. Indeed, it's the only logical explanation. As I said, who'd fear an innocent unarmed Dominican? But of course, Brother, you weren't always that, were you?'

Dunheved grinned as if savouring some private joke.

'You told me how you performed military service as a squire. You are as much a warrior and a killer as any of those you murdered.'

'You said I made a mistake,' Dunheved asked, 'about Leygrave?'

'I never told you,' I declared, 'about the muddy imprint left by Leygrave's boots on that ledge, not in such minute detail. Yet when I discussed his death with you and Demontaigu, you mentioned it. How did you know?'

'I . . . I think you did . . .'

'Mathilde.' Isabella's voice held a sharp rebuke. 'Finish what you have begun.'

'And so to Duckett's Tower at Tynemouth,' I declared. 'A place of intrigue and terror. I always wondered, Brother, why the king's confessor should accompany us. Undoubtedly you persuaded the king that his queen needed you. His grace was so distracted, he would have agreed to anything.' I paused.

'I understand your concern, but murder was your principal motive. Undoubtedly at Tynemouth the Aquilae, unbeknown to any of us, had been in secret, treasonable communication with Bruce's raiding party. They were responsible for those signals sent from the night-shrouded walls of the castle, as they were for loosening the postern gate. They looked shamefaced enough on that war-cog, and so they should have been. They'd plotted to be safely aboard when the Scots launched their ambush. You had already moved against those malignants. You would have loved to have killed them all, but that was not possible. So you struck at Kennington, one cold, windswept morning long before dawn. Rosselin and Middleton had completed their watch; they'd be cold and tired, even fearful. They and their retainers would be fast asleep.' I shrugged. 'God knows if you drugged their drink and food.'

'I tell you . . .' Dunheved seemed angry, not so much at being accused but more that it was by me a woman. I recognised that arrogance in his soul. I'd glimpsed it before in men who regard women as the weaker in every respect. 'I tell you,' he repeated, 'I know nothing about your potions and powders.'

'Hush, hush.' Isabella lifted her hand.

'I will certainly answer that,' I replied. 'You were in the friary library. You told me you were studying Anselm's *Cur Deus Homo – Why God Became Man*. That was a lie; it was nothing of the sort. The archives of the library clearly described the manuscript you borrowed, a copy of Hildegard of Bingen's *Causae et Curae*.' I paused. 'You had also consulted that before we left for Tynemouth. Such a treatise is a rich source of knowledge you could use against your enemies, be it Kennington, Middleton or the wells of Scarborough Castle. You learnt what sleeping potions or powders to buy, which you undoubtedly did at some apothecary or herbalist here in York. Now, during those early hours of that morning, you slipped as stealthily as a hunting cat into Duckett's Tower. You quietly mounted those steps. As you passed each door, you slipped the hook into its clasp, sealing anyone within. Oh, they could eventually get out, but it would take time and alert you. You reached the top of that windswept tower—'

'And Kennington and his retainers welcomed me like the prodigal son?' Dunheved sneered.

'Undoubtedly! Why should they fear the kindly Dominican who could not sleep? Who'd brought up a wineskin to share with them during their lonely, cold, bleak watch? At Scarborough I glimpsed you do the same, edging along the parapet giving the defenders a drink from your wineskin. On Duckett's Tower you would be most welcome. You'd seal the door, slipping the hook into its clasp, then offer these trusting, tired men a gulp of rich claret, blood-warming and comforting. They'd drink, and within a short while, be fast asleep. How long would it take to hurl those bodies over the battlements? A strong man like you, Dunheved – not long? You callously lifted each wine-drugged body over and let it drop.' I paused. 'What, in no more time than it would take a scholar to count to ten.'

'I could have been discovered.'

'How, Brother? Each door was clasped, as was the one at the top of the tower. If anyone saw you come up, you would have changed your plan. If anyone disturbed you, you would have enough time to pose as the innocent who'd climbed to the top of Duckett's Tower to find that all were gone. If you were seen as you went down, you could so easily dissemble, an innocent Dominican who'd climbed Duckett's Tower to discover its guards had disappeared. Naturally,' I added, 'there was danger, a risk in that short space of time when you hurled those bodies to their death. Reflect, Brother Stephen! What real danger did you face apart from that brief killing time? Everything else could be so easily explained away.'

The sound of Isabella's squires politely requesting one of the brothers not to enter the garden made me pause.

'Kennington's death,' I resumed, 'broke the spirit of the Aquilae. They looked for protection from their lord, but Gaveston himself was under threat from the earls. Middleton was your next victim. A superstitious, scrupulous young man, hounded by guilt, he received little comfort or sustenance from either Rosselin or Gaveston. Subject to all forms of soul-disturbing fancies, he took to visiting the Chapel of Our Lady in Scarborough Castle very early in the morning. You noticed that and, once again, assumed the role of the sympathetic friar, the trusted priest, the ascetic confessor. One morning you were waiting for him. You moved the mercy chair round – which you never put back – you drew him into conversation even as you decided on his death, whatever regrets Middleton confessed. The rope was ready, whilst beneath your cloak you carried that small wineskin of tainted claret.'

'The door was locked from within.' Dunheved's interruption was more of a jibe than a question.

'Patience,' I retorted. 'You locked the door. You gave the agitated Middleton words of comfort and a few gulps from that wineskin to calm his humours. I doubt if Middleton had had a good night's sleep since Tynemouth. He was agitated. The wine and potion you'd distilled would soon soothe him, and a drugged man is easy to hang. The noose was slipped around his neck as his body slumped in the chair. You climbed the ladder, looped the other end of the rope round the beam and hauled him up slowly but surely. If Middleton revived, what hope did he have? If he did wear a war-belt you removed that, hid it under your cloak. Whatever, he had no dagger, nothing with which to cut himself down, whilst any struggle would only tighten the noose further. You mentioned the locked door, Brother?'

Dunheved just blinked and glanced away.

'I shall tell you how you did that. You took the key from the sacristy door. You placed it on the floor as if it was from the door to the church; that one, however, you kept. You waited until Middleton was dead, placed the usual mocking message on his corpse and left, locking the door and taking the chapel key with you.'

'I could have been discovered.'

'When?' I demanded. 'You could have hastened to the door and unlocked it. You could claim you came in only to discover what had happened. Terrified lest the assassin return, you locked the door whilst you tried to assist poor Middleton.'

'Those keys?' Isabella asked. 'They were changed?'

'Oh yes. Brother Stephen, you gave extreme unction to your first two victims but you left Middleton to Demontaigu.

Whilst he administered the last rites you became extremely busy inspecting the main door as well as that to the sacristy. I recall the scene distinctly. That's when you picked up the sacristy key, which looked so much like the one to the church, and changed them over. In all the chaos and mayhem, no one would notice you slip the sacristy key back because no one really cared.'

'I could have been seen leaving.'

'Again a risk – but you'd open that door a crack. Peer out. The path to the chapel was a mass of pebbles that would betray sound. The morning sea mist provided a cloak of secrecy. You could slip out and lock that door in the blink of an eye.'

'Someone might have noticed the sacristy key was missing from its lock.'

'For the love of God, who'd notice that when all eyes were on poor Middleton? Who'd even remember there was a sacristy key?' I shrugged. 'After all, you returned it swiftly enough!'

'And Rosselin?' Isabella demanded. I wondered how much of this she knew. Had she been party to all these deaths? I decided that would have to wait.

'Rosselin,' I continued, 'was by now a broken man. Gaveston had neglected him.'

'Why?' Isabella broke in.

'Because Gaveston, in the last resort, cared only for himself. The best he could do was to provide poor Rosselin with one of Ap Ythel's archers, but you, Brother Stephen, took care of that. Rosselin hid away, particularly from any high place. The night the tocsin was falsely sounded and the beacon fire lit? You were responsible for that, as you were for everything else that went wrong in that castle: the pollution of the wells and food stocks. An easy enough task. Poison in the rat runs, some oil and kindling in those bone-dry cellars.'

'And Rosselin?' Dunheved remained unabashed.

'Oh, the tocsin was sounded. The alarm raised. Everyone flocked to the battlements. You acted swiftly. You called Ap Ythel's guard away.'

'I am not Welsh.'

'Who said the voice was Welsh?'

'I heard . . .'

'Perhaps you did, Brother Stephen. I am French, but I can still mimic Ap Ythel's Welsh accent. I often do when I tease him. Her grace has witnessed that.' I pointed at Dunheved. 'You did the same that night. You are a good mimic, Brother. I heard you here in the rose garden imitating the troubadours and jongleurs. Indeed, you are a true mummer. You put a mask on and take it off depending on the circumstances. You called that guard away. He would not need much encouragement; after all, everyone was in high expectancy. Had the earls arrived? Had the king? Once he was gone, you hurried up the steps to Rosselin's chamber. In your wallet you have a key. It may have been from Middleton's chamber or elsewhere in the castle; they all look alike. You intended to pose the same mysterious riddle as you had in the lady chapel. You knocked on the door. Rosselin, sodden with drink, was befuddled. He peered through the grille and saw the kindly face of the Dominican priest. What did you tell him? Good news, that the king was approaching?'

290

Dunheved just smiled faintly. 'Rosselin trusted you enough to open that door. You bustle in all friendly. You urge him to join the rest on the battlements. You pick up his cloak and war-belt as if to help him. Rosselin turns to receive his cloak, but you drop that, pluck the dagger from his war-belt and plunge it into his side, a killing blow up under his ribs, into his heart. You drag him to that open window, pull him on to the ledge and hurl his body into the night. A brief time, no more than a few breaths. You then place the false key on the table and take the chamber one. You lock the door from the outside and join us on the battlements, where you are careful to single me out.

'The next morning you ensured that Demontaigu gave the corpse the last rites while you joined us in Rosselin's chamber. You pretended to collect his possessions into a basket. Once again, in the blink of an eye, you changed one key for another. Your vengeance was now complete. All five Aquilae had been executed in a way that suited their lives, falling from glory to a grisly death. The siege began. You found it simple enough to break the bruised reed. The garrison was unnerved by strange calls and sounds. It was an easy task for a Dominican knowledgeable about witches and warlocks. The well was polluted, the food stocks burnt – all your doing. Who would suspect a Dominican priest, a royal confessor?'

'You did!' Dunheved taunted. 'Surely the Aquilae would have?'

'No, no!' I retorted. 'The Aquilae, in Rosselin's words, were broken. They had been involved in the most horrid treason. They were trapped in it; there was no going back. Resented by most, deserted by their lord, who could they turn to? Rosselin was even reduced to begging for my help. They were like sheep without a shepherd, alone, vulnerable to the ever-watching wolf: you!'

'And afterwards,' Isabella asked, 'the capture of Gaveston?'

'God knows, your grace. I have little proof. I believe Pembroke was honest and true enough. Beauchamp of Warwick and the others needed little encouragement to seize Gaveston. Did you, Brother, send an anonymous message to Warwick telling him to follow us? You had the opportunity for such mischief when you took Gaveston's acceptance to Pembroke. Did you leave similar messages at taverns where we paused before arriving at Deddington to lodge for the night? Warwick would do the rest. He lured Pembroke away, leaving Gaveston vulnerable, but there again, you realised, as I did, that once he'd separated from the king, Gaveston was finished. I am sure you secretly worked to achieve that. Did you advise or encourage the king to choose Scarborough as the best place for refuge, when in fact it certainly wasn't?' I glanced quickly at the queen. 'Though God knows what further encouragement persuaded him to separate himself from his favourite.'

Isabella did not flinch. Ah, I thought, when will she reveal her own role in all of this? Dunheved, tapping his sandalled feet dramatically against the paving stone, abruptly rose and smoothed out his robe.

'I'm a priest,' he cleared his throat, 'a cleric. I claim benefit of clergy. I cannot be tried by the king's courts.'

'His grace can certainly be informed.'

Dunheved smiled patronisingly at me.

'About what?' He sat down, hands clasped. 'Did I not tell you, mistress?' He smiled. 'I heard the lord Gaveston's confession.'

'Which cannot be revealed,' I taunted.

'On the night before he was taken, he confessed to me after absolution that he'd killed all the Aquilae in the very same way you have described to me.' Dunheved chewed the corner of his lip.

'Check and check again,' I whispered. 'Every piece I move, you block. Oh, I know you, Brother. You'll demand to be tried by Church courts, which are more lenient. You'll claim your innocence and point to Gaveston, using the very evidence I have now supplied you with. You'll cause enough confusion, sow enough doubt to nullify proceedings completely, and of course, the king would not like to see his confessor being exposed to public shame.'

'More importantly, mistress,' Dunheved pointed at me, 'you could become a laughing stock, the wench who laid false accusation against the king's own confessor.'

'Be careful, Brother,' Isabella whispered hoarsely. 'Be very, very careful.'

'Your grace,' Dunheved murmured, 'I'm simply saying what others would say. Gaveston killed his own for his own selfish reasons. He was totally bound up with himself. We all agree on that. He was evil and has now gone to his just reward. A man, your grace, let me remind you, who tried to betray you to the Scots, the king's mortal enemies; who put your life and that of your unborn child at risk.'

'And how will you account for Brother Eusebius?' I accused. 'Strange,' I gestured at him, 'in all our meetings you rarely asked me about him. At Tynemouth when I mentioned his death, you ignored me and abruptly asked about Kennington. Why, Brother? Did you feel guilty, or were you cautious lest any discussion might betray a mistake on your part? After all, you were nearly trapped when I went down to the charnel house. You had to flee, locking that trap door behind you. Brother, you were dismissive of me; I was someone to be patronised. A stupid snooping maid who could be frightened, as you tried to do when I went into the belfry after Lanercost's death. You began to sound those bells.'

'Brother!' Isabella hissed. 'Mathilde is of my household, my chamber!'

'Poor Eusebius,' I continued. 'You considered him a fool, but he was sharper. He, in fact, gave you the idea for that mocking verse about the Aquilae flying so high. He mentioned to me how Theobald the lovesick novice tried to fly like an eagle. You befriended Eusebius, but he glimpsed things out of place. He nourished his own suspicious about you. Perhaps he hoped for more silver from you. He referred to himself as the bat and asked his prior if a bat could be more cunning than a dog. He was making a play on the name of your order: *Domini Canes* – Dogs or Hounds of the Lord. He also talked of *lux et tenebrae* – light and darkness – a reference to your secret ways, as well as to the black and white garb you wear. Eusebius thought he was safe. He revelled in the game. He etched a drawing on the wall of his closet in the bell tower: a bat and what looked like a hairy dog or leopard. In fact it was a wolf in sheep's clothing. A reference to you, because Eusebius was sure he'd glimpsed you hurrying through the Galilee Porch on the day Leygrave was killed. He turned menacing. You gave Leygrave the last rites. Eusebius was close by. He babbled to me, intimating that he knew more than he'd confessed. In fact he was secretly threatening you. You overheard and decided to silence his chattering tongue. You followed him down into the charnel house and crushed his skull with a bone. You removed from his tray any coins or medals you'd given him, including a button on a shard of cloth from the livery of the Beaumonts, and left that as a distraction.' I shrugged. 'The Beaumonts were a mere irritation, fearful of being distanced from the king and what he might be plotting regarding their precious estates in Scotland. They were only concerned about themselves. I nearly caught you that day down in the charnel house. Little wonder you joined me and Demontaigu to judge what progress I was making. Very subtle! To be the hunted who could join the hunters whenever he wished and discover what was being plotted.' I sighed. 'So, Brother, how do you plead about poor Eusebius?'

'You have no real proof.'

'True,' I conceded, 'as I have no real evidence you murdered the Pilgrim. He came here disguised as a Franciscan. He wanted to tell me a secret. You saw me talking to someone garbed as a friar. We later left the Priory and went down Pig Sty Alley to the Pot of Fire. Believe me, Brother, the murder you committed that evening was most callous. You considered the slaying of the Aquilae as just punishment. Brother Eusebius had to be silenced because of what he might have seen and heard, but the Pilgrim was mere chance. You were concerned lest some Franciscan here, apart from Eusebius, might also have seen or heard something untoward. You dared not strike at me or mine because of her grace, but the Pilgrim was a different matter. You took a crossbow and waited for us to return, to step into that pool of light. You killed the Pilgrim and slipped away. You murdered another human being for no other reason than just in case . . .'

Dunheved shook his head and made to leave. Isabella whispered something hoarsely in a patois I could not understand, but I am sure she told him to go. The Dominican had lost some of his quiet arrogance. He rose and bowed to the queen.

'Your grace, I beg you to excuse me.'

'You are certainly excused, Brother.'

'I would like words with Mistress Mathilde.'

'If she wishes words with you alone, Brother, you may both withdraw, but Mathilde must return unscathed.' She gestured quickly at me as a sign to go with Dunheved.

I did so, following him into the next enclosure of the rose garden. Behind me I heard the queen calling for her squires. Dunheved walked over to the wicket gate leading towards the Galilee Porch of the friary church. It was twilight, the hour of the bat. Flittering black shapes darted through the half-light. Dusk time, when the demons walk and the gargoyles and babewyns allegedly turn to flesh so as to prowl through the world of men. A fitting time to confront an assassin with a fair face and foul heart. Dunheved turned abruptly at the gate and peered at me.

'What I did,' his words came as a hiss, 'was for the king, the Crown and the welfare of this realm.'

'True, Brother, but it could have also been done by usage

of law. The Aquilae might have provoked God's vengeance, but helpless Eusebius, the poor Pilgrim, Kennington's two retainers? More importantly, Brother,' I stepped closer, 'you relished your role. You enjoyed it. I doubt if this was the first time you'd killed. I am sure it will not be the last.'

'The king would never believe you.' Dunheved was now blustering. 'Nor will any court, be it the king's or the pope's.' He shook himself as if casting away any doubt or guilt. 'I did God's work.'

'Which makes you truly dangerous, Brother. No man is more sinister than when he decides that God has selected him to deal out death and judgement according to His whim. You can go,' I continued. 'The king will not know, but God knows. You, Brother, revelled in wielding the power of life and death. You have moved from strength to strength, exulting in what you do and what you have done. You walk a gorgeous path of power, or so you think, but those you murdered glide through the dusk either side of you. One day they will hold you to account.'

'Mathilde,' Dunheved smirked, 'you should have been a religious.'

'Like you, Brother?'

Dunheved shrugged, mockingly blessed me and was gone.

I walked back to the queen. She dismissed her squires and patted the seat next to her.

'Mathilde. You do have questions? I know you are brimming with them. Did I know? Dunheved told me in confidence what he'd learnt from Lanercost. He said for me to watch, as God would punish the Aquilae. I did not really care.' Isabella played with a ring on her finger. 'I could not voice, even to you, my worst suspicions. Was Gaveston really plotting my destruction? Above all,' tears brimmed in those beautiful eyes, 'was my husband? I decided to resist, to turn the king's heart from Gaveston and his coven.'

'They admitted as much,' I intervened. 'Both Rosselin and Gaveston said you were more subtle than a serpent. Gaveston confessed I had saved him from great sin, namely your death and that of your unborn child. Rosselin and the rest also came to regret their plotting, but it was too late. They must have been mystified as to who was their hidden enemy. You? Gaveston? The king?'

'My fears haunted me,' Isabella murmured. 'In the end it came down to power. Edward had to decide to save either himself, me and our child, or Gaveston. He made his choice.'

'Your grace could have taken me into her confidence.'

'What about?' Isabella whispered. 'That Dunheved was a killer? I only began to suspect him after Scarborough. For a while I thought Gaveston was killing his own. I became absorbed with him. I could not believe he would plot such wickedness; well, not till Tynemouth, and that was proof enough. I questioned Dunheved on his return from Warwick about whether he had had a hand in the death of the Aquilae. He denied it, blaming Gaveston. Dunheved will never admit his crimes, not to me or to the king. You he despises as some kitchen wench not worth bothering about. I did not really care for the Aquilae. After Tynemouth I was concerned only about my child. I confronted Edward.' She turned blue eyes brimming with tears. 'He did not deny that it was possible Gaveston might wish to hurt me.'

'Did you threaten the king?'

'Yes, Mathilde, I threatened the king my husband, the father of my child. I taunted him with the allegation that Gaveston knew about the changeling story. Was Gaveston, I screamed, blackmailing him? Edward remained silent.' She sighed. 'Now, as you know, French ships, alerted by the growing crisis, appeared off the coast. In Whitby I communicated with the seigneur of the flotilla; the master of the *The Wyvern* was my emissary. He brought letters from my father offering assistance. I responded that, if necessary, I would flee England on board a French ship.'

'But you decided against that.'

'Yes, Mathilde, I travelled to York. I pleaded with my husband to separate from Gaveston and allow him to go to Scarborough Castle. Anywhere, just away from us. I urged Dunheved to support me, and he did. I also told my husband that if Gaveston did not go into exile, I would.'

She smiled at my surprise.

'I threatened to take sanctuary in Holcombe church, then ask to be escorted to the nearest port to take ship to my county of Ponthieu. Once there, I would don widow's weeds, enter a nunnery and claim that, until Gaveston left England, I had no husband.'

'And Edward would have been publicly humiliated?' I declared.

'True,' Isabella agreed. 'Both I and his son would be beyond his power. What else could I do? Gaveston had been with us for four years, Mathilde.' The queen's lips grew tight, her words coming out in a hoarse whisper. 'For four years I put up with his foolishness, his arrogance, his provocation of the earls. I let him wine and dine, dance and strut, but I watched his eyes. As I grew older, he began to resent me. He feigned great pleasure that I was pregnant, but he didn't hide it so well. Lanercost's confession to Dunheved simply confirmed my own deep suspicions. My husband was deeply shocked. Mathilde, his love for Gaveston never really threatened me, but when he saw it might . . .'

'So the king let Gaveston go to his fate?'

'Yes, Mathilde, you have it in one. I begged him to let God dispose. Edward grew more malleable after Tynemouth. To be truthful, he was also tired, eager for change, for a respite, wary of Gaveston's growing obsession. In the end,' Isabella pulled a face, 'the king simply did nothing. He let events manifest God's will.'

'But now Gaveston is dead, the king may change?'

'No, no,' Isabella declared. 'Edward takes great comfort from the thought that Gaveston wove his own fate. He recognises that, as he does the fact that I had no choice but to defend myself. So . . .' She turned away.

'And Dunheved?' I asked.

'Brother Stephen will no longer be my confessor, Mathilde. I never suspected he was a killer until I heard what happened in Scarborough and afterwards. I shall distance myself from him. He remains the king's confidant. God knows, no action will be taken against him. Edward will simply not want to know. Moreover, the king will be eager to test his new freedom, rejoice in his power, exult that his lovely wife bears his heir. As for the future . . .' She grasped my hand. 'Mathilde, *ma fille*, finish your business here, then join me at the abbey early tomorrow after the Jesus mass. Let this matter rest.'

Then she was gone, in a swirl of fragrant perfume, calling for her squires. I walked out of the rose garden into the darkened friary church so full of brooding memories, haunted by the ghosts of those slain. I made my way up to the lady chapel and lit tapers for those murdered souls and for my own beloveds. The flames danced against the darkness. I glanced up at the serene, beautifully carved face of the Virgin and intoned a poem my mother had taught me: *Tu as mis au monde le Sauveur de l'Univers. Benie sois-tu, Marie . . .*

Ah well! Now sheltering here in another Franciscan house, I gaze down through the murk of years past. I glimpse in a glow of golden light the beloved faces of those long dead. I also see Dunheved's. Oh, Brother Stephen Dunheved! We like to think of God's justice as in some miracle play, shooting out like an arrow or flashing like a barb of lightning. Of judgement falling immediately. Of sentence being imposed swiftly. Life isn't like that. Time creeps, and so does God's judgement. Dunheved's day of doom eventually arrived, as it did for all the others: Lancaster, Pembroke, Hereford and Warwick. The murdered dead caught up with Dunheved at Berkeley Castle some fifteen years after those hurling times at York. I was there when he was brought to judgement. My face was the last he saw before they bricked him up, sealing him into a living tomb, where his body now rots. But that was for the future, when the furies once again massed like black clouds, low and threatening, before God's judgement lashed down like rain to wash away more of man's sin.

Author's Note

The events of this novel are closely based on fact and are described by contemporary chronicles, particularly the *Vita Edwardi Secundi – The Life of Edward II*. I analysed this period in my DPhil thesis on Isabella for Oxford University some thirty years ago, when this story first took root!

- The development of medicine and its practice by women is well attested. Indeed, the role played by women in medicine flourished until it was declared illegal by the despotic Henry VIII in 1519.
- The destruction of the Templar order occurred as described. Many accounts allege how Templars took refuge in Scotland and even played a decisive role in Bruce's great victory over Edward II at Bannockburn in 1314.
- Edward II and Gaveston did shelter in the north during the spring of 1312 and secretly negotiated with Bruce. Lancaster and the other earls did pursue

them both. Isabella was trapped at Tynemouth and had to fight her way out. Some chroniclers place this in 1312, other 1323, and a few claim that such an escape occurred twice. Indeed, James Douglas, Bruce's war leader, hatched other plots to seize Isabella throughout Scotland's fierce guerrilla war against England.

- The Beaumonts, I believe, are faithfully depicted here. For the next sixteen years they kept close to the Crown, eager to save their estates in Scotland. Isabella's household book for 1311–12 still survives and depicts the Beaumonts as her close kin. Later on, the queen championed Louis to become Bishop of Durham.

- Gaveston's fall is accurately described. Something hideous occurred at Scarborough that forced him to surrender. *The Life of Edward II* claims he ran out of food, yet the castle had been well provisioned. Pembroke's custody of him was benevolent, but we will never know if that earl's hasty flight to visit his wife was contrived or a genuinely stupid mistake. Gaveston was seized and executed by Warwick and his allies, as described by Mathilde. Edward II's reaction to his favourite's death was strangely muted. He called Gaveston a fool, and only much later did he kindle his angry hatred against the earls, especially Lancaster. Isabella's separation from her husband during the crisis was also very curious, bearing in mind that she was pregnant. Years later, in her struggle against Despencer, Isabella actually did flee to France and don widow's weeds.

- The Pilgrim from the Wastelands story – both the horrific physical clash between Edward I and his son and the story of Edward of Caernarvon being a changeling – is based on contemporary sources.
- Finally, Brother Stephen Dunheved, the Dominican confessor to Edward II, was a real and very sinister figure, whose murderous intrigue was to play a prominent role in the murky, bloody politics of Edward II's reign.

Paul Doherty
September 2008
Website: www.paulcdoherty.com